# Waltzing at Midnight

# Robbi McCoy

Bella
BOOKS
2009

Printed in the United States of America on acid-free paper
First Edition

Editor: Cindy Cresap
Cover Designer: Linda Callaghan

ISBN 10: 1-59493-153-4
ISBN 13: 978-1-59493-153-6

# Acknowledgments

Perpetual thanks to my diligent reader and life partner, Dot, for her insightful suggestions, gentle criticisms and continuing interest and patience. Many thanks also to Marianne Garver for her thoughtful opinions and for lifting my ego with grace and humor.

## Dedication

To Gladys, for your many gifts of words and the delight that you took in each of my successes.

## About the Author

Robbi McCoy is a native Californian who lives in the Central Valley between the mountains and the sea. She is an avid hiker with a particular fondness for the deserts of the American Southwest. Robbi's previous publications include numerous articles and short stories and two books, a hiking guide, *Geology Trails of Northern California* (Gem Guides), and *Late Bloomers: Awakening to Lesbianism After Forty*, a collection of coming-out stories. She also enjoys gardening, culinary adventures and the theater, and is the author of several ancient computer games. An English major with a minor in computer science, she works full-time as a software specialist and web designer for a major West Coast distribution company. *Waltzing at Midnight* is Robbi's first Bella Books romance.

# Chapter One

I wasn't normally someone prone to panic attacks or even excessive nervousness, but ever since I had started working on Rosie's campaign, almost from the first day, in fact, I had caught myself more than once feeling that something big was about to fall on my head. A rush of adrenaline, followed by a fierce sensation of immediate danger, caused me to mentally, and a couple of times literally, duck. It was disconcerting. It was hard to ignore. The adrenaline was real and the heart palpitations which followed were notable. There was something about the atmosphere at campaign headquarters that made me unusually wary.

When I mentioned this to Faye after the first couple of weeks, she dismissed it as a normal response to the high level of excitement in the office. I wasn't used to such energy. My life was usually so quiet. I think what she meant was that my life was hopelessly dull. I decided she was right. The feeling of anxiety was uncomfortable and it remained with me, but I tried to turn it into something positive and direct it toward the work we were doing.

After two months, I was no longer distracted by this sensation, which was, I decided, a natural reaction to being so far removed from my comfort zone. But it was still there, an uneasiness that nipped at the edges of my consciousness almost all the time whether I was at the office or home with my family.

"Thank you so much, and remember to vote on November third," I said into the phone for about the thirtieth time already today. Getting people to the polls was our main goal. The 2007 election had no big issues, no presidential race, nothing pressing to coax people out. There were a handful of bonds, some city council seats, a couple of propositions which weren't especially controversial and the mayor's race. This was probably a good year for cutting my political teeth.

Clark, Rosie's campaign manager, met the UPS truck outside at the curb and was just coming back in carrying a box. "This is the new batch of buttons," he said, dropping the box on his desk.

Ginny, our regular UPS driver, followed him in with a hand truck and three more boxes.

"Let's see them," I said, coming over to Clark's desk. He was tearing one of the boxes open while Ginny and I waited.

"Yeah, let's see," Ginny said, peering expectantly over Clark's shoulder.

Ginny, a woman in her early thirties, showed up each day with our deliveries in her brown shirt and shorts and then volunteered for Rosie's campaign on her days off. She wore her long blond hair in a ponytail through the back of a baseball cap. It swished about a lot because she was always on the run, jumping in and out of her truck. Clark produced a handful of buttons and passed them over to us.

Rosie's image appeared in the center of the button, smiling, waving. Around the outside, in red lettering, were the words "Vote For Rosie—Knock Kiester on His."

"I like that," I said, pinning one on. "He should have changed his name if he wanted to be a politician."

8

"It hasn't hurt him much, though," Clark pointed out. "Making people remember your name is half the battle. You couldn't really forget his, could you? So we'll use that to our advantage."

"Give me a bunch of them," Ginny said. "I'll pass them out to everybody on my route today."

Clark gave her a box of buttons, signed her paperwork, and then she was out the door, ponytail swinging.

There were three of us in the office this morning, me, Clark and Tina. Tina was the company receptionist, so she was here full-time, but the rest of us were volunteers for Rosie's campaign. As the day wore on, more volunteers came and went as their schedules allowed. We had converted Monroe Advertising into campaign headquarters, pretty much curtailing business as usual. The closer we got to election day, the less likely any advertising business would be happening here. Rosie had sent her other regular employee, her graphic artist, home to telework for the remainder of the campaign so he wouldn't be stumbling over us.

Rosie charged in about ten o'clock, looking invigorated. Despite the brutal pace of her schedule, she seemed to have limitless energy. "Good morning, all," she called, her presence filling the room. Then, taking Clark firmly by the shoulders, she said, "Clark, everything's coming up Rosie!"

"I know," he said exuberantly.

"Why don't we have a button that says that?" I asked.

"Good question, Jean," Rosie said, spinning around to look at me. "Clark, see what you can do. Let's try to keep line two free today, okay? I've got to return some calls. I've got a business that's going down the drain in the midst of all this campaign folderol."

Rosie shut herself in her office, leaving us to the task of selling her to the voters. The momentum was building, along with the exhilaration we all felt knowing we were going to win. The volunteers were in a high-energy state. The candidate was soaring.

Through the window between Rosie's office and the reception

area, I could see her at her desk, talking animatedly into the phone. She was an attractive woman, made even more so by the jubilant personality that radiated off her. Her light ash brown hair was graying around the edges, cut short, lying naturally with no part. She didn't wear much makeup, but she didn't need to. She had clear skin and round, expressive brown eyes. The usual creases in the forehead and on either side of the mouth, and the usual softness of features that come with age gave her an experienced, intelligent look, the look of a woman who deserved respect. You saw a lot of her front teeth because she was always either smiling or talking expressively. She was open, natural and genuine. I had never known such a charismatic woman, and she made me feel extraordinarily dull by comparison.

Rosie had been pushed into running for mayor of Weberstown, shamed into it by her friends and colleagues who insisted that the only place she could really do the work she wanted to do for the city was at the helm. That's what I'd been told, anyway, since I hadn't known Rosie before I walked through this door to volunteer. Now it seemed impossible to me that I hadn't at least known about her. She was involved in practically everything that happened in this town, in every arena, especially the arts, to which she seemed particularly devoted. She was a woman at the top of her game, by anyone's standard.

It hadn't even occurred to me, living out my self-centered life among my small circle of acquaintances, that elsewhere the town was bustling with all of this activity. I had learned more about my town in two months than I had in forty years. And I felt ashamed that I hadn't previously given a thought to people like Rosie who worked tirelessly without my gratitude to improve and preserve my way of life. There were just a handful like her, but together they exerted enormous influence over how our community grew and prospered while the bulk of the citizenry did nothing or, worse, just complained. I hadn't been doing my part all these years, that was apparent, which was doubly embarrassing considering that I was a native and Rosie was an out-of-state transplant.

Rosie had a rare gift, the power to motivate people. If she

could motivate me, who wouldn't she be able to motivate? The more involved I got with this campaign, the more compelled I felt to be active myself, the more desperate I felt to accomplish something, as though I was in a foot race at the back of the pack, falling further and further behind. The momentum here was so unforgivably fast. With my limited skills and even more limited experience, there wasn't much I could do of importance, but, certainly, helping to get Rosie elected would be something that would have important consequences.

After spending Monday at headquarters working the phones, I went door-to-door Tuesday, peddling Rosie to stay-at-home moms, retired people and the unemployed who were home watching truck driving school ads on TV. If no one answered the door, I left a flyer.

"I hope we can count on your vote," I said to a young woman with a wide-eyed toddler peering around her legs. Then I was back into the street.

It was a hot October day just over a month away from the election. This wasn't my neighborhood, but was similar with its rows of California tract houses with painted cedar siding, three-car garages and no side yards, a respectable middle-class residential area. City-planted ash trees lined the street on either side. A dog barked at me from behind a six-foot redwood fence. I'd never have thought I'd be out knocking on strangers' doors, but I was enjoying it. It was easy enough to hand out leaflets and talk up your candidate, especially if you really believed she was the woman for the job. When I started, I didn't have much of an opinion, but a couple of weeks later, I was thoroughly convinced that Rosie was that woman.

And what would I be doing otherwise right now at one o' clock on a Tuesday afternoon? Groceries? Dry cleaners? Things that needed doing, I supposed. It was beginning to get on Jerry's nerves, my volunteer work. He wanted me home when he came in, and, as I'd only recently realized, he wanted me receptive to his mood, to a discussion of his day, not preoccupied with my own day's events. He definitely didn't want me to talk about them, cutting into his time, as it were. The jobs I normally took, low-paid office work, didn't detract that much from my home life. Those jobs left me mentally unencumbered and home to greet Jerry when he arrived. Amy, too, wasn't getting the attention she was accustomed to, but this was temporary, would be over soon, and then I would quit neglecting my family. Now that Amy was in college, though, and really didn't need her mother hovering about, this work of mine was doing her no real harm.

"Oh, yes," an elderly man said after I introduced myself. "We're going to vote for Rosie. You bet."

"Can I put a sign on your lawn?" I asked. He agreed, helping me hammer in the stake.

We were going to win, I could feel it. Rosie for Mayor signs littered the streets of Weberstown, welcoming me everywhere I went. As I turned into my street at the end of the day, a six-foot sign planted in my front yard waved me into the driveway, testifying to my family's political involvement. Just across the street the Strattons boasted an equally impressive endorsement of opponent and incumbent, Hugh Kiester.

I hurried into the house, my feet aching, and threw together a meal of tuna salad sandwiches, ready just in time for Jerry's arrival. He came over and hugged me at the kitchen counter, the stubble on his face scratching my cheek. "How was your day, hon?" he asked.

"Fun. I did the door-to-door bit."

"I'm a little worried about you walking the streets in strange neighborhoods."

I stuck a plate in front of him and gave him a paper napkin. "I've got my mace." I put the sandwiches on the table and sat down. "We're up in the polls again. Rosie's got it nailed. I'm so excited!"

He smiled affectionately, crow's feet appearing around his light brown eyes. "Yes, you are. This work seems to have done you a lot of good." He bit into a sandwich. "It hasn't improved our meals any, but I guess if it makes you happy, it's a good thing."

Happy? Is that what this is? I asked myself. Wasn't I happy

before?

"Maybe you should consider finding a full-time job after the election," Jerry said. "Something interesting, not like those things you've done before, but something that would absorb you like this, push you a bit."

"I thought you were feeling neglected," I said, taking a sandwich.

"Well, it was a selfish attitude. Jeannie, I've been watching you lately, and I've made some observations." He stopped eating and looked at me purposefully. "Maybe you didn't realize it—I know I didn't, but a couple of months ago you were a miserable woman."

"What?" I objected. "I was not miserable."

"I think you were. And now you're not. Think about it. You're so full of life now, so enthusiastic about what you're doing. It's fun to watch. Amy thinks so too. Ask her."

I said nothing, thinking about what he said. Yes, I felt different, more energetic, more anxious to get up in the morning and get going. I might have been bored before, but certainly not miserable. I was happily married to a successful CPA with two well-adjusted, healthy children, one of them cavorting across Europe, one of them still at home, attending our local community college. What was there in this scenario that could possibly make me miserable? I just needed something of my own to do, probably, especially with the kids out of the nest, if not literally, then at least emotionally.

Yes, Jean, I thought, you're a cliché—a forty-year-old wife and mother with the kids grown, feeling left out of the world and desperate for a life of her own.

"Where is Amy, by the way?" Jerry asked.

"Still at school, I guess."

Jerry got a bottled beer out of the refrigerator and twisted off the cap. I was reminded of the time before we were married when he had opened a beer with his teeth to impress me. You could still see the chip, small, but right there on the edge of his front tooth.

"What are you smiling about?" he asked.

"Oh, nothing. Maybe I should go to college," I said, "one of the business colleges or the community college."

"Yeah, you and Amy could trade notes." He sounded amused.

"I'm serious. Why shouldn't I go to college?"

"No reason. You're an intelligent woman. I guess we can afford it, at least the junior college. You've got until January to decide on a major. Pick something lucrative, okay? If my wife's going to get a career, I'd like it to pay. Not like this campaigning stuff. You're working more than forty hours a week with nothing to show for it. At least at that dentist's office, you brought in a pretty decent paycheck."

"There's plenty to show," I countered. "And next month when Rosie's elected, it'll show well enough."

"I hope she appreciates what we're going through," he said.

I mussed his thin hair. "Poor lamb."

At ten o'clock, I confiscated the remote control from Amy and switched to the local station to watch Rosie in a debate against Hugh Kiester. The third candidate, Mike Garcia, wasn't considered a serious contender and had not been invited. Rosie appeared behind a podium in a broad-shouldered red jacket and white blouse, precisely groomed and made-up, every light brown hair in place—and the gray ones too—her cheeks slightly ruddy, her lips bright red, a smile on her face, as usual. I smiled too, remembering her complaining to Clark about having to wear lipstick on camera. She didn't like it, thought it made her look like a clown, but everyone insisted that there was no choice in the matter, that's just the way it had to be, like a law of physics or something.

"She's a good-looking woman," Jerry said.

Yes, I thought. She's beautiful.

Kiester was droning on about his public service career, about how qualified he was for the position. "My opponent has no experience dealing with the complexity of big city finances," Kiester said. "I ran a multimillion dollar company for fifteen years, and I've been working in city government for eight years, as a member of the planning commission and then as mayor. I know how to make long-term plans for our future growth. As mayor, you have a responsibility to deal with public funds wisely and with foresight."

"The city is practically broke," Rosie said. "Are you bragging about that, Hugh? During your term, the monies have been so badly mismanaged that if Weberstown were a charity, it would be criminally prosecuted for fraud. The reserve was in the millions of dollars when you became mayor. Today there is no reserve to speak of."

Rosie's manner was spirited and good-natured, as though she were enjoying the game. She was relaxed. He was tense and on the defensive. You could tell he was frustrated, had no means to slow the momentum of phenomenal Rosie.

"And on the issue of planning for the future," she said, "the plan submitted by your planning commission last month, a year late and forty million dollars over budget, is doomed to be voted down by the council. It's unrealistic and even in opposition to the county and state plans. Environmentalists and state offices are hollering bloody murder. But I've got to give you the fact that it's farsighted. Fifty years! No other city's plan has been able to see that far into the future, Hugh. Maybe you ought to rent out your crystal ball."

I smiled along with Rosie as she and the camera turned to Kiester, whose face was contorted into a grimace trying to become a smile.

"Isn't he a jerk?" I said. Jerry patted my arm to placate me.

The mediator asked about job creation. This was one of Kiester's vulnerable areas. Rosie was going to smear him. I was definitely enjoying myself.

"Bringing new jobs to our county is one of my top priorities," Kiester said. "We have implemented several new programs to make this area attractive to business, including the one-stop permit office which will open in January. In the recent past we've asked new and expanding businesses to shoulder too great a percentage of support for our infrastructure. I've ordered the council to review the business tax structure and look into the fee system, land use and environmental regulations, and several areas where we might ease some of the burden away from businesses willing to locate here and employ our citizens. Two companies which will employ a total of two hundred and eighty-five people have committed just this month to relocating to our city."

When it was Rosie's turn, she sparkled at the camera and said, "If you can't get a job done, take credit for somebody else doing it. The two relocating companies the mayor refers to were secured through the negotiations of the Vision Partnership, a cooperative of civic leaders and businessmen and women, of which I am the director. The Partnership was formed because we're deeply concerned about the lack of jobs in our community and we've been unable to move city government to act. One of the reasons we haven't been more successful is that businesses are alienated by the apparent apathy of city government in assisting them. The regulations are oppressive, the taxes are restrictive, and the red tape involved in getting licenses and permits is prohibitive. Not a single piece of legislation has been passed in the last two years to ease these constraints, and the one-stop permit office, which we've been pushing for at least three years, has been too long coming."

Rosie gestured in a relaxed manner with her hands, talking into the camera as though she were addressing a friend. She was so good at this! "And, as the mayor has just told us," she continued, "he has finally asked the council to review some of the restrictive policies, policies he promised in his previous campaign to revise. How many terms do we give Mr. Kiester before we get some results? Since he took office, twenty-two private-sector employers in the city have shut their doors. Four hundred and twenty-one people lost jobs." Rosie paused for effect. "No, he didn't cause an atmosphere discouraging to business, but neither did he do anything to improve it. As far as I'm concerned, the single most urgent issue for this community is unemployment. Put people back to work and you'll reduce crime. Bring more business to town and you'll increase the tax revenue. I've shown my commitment to this issue through the creation of the Vision Partnership. Mr. Kiester has shown his lack of commitment through inertia." Rosie glanced at Kiester, the camera dutifully following her lead. He coughed nervously. Rosie continued. "We need to inject some life into this lackadaisical government. We need to get off our Kiester." Rosie hit the podium with her fist. I laughed out loud.

"Isn't she something?" I said after the debate.

"Mom," Amy complained. "Enough already. People are gonna think Rosie's your GF or something if you don't cool it." My daughter got up from the couch, standing to her astonishing five feet nine, her lanky form slumped at the shoulders. Both of my children were tall, unlike me, and Amy was having a hard time accepting her attributes. For her sake, I hoped she had reached her full height. Already she wore only the flattest shoes she could find and her posture was suffering. Despite her awkwardness over her tall frame, however, she wasn't the least bit shy.

"Well, don't you think she's impressive?" I said. "She's the perfect role model for someone your age."

Amy sang in a mocking voice, "She's the tops, she's the tower of pizza."

"Pisa," Jerry corrected.

"Really? I like it my way." Amy tossed her head to throw her long hair out of her face.

"Hey, princess," Jerry said, "how about taking all these newspapers and putting the bins out for pickup?"

"Yes, my lord and master," Amy said with a low bow. "Your wish is my command."

"Jerry," I asked, as Amy took an armload of newspapers from the room, "are you going to vote for Rosie?"

"You know I am," Jerry said. "You'd probably kick me out if I didn't."

"But wouldn't you vote for her anyway?"

"Probably. It's hard to know with you campaigning us to death. We're getting a biased view."

17

"Well, if you just look at the facts—"

Jerry held up a hand. "Whoa. Let's not. I'm going to bed. Are you coming?"

I nodded. "I'll be there in a few minutes."

As soon as Jerry had gone, Amy returned, flung herself on the couch and switched stations to tune in to some reality show. "You're pretty sure Rosie's going to win, Mom?" she asked.

"How could she lose against that imbecile?"

Amy tossed her long hair yet again and leaned her head on the back of the couch. "Yeah, she'll probably win. Kiester is so gross. People are tired of seeing his face."

This girl understands politics, I thought. "Don't stay up too late. School tomorrow." Before going to bed, I cleaned off the kitchen counter, except for the pile of Rosie propaganda at one end. There she was smiling up at me from a flyer with that magnetic personality. Seeing her image there, I couldn't help but smile myself.

From the moment we met two months ago, I'd felt the special energy she radiated. "Welcome aboard, Jean," she had said, shaking my hand heartily. Her presence was powerful. When she looked at you, you knew she was seeing you, really seeing you. And she was honest and intelligent, so much more intelligent than Kiester. I didn't suspect, when Faye coerced me into volunteering, that I would end up believing so firmly in my candidate, that I would want so much for her to win. I'd always assumed, like most people I knew, that politicians were self-serving manipulators. Rosie was exactly the opposite. She acted out of altruism. Her business, and the business of the community, seemed to be what she lived for. With no husband, no children, she gave herself over to public life.

Faye thought it would be good for me to get involved in something. "And you'll be setting a good example for your daughter," she said, a timely example, since this was Amy's first election. That's the way, Faye, hit a mother where it counts. I had argued at first about not having the time, about not knowing anything or even caring about politics. For the sake of our long friendship, for the only friendship that I had kept from high school, I finally relented and agreed to work a couple of hours a week for the Rosie campaign.

That couple of hours a week had turned into a full-time commitment. No, I wasn't earning any money, but I was definitely having fun. The best part was that it wasn't just something for me, like a hobby. It was something important. I felt different. I felt renewed, as if on the verge of a whole new life, a life that would be so much more meaningful than what had come before it.

# Chapter Two

During lunch, a peanut butter and jelly sandwich for me, eaten between phone calls, Rosie called me into her office. "How's it going?" she asked, looking up at me with the expectation of good news.

"Great."

"Glad to hear it. Jean, I need a favor. I'm speaking this afternoon at the Women's Center, and I've dribbled coffee on my scarf." She showed me a small stain on the cherry-colored silk scarf around her neck. "I hate to ask, but do you think you could get it cleaned by two?"

"I'll do my best."

"You'd probably be better spent here, but Tina's out and I've got another meeting in a few minutes."

"I don't mind. You can't give a speech with a coffee dribble. We want you to look your best at all times."

She untied the scarf and handed it to me. "Other than that, how do I look?"

She stood before me in a black and tan suit, black slacks,

two-tone jacket with gold buttons, cream-colored shell, a string of colored glass rectangles on her chest—red, pink and clear iridescent tablets that sparkled as she moved. "Fantastic," I said.

"I'll be glad when this election is over so I can relax a little bit about my appearance. Clark almost had a stroke the other day when he saw my earrings were on the wrong ears."

I knew Rosie was taking special pains to look good all the time these days. In the two months that I had known her, I hadn't once seen her looking anything less than meticulous, every hour of the day and night. "Compared to me, you always look like you just walked out of a magazine," I said.

"You haven't seen me at home with the horses, Jean. Besides, I think you're very attractive. You have the sort of figure and features that don't need a lot of enhancement, a quite natural beauty." She looked into my eyes momentarily, then clapped her hands together, saying, "Well, let's get going. I'll be back for the scarf at one thirty."

"Right," I said. I flew out to a dry cleaners and waited while they cleaned the scarf, arriving back in time to tie it around Rosie's neck before she left. I arranged it carefully, puffing it up, leaning it toward the right so that it draped gracefully over her shoulder and covered the top of the jacket lapel. She stood about two inches taller than me, about five-seven. I caught her scent momentarily, light, floral, perfectly subtle. Soap, I thought, or body wash, even shampoo. Not perfume. It was too faint. When I had finished with the scarf, I noticed Rosie's amused expression.

"You do that very well, Jean," she said. "And very thoroughly. Thanks. Leave me a note so I'll remember to pay you back for the cleaning." To the office at large, she said, "Well, gang, I'm off on another vote-gathering safari. Keep up the good work. There's no stopping us now."

At four o'clock, Clark asked me to go to the mall to take over the booth for a couple hours. I called home before leaving. Amy answered. "I have to work late," I said. "Do you think you can make something for your dad's dinner?"

"Well, I could call out for pizza."

"There's a package of chicken breasts in the refrigerator. How about baking them?"

"I could pick up Chinese," she suggested.

"Just put them in a dish and turn on the oven. You don't even have to put anything on them."

"But I've got to touch them."

"Yes. Rinse them off and pat them dry with a paper towel. Then maybe sprinkle a little soy sauce on, or Italian dressing. Be creative."

"Now, Mom, you just said all I had to do was put them in a dish."

"Come on, Amy, help me out. You can use the bag of salad in the fridge too."

"All right, all right." In a puckery British voice she said, "And then I'll whip up a cherries jubilee for dessert, dah-ling. And what would you say, my dear, to an unassuming little California fumé blanc, Kenwood perhaps, or Beringer?"

"Thank you, dah-ling," I said, then hung up.

The booth at the mall was decorated with red, blue and white paper streamers. While in it, I wore a white straw hat with a blue and red ribbon trim. On the front of the booth was a picture of Rosie, the one with the broad, teeth-flashing smile. I was talking to a young man and his wife when Faye came along to relieve me. The couple had asked about Rosie's plan for revitalizing their downtown neighborhood.

"Rosie plans to offer low-interest loans and tax incentives for new businesses and renovation of existing ones," I said, "and she'll expand the Neighborhood Pride program into downtown shopping areas and the waterfront. But let me ask you a question. Why are you shopping here instead of downtown, closer to home?"

The two of them looked at each other and then back to me. "I don't feel safe downtown at night," the woman said.

I noticed Faye leaning against the table, pushing her white hat on over her dark brown curls and grinning at me.

"That's one of the biggest problems," I said. "A small business downtown can expect to get burglarized on a regular basis, and the crime level discourages customers. Rosie has a plan that unites the local residents and business owners in creating enclaves of well-lit, well-patrolled, clean shopping areas like small town Main Streets." The idea of an old-fashioned Main Street made them smile. I spoke to them a few minutes more, then sent them away with visions of malt shops and dime stores, certain of their vote. I removed my hat and smoothed my hair.

Faye, who owned a travel agency, did what she could for Rosie's campaign during her slow times and off hours.

"You sound like you know what you're talking about," Faye said, pulling up the folding chair beside me. She slipped her shoes off under the table and sighed.

"Rough day?" I asked.

"No, just the shoes. Obviously, men design women's shoes to keep us in our place. How can we possibly excel at anything with crippled feet?"

I pointed to my sneakers. "You're a modern woman. It's your choice."

She nodded. "Depends. You're married. You can afford to be good to your feet. For those of us still prowling through the jungle hooting out the mating call, all the plumage is strictly necessary."

"Mating call?" I scoffed. "Since when? You've already turned down everybody in town."

She shrugged. "I'm getting old."

Since Faye was exactly the same age I was, I wasn't sure I liked the sound of that, but, at forty, she probably was having to reassess her lifestyle a bit. She'd never been married and had no children. She'd had a lot of fun, at least that's what she claimed, but maybe it was getting tiresome. One thing I did envy about Faye's lifestyle was how much traveling she'd gotten to do. That was the point of being a travel agent, she'd told me. She had been all over the world, literally, to every continent except Antarctica. And now she was talking about that as well, just to complete the list. She had arranged a few trips for me and Jerry, twice to

Mexico, once to Hawaii, but that was the extent of our travels. I wasn't sure why. Lack of energy was about the only excuse I could come up with.

"I guess you can run along now," Faye said, "as much as you seem to be enjoying yourself. Which I am glad to see, by the way. It's put some life into you, this work."

"Yes, so people keep telling me. I'm beginning to wonder if I was one of the living dead before."

Faye laughed. "Well, it wasn't that bad, I'm sure. I just meant that you seem really involved, you know. You sounded just now like you really care about this election."

"Well, I do care, actually. More than we could have guessed. It's Rosie, of course. She's such an inspiration."

"Oh, sure. I told you you'd like her."

Faye had known Rosie about five years. Their businesses brought them into some of the same circles. And, like Rosie, Faye had it in for Kiester. It was, in fact, originally Faye's idea to run Rosie for mayor against him. They had started talking about it almost as soon as he was elected, as a sort of joke at first, but eventually in a serious mode, because the more people she mentioned it to, the more support the idea received. Other people with money and influence started taking up the idea. And now here we were, turning it into reality.

"Are you on your way home, then?" Faye asked.

"I think I'll look around a while. Amy's cooking dinner, more or less. Can I get you something to eat?"

"No, thanks. I stopped at the food court on the way in."

I went browsing through the stores and ended up in Macy's where I tried on several pairs of tailored pants, jackets and blouses, the sort of clothes I had so little of. I'd never needed this kind of smart business clothing before. I guess I didn't really need it now, either, because the attire for the campaigners was extremely casual. But Rosie, with her elegant wardrobe, was making an impression. I ended up buying a wool jacket in a fine, patterned weave of wheat and tan. And, in an adventurous mood, I bought a scarf to accessorize it.

In the full-length mirror of the dressing room, I tried the jacket on over my white blouse, which didn't work at all, so I bought a new blouse as well. Then I surveyed myself in this chic, conservative outfit, pleased with the professional look. I should probably cut my hair shorter, I thought. It was stylish, though, chin-length, nice highlights. But even with this part on the side, the bangs wouldn't stay behind my ear. I was forever sweeping them back. How would you look in a style like Rosie's, I asked myself. Something shorter, neat, requiring no fuss. Or maybe just parted in the middle. I ran my fingers through the center of my hair, creating a new part and adding a little unintentional mess in the process. There, I thought, now I look like Meg Ryan. Well, that wasn't half bad.

Looking at myself in the mirror, I had that feeling again, that gripping anxiety that clutched at my throat. I shook it off and made my purchases.

The next day I wore my new jacket and blouse, my navy slacks, navy pumps and the silk scarf around my neck. I put my makeup on with more than the usual care, not wanting to waste the effect of my new and extravagantly expensive clothes. I parted my hair in the middle and gave it a bit of a tousled look with some gel. When Jerry came in to say good-bye, he said, "You look great. A special occasion?"

"Well, you know," I said, "meeting the public. Representing the candidate. Want to make a good impression."

"You've changed your hair."

"A little."

"Lookin' good," Jerry said approvingly.

I realized I was not intending to be out meeting the public this particular day, but if a girl's got new clothes, she's going to wear them.

Rosie, in a rush as usual, came through the office twice during the morning. The second time, as she signed some papers on Clark's desk, she glanced at me and smiled. "Jean, you look very nice today."

"Thank you," I replied, pleased that, as busy as she was, she'd noticed.

"Yes, I love that jacket. And I like your hair that way. Really cute."

I felt a hot rush in the face. A blush? How silly.

Clark got off the phone and said, "Rosie, the public employees' union has endorsed you."

"All right!" Rosie said, slapping his outstretched hand. "I'm a locomotive." She chugged into her office, pulling the handle on an invisible whistle, euphoric. It was contagious, Rosie's joy. We were all grinning.

Saturday I took Amy with me to Elmwood Park to work the crowd that came out for the free lunch and jazz concert we sponsored. Faye, under a chef's hat, grilled hotdogs. I sent Amy to pass out buttons while I gave out slogan balloons to the children. Because it was the weekend, we had several volunteers available to work the crowd. Ginny, the UPS driver, had signed on to work, as well as Clark, and a couple of others.

Five musicians sat on a portable stage under the oak trees, belting out Dixieland jazz. Rosie, in one of our white straw hats, climbed up on stage with them during their third number. She spoke into the microphone. "Welcome, everybody," she said. "I'm Rosie Monroe and I'm running for mayor! Don't worry, I'm not going to make any speeches. I just wanted you to know who's paying for lunch. Enjoy the music and be sure to vote."

After Rosie replaced the microphone, the bandleader took her by the arm and handed her his saxophone, entreating her to play. She waved him away, but he persisted, and a few moments later she was blowing away along with the others through a bouncy rendition of "Brown Sugar Baby."

"Wow, she's really good," I said to Faye.

"Yes, I've heard her play before. I think she might even be in a band." Faye served up another hotdog, chips and beans lunch to a potential voter.

Ginny walked up while Rosie was still playing, followed by a girl in jeans, a denim vest with a black tank top under it, an extremely close-cropped, boyish haircut and a multitude of earrings in each of her ears. "Hi, guys," said Ginny, her ponytail threaded through an Oakland A's baseball cap. "Sorry I'm late. Give me something to do. I brought my girlfriend, Aura, to help out."

Faye and I looked at each other with the same implied question about the name Aura, then Faye said, "You could really help if you'd do a little clean up detail, like empty the trash cans and keep the picnic tables clear. Put on these T-shirts, though, okay?" Faye indicated the Rosie for Mayor T-shirts at the end of the table.

"Okay," Ginny said, looking through the shirts for a couple of good fits.

After her musical number, Rosie arrived at the lunch table, excited and wide-eyed. "How are my little soldiers?" she asked, slinging an arm around Faye and giving her a squeeze.

"We're slinging hash, General," Faye said. "Bribing the voters with beans."

"How about slinging some my way? I'm starved." We made up a plate for Rosie while she greeted the people around us. She gave Ginny a friendly hug and, from where I stood, it looked like she was getting introduced to Aura.

"What's Ginny's connection with Rosie anyway?" I asked.

"She told me they've been friends for years. I don't know the circumstances. But Rosie has friends everywhere. And it's a good thing. That's how elections are won."

Ginny and Aura pulled on T-shirts and both of them immediately rolled the sleeves all the way up, baring their arms. As they left, Rosie returned to us and sat at the end of the table to eat. I noticed that she ate like she did everything else, with gusto and without self-consciousness. "Do you think we'll have enough stuff?" she asked, chomping off a third of her hotdog with one bite.

"We might have to replenish the chip supply," Faye said. "I can send Clark to the store."

"This was a great idea," I said. "A lot of people showed up."

Rosie wiped her hands on a paper napkin. "People will always show up for a free lunch. We'll have to do this again."

As Rosie finished her meal, Amy came by wearing Rosie buttons on both ears and five of them down the front of her T-shirt. While walking toward us, she was looking at her phone where her thumbs were moving at the speed of light, texting. I saw that she was approaching a sidewalk and called her name, hoping she'd look where she was going, but it did no good because, of course, she had her ear buds on and was listening to music as well. Without looking up from her phone, she somehow detected the sidewalk and stepped onto and over it without incident. She looked up only when she had come within a few inches of the grill.

I put my arm around her, saying, "Rosie, I'd like you to meet my daughter Amy."

Rosie shook her hand. "It's good to meet you, Amy. Your mother is one of the most ferocious campaigners I've ever seen, so I'm not surprised she's gotten you into the act."

"I've been passing out buttons," Amy said. "This is so cool. Everybody's really up, so hyped. Mom, too. Just look at her. I hope you win, Rosie." Amy suddenly changed voices, deeper and deadly serious. "I'm sick of those fat-bellied, bald-headed old men sitting around farting and belching and spewing up garbage. What we need is a woman at the helm, a woman, I say, to lead us into a brighter tomorrow." Amy looked skyward. "A woman with vision and clarity of purpose," she said, hitting the air with her fist, "a woman…who can play the saxophone!"

Rosie snorted. "Want a job as a speechwriter?" she asked.

Amy beamed.

# Chapter Three

Monday afternoon six of us were working at the office, gearing up for the final weeks before the election. Although time was growing short, none of us were worried about that. The election was in the bag, so the sooner it happened, the better.

In one corner of the room, a large flat-screen television was turned on, as usual, to the local community access station. Someone I didn't recognize, some young woman, was interviewing Holloway, the district attorney, at the courthouse. I was on the phone with a potential voter, so I wasn't listening to what Holloway was saying, which I probably wouldn't have anyway, since he was supporting Kiester. As I understood it, those two were cronies from way back.

Just as I hung up the phone, I heard Holloway say, "Hugh's position on these issues is well known, but I don't know what we can say for sure about Rosie. Voters have got to be wary of the scary liberal politics typical of the homosexual community, and therefore likely to be held by Rosie, who, being a lesbian, would have to be sympathetic to those views to some degree."

I gasped. Then I looked around to see if anyone else was listening. Faye was. She had stopped in the middle of the room and was staring at the TV, immobile. Clark was trying to clear a paper jam from the printer.

"Clark! Clark!" Faye yelled, pointing at the TV. Clark turned and looked, as did everyone else in the room.

"But Rosie will have to answer that question herself," Holloway continued. "I can't say I really know her position on amnesty for illegals."

"What?" Clark asked, annoyed. "What's the problem? Rosie's position on that is—"

"No!" Faye practically hollered. "He just called Rosie a lesbian."

Clark looked from one to the other of us and then said, "What? Why did he say that? Some kind of slur? Like dyke? Did he say 'dyke'?"

"No. It wasn't like that." Faye shook her head.

"It was very matter-of-factly," I said. "He said 'lesbian,' like a member of the homosexual community, like that. As if it was just something everybody knew."

Clark looked completely baffled. "I don't get it. I mean... This is absurd! What the hell did he say that for? What kind of game are they playing? I've known Rosie for nearly ten years, and—" Clark had gotten red in the face.

"Where is she?" Faye asked.

"Fund-raising luncheon," Clark said, still looking stunned. He shook his head. "This is just some pathetic trick. They have no way to attack us, so now they're making stuff up. This will come back to haunt him. His smear campaign will bring him down once and for all!"

"I'm confused," I said. "What does homosexuality have to do with amnesty for illegal aliens?"

"Nothing!" Clark snapped. "Which makes it pretty obvious what they're up to."

All of us were probably thinking the same thoughts then, dredging up our knowledge of Rosie's personal life. She had been divorced long ago, had no regular male companion that we had heard of or seen. But no woman either. One evening I'd seen her escorted by a nice-looking, silver-haired man who opened the car door for her and walked into the restaurant with her arm in his. I had paid attention because I was curious, because Rosie never said a word about her personal life. Not like the other candidates who trotted out as many children and grandchildren as they could gather around them to show the world they had "family values," as though procreating were proof enough.

We'd all been given a biographical sheet so we could answer questions from voters. It listed the basic facts about Rosie's life. Place of Birth: Portland, Oregon. Age: 51. Years of Residence in Weberstown: 30. Education: BA in Music, MA in Art History from UC Berkeley. MBA from the University of the Pacific. Marital Status: Divorced. Children: None. There was then a long list of organizations of which she was a member.

Wow, I thought, there's no information on that sheet that would tell you anything about her. It was useless. It was worse than useless.

The phone rang and I answered. "Hi, Jean," said the caller, "this is Gary from the *Sentinel*. I'd like to talk to Rosie."

"She's not in. Can I take a message?"

"I've just heard that Mr. Holloway of the district attorney's office claims that Rosie's gay." I groaned silently and gave Clark a pleading look. "Can you confirm Holloway's statement?"

"Who is that?" Clark snapped. I handed him the phone, relieved to give it up. "Gary from the *Sentinel*. About the ..." I pointed at the television.

Into the phone, Clark said, "It's a dirty trick. I don't want to see anything about it in print, do you understand? It's a vicious lie. If you print this, we'll sue." After surrendering the phone, he stood quaking with rage. "Call Rosie's mobile," he said to Faye. "Tell her I'm on my way to pick her up. Don't make any statement about this to anybody. And don't let anyone in. I'll be back as soon as I can. Then Rosie will straighten this out."

After Clark had gone, I sat with Faye to wait. "What do you

think?" I asked.

Faye shook her head, looking perplexed. "It's ridiculous. Like Clark, I've known Rosie for years. I've seen her dozens of times out, you know, at events."

"Business-related events?" I asked.

"Yeah, sure."

"You don't socialize with her, then. I mean, you aren't really friends, personal friends?"

Faye looked confused. "Jean, I've never thought about it that way. She was just Rosie." Faye was obviously searching her memory. "I've arranged trips for her, business trips. At public events, she was usually alone or with other people who were part of the group. No, I have never been out to lunch with her, just me, and have never been to her house. I guess, if you think about it, our relationship has been pretty much business only. I never felt that way because she's so friendly, you know. You feel like you know her. When it comes right down to it, I guess I don't know anything at all about her private life. Rosie is so involved in the public life that I just figured that was her private life, that it was all the same thing."

"Well, so what if she is a lesbian," I said. "What difference does it make?"

"Looks like it makes a difference to Clark. He seems pretty upset about it. I guess he figures it will lose us votes. I mean, think about people like your parents. It would make a difference to them, wouldn't it? I know it would make a difference to mine."

"I don't know," I said, thinking about my parents and how this subject wasn't something we talked about. I really couldn't say if they would change their vote over something like this.

I proceeded to deal with several callers who wanted me, when I told them Rosie was out, to confirm or deny the rumor. After an hour of avoiding saying anything, I got a call from someone asking, "What do you know about Rosie and Catherine Gardiner?"

"Nothing," I said truthfully. I had never heard of her. Was this another land mine about to explode? "Does anybody know who Catherine Gardiner is?" I asked after hanging up.

"I do," Faye said. "Why?"

"They're asking about her now."

Faye bit her lip. "Oh, no."

"Who is she?"

"She's a poet, a radical lesbian poet. Lives in San Francisco, I believe, or Marin County."

"Do they know each other?"

Faye shrugged. "If the press has made that connection, they must. Oh, God, the walls are tumbling down."

I felt frantic, like I should find a way to save the day. But what could I do? Rosie would know what to do. She would march in and take charge and blast Kiester right back with both barrels.

Clark finally came back with Rosie. They came in from the alley through the back door. Rosie seemed calm, but serious and distant, subdued in a way I'd never seen her. I told her about the Catherine Gardiner question. She closed her eyes and took a deep breath. When she opened them again, she said, "That woman lives for controversy. She doesn't have a subtle bone in her body. If they talk to her, we're doomed."

"Can you talk to her first?" I asked, frantically trying to keep up, to understand what we were doing, what the situation was.

Rosie tossed up her hands. "I can try. Please, no one leave. I'd like to speak to you before you go." Rosie went into her office to make the call.

"I guess it's true," Faye said fatalistically. "I had no idea. One has to wonder, then, how *they* knew."

Clark shrugged. "She didn't say anything. Just sort of caved in when I told her. It appears to be true."

My head was whirling. I sat, trying to force myself to think clearly. How big a disaster was this?

Clark, his tone accusatory, asked, "Did anybody here know about this?" No one admitted it if they did. We were all silent then, waiting for the other shoe to drop. The phone rang, but nobody answered it. We just sat around like deflated balloons.

I saw the lighted button on Rosie's line go out. She was off the phone. When she returned, she leaned against the edge of a desk, facing us squarely, her expression solemn. "As you all know," she said, "the Kiester camp has just outed me. The press has seized upon the news and will no doubt make it a headliner. They're working very fast, too fast, in fact, to head off." Rosie stopped, took a deliberate breath, then said, "I don't know how they're getting their information, but they've got a reliable source. They've contacted a friend of mine, a woman known for her radical politics. My association with her will be damaging." Rosie lowered her gaze, looked at the floor. Without the characteristic sparkle in her features, the lines on her face no longer added interest. They just made her look tired.

"I'm truly sorry about this," she said. "I know how hard you've worked. I hope you know how much I appreciate it." I wanted to comfort her but held my place. It was obvious how gut-wrenching this was for her.

After a moment of silence with glances all around the staff, Clark said, "You should have told me. We could have prepared, linked you up with a man, for God's sake. We could have dealt with it up front somehow. Even if you had been out from the beginning, we would have had the upper hand. There are so many ways this would not have been a problem. This way, you just handed them a bomb and said use it at your convenience."

Rosie faced him. "I've always tried to keep my personal and professional lives separate. This is just so irrelevant." She paused. "I didn't think it would come out. It's not generally known, and I know Kiester didn't know. Someone's tipped him off." Rosie shook her head. "I didn't think he would go this low in any case. This is a conservative town. I didn't think the public would be comfortable with the subject. I mean, why bring it up? I'm single, nobody lurking in the wings. I thought it was worth the risk just not making an issue of it."

"But would I have thought so?" asked Clark. "Would I have busted my ass trying to get you elected if you'd told me this up front? It's completely naïve to think that you can keep your personal life out of politics."

She looked contrite. Rosie on the defensive was an uncomfortable sight. "Yes, you're right," she said. "I'm sorry to all of you. I'm afraid this is going to hurt us."

"You're damned right it's going to hurt us," Clark said. "It's going to kill us. To successfully run a lesbian for mayor in this town would be tough under any circumstances. But to have it sprung on the voters three weeks before the election, well, there's just no way. They're going to feel like you betrayed them."

"Yes, I know. Kiester's going to win after all."

"You're giving up?" I asked, astonished.

Rosie looked at me sympathetically, as though I were the victim somehow. "Jean, we've lost."

"But we haven't lost yet," I said. "This morning you were the hands-down favorite. And we don't even know what the media will say. They might not say anything. And even if they do, it might not matter that much to people."

Rosie smiled sadly, affectionately. "Jean, you don't know where you're living. We may be just a hundred miles from San Francisco, but we may as well be on another planet. The people here have their roots in farming. They're conservative and they have traditional views. In any election ever held here where an initiative was on the ballot for gay rights, for abortion, for any of the typically liberal issues, every county in the Central Valley has always voted on what I would call the unenlightened side. That's just a fact as irrefutable as knowing that California as a whole will always vote Democratic. This city isn't ready to elect an openly-gay mayor. But, okay, we'll watch the news before we throw in the towel. It's almost five. Kiester will know how to spin this to his advantage. There's no way he's going to let it go."

"You should have told me," Clark muttered again.

Rosie was right. It was going to be a headliner. We didn't have long to wait before her photograph was displayed on the screen along with the repetition of Holloway's remark. Then they played a brief interview with Catherine Gardiner, who slid past their questions, saying, "Sure, I know Rosie. She deserves the job. I'd vote for her myself if I could, if I lived there, in that town. What's that town she lives in again?"

At this, I noticed the briefest of smiles slide over Rosie's lips. Catherine Gardiner was a sharp-featured, wiry woman. She was wearing an absurd, ankle-length denim skirt and a peasant blouse. Her long, wind-blown hair was dark gray, caught on one side haphazardly in a silver barrette.

"How would you characterize your relationship?" asked the reporter.

"As a friendship," Catherine answered, sounding as though she'd said exactly what she'd been told to say. Her tone was sly, faintly mocking.

"Ms. Gardiner," he persisted, "you're well known for your radical views. Does Ms. Monroe share these?"

"Oh, no." Catherine laughed ironically. "Not in the least. Rosie builds things. I tear them down. We couldn't be more different."

Next on was Hugh Kiester, pretending innocence. "It was an unfortunate comment," he said. "I had a little talk with Holloway about it just a while ago. I think we should stick to the issues and stay away from personal remarks. If Rosie wants to keep her homosexuality under wraps, she should have the right to do so. Although some voters may feel they have a right to know such things, I don't happen to agree."

"The bastard," Clark snarled.

"Rosie Monroe was unavailable for comment today," the announcer said. "And none of her staff would confirm or deny the rumor."

Rosie switched off the set. "Well, there it is."

"It isn't that bad," Clark said. "Your friend did fine. There was no confirmation there. They don't have anything. I'll arrange a press conference for you for tomorrow. You'll deny it and we'll put this to bed."

Rosie shook her head. "I can't do that."

"Why not? It might save this campaign for us."

"I can't do it because it'd be a lie."

"Dammit, Rosie, you can't always tell the truth in politics.

36

You do what's best. Anything that can get you elected is best in this case. Deny it. You said yourself that you're not involved with anyone, so what difference does it make?"

"It won't work, Clark. They'll keep prying. They'll find something."

"What will they find? Come on, Rosie. Other than this poet woman, who apparently won't squeal, what will they find?"

Rosie, exasperated, glanced around the room. When her eyes met mine, I saw how pained they were. "Clark," she said. "I'm fifty-one years old. I've led a full life. If they look for it, they'll find something. I'll talk to the press tomorrow, but I won't lie."

"You're not going to admit it? Do you know how bad that will look? It will look like you've been hiding it. Hiding being gay is worse than being gay."

"I don't know what I'm going to do. Arrange the press conference, will you, please? Faye, do you think you could find out what was on the other stations? If they had anything more?"

"Sure. I'll give you a report first thing in the morning on my way to work."

Faye said good-bye, and after Clark made a few phone calls, he left too, obviously disgruntled. Everyone else was gone by then except Rosie, who was in her office with the door closed. I decided to see if she wanted to talk. Most of the time she seemed awfully tough, but people are like that in their public roles. I knocked on her door. "Come in," she called. She sat at her desk, typing on her laptop. She looked up at me over the top of reading glasses.

"Hi," I said. "Everyone's gone."

"Except you."

"What are you doing?"

"Trying to find a way to say nothing. It's not one of my talents. I tend to get right to the point and say what I think. This time, that wouldn't help much. Have you got any ideas?"

"You're still the best candidate, Rosie." I sat in the straight-backed chair next to her desk. "You're still honest and hard-working. People won't change their minds about that."

Rosie shook her head. "Jean, wake up. I'm pleased to see that you haven't changed *your* mind, but you're not typical. None of my attributes will matter to a certain sector of the public when they hear about this. Those people won't vote for a lesbian, period. If they found out that Christ was gay, they'd become Jews. Oh, sure, I might get a few new votes from the gays and lesbians, but it won't even out. People vote in illogical ways, based on emotions, not facts. You must know that by now."

I nodded. When I looked at her again, she was staring directly at me, her eyes placid. "It really doesn't matter to you?" she asked quietly.

"I don't think so," I said, flattered that she seemed concerned about my opinion. "Your sexual orientation, it's a private issue. It has nothing to do with your qualifications for the job."

"I'm glad to hear you say that. And I think that's the answer. That's the only statement I can make tomorrow. Thanks, Jean. Now get on home to your family. There's no point in putting in overtime here anymore."

"Don't give up, Rosie," I said. She managed a small smile. I left, feeling angry and confused. Was it possible, I wondered, that Rosie could lose the election over this? The Kiester campaign apparently thought so. Otherwise, they wouldn't have played this card. Rosie seemed to think so too, and she knew the political climate of this town better than I did.

By the time I got home, I was overcome with fury toward Kiester. If he had been within my grasp, I would have strangled him. Instead, Jerry met me at the back door with a hug. I was home late, I realized, and hadn't called. But he had heard the news. "I'm sorry," he said. "It must have been a pretty big shock." Jerry led me into the family room where Amy was watching television. They sat on either side of me on the sofa.

"It's true?" Amy asked. "She's gay?"

I merely nodded.

"Go figure," Jerry said. "Oh, well, it just goes to show you. All politicians are phonies."

"What do you mean?" I asked.

"She was pretending to be something she wasn't," he said.

"She wasn't pretending to be anything. She was claiming to be the best candidate for mayor. That's what she was. Is."

"Well, okay, so she wasn't pretending to be straight, but she was keeping a pretty big secret."

"It's irrelevant," I said testily.

Jerry loosened his comforting hold on me. "Okay, okay."

Later, when it was time for the ten o' clock news, I said to Amy, "Switch to channel eleven. I want to see if they have anything to say about Rosie." The late report was similar to the earlier one, except that the reporter questioning Kiester suggested that the rumor was politically motivated, intentional and sanctioned by Kiester himself.

"Of course it was," I said, disgusted.

"That's insulting," Kiester said. "I've been running a fair, issue-oriented campaign. I've known Rosie for years and I like her. She's a good woman. I wouldn't sanction something like this. But it's the sort of thing that's bound to happen. There are obviously people who know about Rosie. Comments are made, often quite innocently. There was nothing malicious about Holloway's remark. It was just unconsidered, said in the wrong place and the wrong time. The way to have avoided this sort of thing would have been for Rosie to be open about it up front."

"He's accusing her of deceit," I said, feeling frustrated.

Then they showed the tape again of Catherine Gardiner's statement. She had apparently said nothing more, but they didn't let that stop them. They dug up an NPR interview from last year and played it over a publicity still of her. They had obviously been looking all evening for something controversial. She was asked her opinion of abstinence as a legitimate part of sex education. Her answer: "Yes, I think abstinence is a valid option to teach high school girls, at least the ones with underdeveloped sex drives. I would also advocate teaching them how to pleasure themselves, which is ultimately the safest form of sex and, for straight women, probably the best they're going to get anyway."

Amy's mouth dropped open and she immediately went into

her Britney Spears imitation, saying, "Oh, my gawd, y'all! That's just not right."

Jerry looked at me accusingly, as if I were responsible, somehow. Well, that wasn't going to help our position much, I thought, regardless of how irrelevant it was. Strange woman, this Gardiner. What was the attraction there for Rosie, I wondered.

"Honey," Jerry said cautiously, "Are you going to keep working on Rosie's campaign?"

I stared at him. "Why are you asking me that?"

"Well, we can certainly vote for her if you want, but I don't want to be seen as a gay rights advocate or something. That isn't one of our issues."

"This isn't about gay rights. What kind of a stupid thing is that to say?" I marched out of the room, angry again. If my own husband was no longer in Rosie's camp, who would be? She was right, apparently, to be pessimistic. People in this town wouldn't vote for a lesbian.

# Chapter Four

I accompanied Rosie to her news conference, waiting inside while she spoke to a half dozen reporters on the steps of her office building. There were some out-of-towners among them, I noticed, based on their camera logos. Our mayoral campaign had apparently gained the attention of neighboring cities. Rosie was dressed smartly, as usual, but her demeanor was diminished.

"Were you and the poet Catherine Gardiner ever lovers?" one reporter asked.

"My private life is not an issue in this campaign," Rosie said. "It has no bearing on my qualifications as a candidate. The insinuation that I've been dishonest by not discussing my sex life is absurd. Has anyone asked the other candidates to produce a list of people they've slept with?"

I watched them hound her and hated them profusely. They were destroying everything we had built up with this heartless assault. She continued her refusal to discuss the only subject they were interested in. It was a short interview. After she had retreated inside, I walked with her to her office, wordless. Though she had stood firm and confident before the cameras moments before, she was a wreck now. She sat dumbly in her desk chair, staring into her lap where her hands lay immobile.

"Rosie," I asked, "will you be okay?"

She didn't answer for a moment, then said, quietly, "It's over, Jean."

"What about the sympathy vote? You're being badly treated."

She laughed shortly. "People are sympathetic with people they can identify with. Besides, it's not sympathy I want to put me in the mayor's office."

"What difference does it make, as long as you get there?"

She continued to stare into her hands, wordless. I stood by the side of her chair and put an arm around her shoulder and held her, thinking how wide-ranging this woman was. A few days ago I thought I'd known her, then had discovered I didn't. Now, did I know her better? Or even less?

"No, it's all over," she said, "all the work and money and hope, gone. This is so frustrating. It's going to be a challenge to get through the rest of this campaign, to put a brave face on it. I feel so badly about letting everybody down."

"But you didn't let us down," I said. "You did everything right. It's those Kiester bastards that did it. Those bastards knew they couldn't win in a fair fight."

She looked at me and smiled sadly. "Jean, you're something of a surprise to me."

"How do you mean?" I asked, releasing her.

"Well, Faye described you as a bored empty nester who needed something to do, who didn't know anything about politics, but could answer a phone and hand out leaflets. Over the past couple of months you've unfolded into a strong, driven woman with remarkable organizational and interpersonal skills, with a tenacious public spirit, a fierce loyalty, a personality that I would never have described as Faye did. Was she putting me on? Does she even know you?"

Embarrassed, I said nothing for a moment. "That doesn't

sound like me," I finally said. "You're exaggerating. Faye's known me since high school."

"I'm not exaggerating," Rosie said seriously. "You underestimate yourself. Although you haven't been with us long, I believe that your being here has made a significant difference. I've watched you soaking everything in like a sponge and somehow instinctively knowing what to do with the information you absorb. You're somebody who can get things done. That might not sound like a great talent, but believe me, it is. It's valuable and it's rare." She paused and smiled warmly at me. "I know it's a meaningless offer, but I'd like you to take over my campaign. Clark's quit. He said it's because I wasn't totally honest with him, but I think it's also because he's not comfortable with the sexuality issue. Will you do it?"

Shocked, I asked, "Me?"

"Well, you needn't be flattered because you'd be minding an empty store. You'd be the clean-up crew."

"Okay," I heard myself say. "Sure, I'll do it. Imagine, me a campaign manager."

I was ecstatic. Jerry wasn't as happy for me as I'd thought he'd be. "Great," he said. "Manager for a loser." Jerry's sarcasm toward Rosie, which had appeared as soon as he'd learned she was gay, angered and embarrassed me. He wasn't the only one who had changed, though. The climate I'd been working in for the past couple of months flip-flopped overnight. The attitude at headquarters was defeat-oriented, and the new polls bore out that pessimism. Rosie's popularity had plummeted. There were other indicators too. Some of the people I talked to were openly hostile. One man on the street even muttered "filthy dyke" as he walked away. He was referring to me. And not only did people withdraw their support, but they made a point of being nasty about it, making sure we knew why. I didn't tell Rosie about the unpleasantness. I didn't have to. She knew how it was. We had lost several of our volunteers too, for various reasons, including sheer disappointment. Or, like Clark, they felt misled because Rosie had kept this fact about herself from them. Ginny, however, was still on board, and I realized that I wasn't surprised about that.

Rosie kept her previously-made appointments, but she made it clear that she didn't want to load up her calendar. She was winding down, merely playing out the hand. In public, she remained the upbeat candidate, but she no longer hid her frustration, at least not from me.

"Every time I walk out that door," she said, "somebody asks me about my sexual orientation. They don't want to talk about crime anymore. Now they want to know if I support same-sex marriage legislation. What the hell does that have to do with being mayor of this city?"

It became clear to me as these issues arose and were discussed that Rosie had adopted a strategy long ago for protecting herself from the homophobic society she inhabited. It was the way she always operated, completely separating her private and public lives. For most of us, that wouldn't happen because there was no need for that kind of privacy. Personal privacy, in fact, was becoming a sort of archaic notion, especially with the prevalence of cell phones, but for someone whose private life had the potential for bringing condemnation, it was probably a natural adaptation and had worked well for her up until now. Having operated that way for so long, she found it truly frustrating to have to deal with the public idea of that private self, with how her two separate worlds were now merging.

That frustration was no more apparent than when other people were dragged through that previously locked gate. One morning I took a call from a woman identifying herself only as "Sue."

"There are reporters asking me questions," she said. "What am I supposed to tell them?" Her voice was quiet, shy.

"Say as little as possible," I advised her. "Just say she's a friend and keep it at that. You don't have to answer anything."

When Rosie came in, I told her about Sue's call.

"How do they find these things out?" she asked, disgusted. "I've already lost the election, so what's the point? Why are they out there harassing my friends?" Rosie stood in the center of the room, looking distraught, watching me. "I can't imagine what's going on in your mind," she said, "what kind of picture you're getting of my life. You're probably wondering if droves of them are going to start oozing out of the woodwork." She wanted to know if I was judging her. She didn't wait for a reply. She walked toward her office, saying, "I think I'll give Sue a call. She's not very good at standing up to people."

It intrigued me that Rosie had kept on good terms with her ex-lovers. They seemed to respect her, the two that I knew about, and she referred to them as her "friends."

Thankfully, no story appeared about Sue. But there were other disturbing reactions.

Three days after Rosie's press conference, I came home to find the banner in my front yard vandalized. In the hand that was raised into a wave, someone had drawn an oversized and finely-detailed dildo in red paint. Standing beside my car and without a thought in my head, I pushed my fist into the driver's-side window. It shattered in the frame into a spiderweb of broken glass. I stood in the driveway, shaking all over, pain shooting through my hand. A moment later, Jerry drove up. He saw the banner and then the window. Rushing over to me, he said, "Are you okay?"

I moved my fingers tentatively and nodded to him. He went over to uproot the stakes of the desecrated banner. I walked into the house, then sat at the computer and wrote a letter to the editor of the *Sentinel*, the knuckles of my hand stinging. When Jerry came in, I kept writing and didn't greet him.

"That was a stupid thing to do," he muttered. "I'm surprised you didn't break your hand." He called a glass shop and arranged to have the window replaced the next day, Saturday.

"Thank you for taking care of that," I said. "You're right. It was a stupid thing to do."

I called Gary at the *Sentinel* and told him I was sending him a letter and wanted to see it in tomorrow's edition.

"I'll see what I can do, Jean. Hey, sorry about…you know."

"Yes, I know."

Saturday morning Jerry brought the newspaper to the

breakfast table, having read my letter to the editor. "Who wrote this for you?" he asked. "Rosie?"

I took the paper from him. "Nobody wrote it for me. I wrote it myself."

"Really?"

"Yes. Why do you ask?"

"It doesn't sound like you. I guess I've never read anything you wrote before, except personal letters. It's very articulate."

"Your compliments are really backhanded," I said.

"Don't you think you're getting a little carried away, Jeannie? If this is a sincere appeal, you're going to be very disappointed when she loses."

I didn't answer him. Instead, I read my letter to see how it sounded in print.

*I'm writing out of appalling disbelief at the reaction of the citizens of my city to the rumor put out by the Kiester campaign that Rosie Monroe is gay. Before that rumor broke, she was leading in the mayoral race by twenty points, her lead climbing daily. And rightly so. Few people have done more for Weberstown than Rosie has. She's worked hard to make this a better place to live for all of us. She's worked largely without recognition or any thought of recompense. She entered politics reluctantly, pushed into it by those who know how much she can benefit this town.*

*We are all aware by now of some of Rosie's accomplishments. She almost single-handedly saved the adult literacy program from shutting down last year. Her Women in Business directorship has allowed that organization to feed and clothe over one hundred homeless children this year alone. Her work with the Weberstown Arts Commission has contributed a renewed energy to the fine arts in our community, and the beautiful new portrait gallery of the museum wouldn't exist without her efforts. I could go on and on, but why bother? Most of us already know Rosie as one of our most valuable citizens. Why have so many chosen to ignore all that now? Because some low-handed, desperate politician whose morals must certainly come into question has slandered her to get your vote? So, am I to conclude that the sleaziest of political shenanigans has worked?*

*Rosie is not an experienced politician. She's a humanitarian and public servant by nature. She's the kind of person I would be proud to have as mayor. I will be very much ashamed if we allow the despicable political machinery of this town to sway us from the right choice. Rosie deserves your support. As an ordinary, middle-class citizen, wife and mother of two, my vote goes unhesitatingly to Rosie.*

"Not bad," I said. "Looks even better in print." Jerry was watching me, I saw, warily.

He finished his coffee and stood. "I've got to go get that window replaced." He took hold of my hand and rubbed his thumb lightly over the most obvious bruise. "What are your plans?"

"I've called Faye. She's giving me a lift to the office, so I won't need your car."

Faye and I arrived at the office before Rosie who, a few minutes later, came in grinning and holding a copy of the newspaper. "Jean, you clever girl," she said. "What a beautiful letter. So sincere, so full of earnest appeal. And the part about being a wife and mother—brilliant!"

"Well, it's true," I pointed out.

"Yes, so it is." She looked momentarily sheepish. "Doesn't quite capture you, though, does it? Well, it's a strong hit at the conscience of the voters, and I thank you, but I don't think it's worth throwing the punch."

"I'm just so angry," I said.

"I know you are. Get over it. It won't help. But I appreciate the effort."

"We need to find a way to deal with this issue, put it behind us and move on," I said. "Your refusal to answer questions about it may be keeping it alive."

"What do you suggest?"

"I don't know. I'll try to think of something."

Monday morning, we got a call from a representative of the National Gay and Lesbian Alliance. Rosie agreed to take it and was on the phone about fifteen minutes.

"What did they want?" I asked when she emerged from her

office.

"They wanted to take up my cause. They wanted to launch a media blitz, put my story in newspapers, magazines, that sort of thing, put a face to the problem. You know, isn't it a travesty that this kindly old grandmother couldn't get elected as her hometown mayor because she's a lesbian."

"Kindly old grandmother?" I asked.

"Okay, I'm exaggerating. But you get the idea."

"What did you say?"

"I said no, thank you." Rosie sat at the empty desk next to mine. "I know that such stories need to be printed, and I considered it, but that sort of publicity wouldn't be good for this town. I don't want our city to be portrayed in the media as a symbol of homophobia."

"I don't understand why you're so concerned about a city that's treating you this way."

"I know you're angry right now, but the town's been good to me, Jean. I've always known that this wasn't San Francisco, or even Sacramento. This town is having its share of growing pains these days. Sexual orientation is not the only issue that these people are struggling with. Sometimes we've had a tough challenge to convince people that the town needs things like an arts commission, for instance, or that it should pay for a museum exhibit when crime and unemployment rates are high. They don't understand the connection. I thought I could really do something for this city as mayor."

She was more forgiving than I was in the light of all of the insults we were encountering, but it occurred to me that Rosie, having been gay all her life, had a lot more experience with homophobia than I did and had probably learned a little bit about how to let it roll off. That was not an easy life, I imagined. It was certainly not the path of least resistance. Nothing like mine, in fact. I had followed the easiest possible path. I had married my last boyfriend out of high school and had easily flowed through twenty years of normalcy without anyone ever challenging or questioning me, least of all myself.

Rosie's next scheduled interview was on a local cable TV talk show hosted by David Foster. She asked me to cancel it.

"Why?" I asked.

"I'm tired of evading the issue of my sexual orientation. Foster is bound to ask me about it. He's not a particularly kind interviewer."

"Maybe you should quit evading the issue," I said.

"What do you mean?"

"Answer his questions."

She said nothing, appearing unsure.

"What have we got to lose?" I asked.

"Let me think about it. There's not much fight left in me, Jean. I'm tired. A couple more weeks and we can get on with our lives. After this, I'm going to try to rest up for a while. How about you?"

I stuttered. "Uh, I don't know." Soon it would all be over. The idea panicked me. I'd have to find something else to do. "My daughter gave me a copy of the course catalog from her college," I said. "I've been looking through it, trying to decide on a practical, job-oriented class. I'm just not sure what would make sense." I produced the catalog and handed it to Rosie.

"Something to do with business, I guess." Rosie flipped through the pages. "How about beginning economics? That's a practical, useful starting point."

"I don't know. I think money matters are beyond me."

Rosie stared. "Jean!" She picked up the ledger on the edge of my desk. "What do you call this? For a month, you've been keeping the books for my campaign. This is money matters."

"But all you need to know to do that is how to add and subtract."

She frowned and put the ledger down. "I wish you'd quit underestimating yourself. It's getting on my nerves." Rosie, irritated with me, went into her office and shut the door.

Was I underestimating myself? I opened the ledger and looked at the columns of handwritten figures. We should be doing this on a computer, I thought. And then I remembered that

I didn't know how. That evening I sat in the den at our computer with one of Jerry's Excel books and Rosie's campaign ledger and began to teach myself how to build a spreadsheet.

Amy came and looked over my shoulder. "What are you doing, Mom?"

"Teaching myself Excel."

"They've got a class at school."

"I can't wait that long. Do you know this, Amy?"

"Nope. Don't know it, don't want to know it and don't care."

When Jerry got home, he answered a couple of questions for me, but became almost immediately impatient. "Now look what you've done," he said, pointing to a cell on the grid. "You've got a circular reference. It won't work that way."

"Instead of trying to make me feel stupid," I said, "why don't you help me?"

"I wasn't trying to make you feel stupid."

"Well, you are."

"Fine. Do it yourself." He left me alone, for which, I realized, I was grateful. His help was tinged with criticism. So I looked up "circular reference" in the online help to see what kind of sin I had committed. After a couple hours, I was beginning to understand how the thing worked. It wasn't so complicated after all. In fact, it worked almost exactly the same as it did on paper.

At ten o' clock, Jerry came in, saying, "Are you going to be playing with that thing all night?"

"I might," I said coldly. He came up and looked over my shoulder. I was filling in figures now, having completed the formulas.

"That's not bad," he said, "for a first attempt." How gracious he was. "May I make a suggestion?"

"Yes."

"Change this formula from a simple addition to a sum. If you need to add another row later, you won't have to recreate the formula."

It was a good piece of advice. I made the change. I'd apparently gained enough of his respect to be worthy of legitimate help.

"And here," he said, "instead of putting the percent into the formula, put it off in a single cell somewhere and reference it as an absolute. That way, you can change the percent in the one cell and it will automatically change in all these formulas."

We continued refining my design until about eleven when Jerry persuaded me to stop and come to bed. I had reached the point where I was satisfied, more than satisfied, with my accomplishment. I'd always assumed such things as spreadsheets were incredibly dense and mysterious. But if you took it a step at a time, patiently, it was pretty straightforward.

"Not to everyone," Jerry said, undressing. "We've got people at work who can only use a spreadsheet that somebody else designed. And that's after months or years. In one evening, you've gone far beyond them. I'm very impressed."

I fell asleep with a great sense of urgency, anxious for tomorrow to come, as though I had been wasting my time, wasting my life. I wanted to do things. I didn't know what, but something, something new, something that mattered. I was only just beginning to understand how much a single individual could accomplish. I had so much time to make up for.

# Chapter Five

Faye and I were working out on side-by-side elliptical trainers at the gym, which we only occasionally managed to do together because of schedule conflicts. After a good forty minutes, we had both had enough.

"We may as well face facts," Faye said, as we walked to the locker room. "Rosie's gonna lose."

"It seems so unfair," I said.

"It makes you feel differently about her, doesn't it?" Faye asked. "Knowing about this. I mean, it shouldn't matter. But it does."

"Yes," I said, not really agreeing with Faye in the way she would assume. "How do you feel different?"

We changed into our street clothes while we talked.

Faye pulled off her tank top and wiped her face off with a towel. "I don't know. I mean, I like Rosie. I think she'd make a first-rate mayor, even president of the country if such things were possible, but I am always aware of…I mean, just knowing that she has sex with women…"

"She doesn't do it in front of you," I said. "She doesn't talk about it."

"I know. But you just know it. It makes a difference."

After we left the gym, I said good-bye to Faye at her car. Knowing about Rosie did make a difference. To me too. But I didn't know how, exactly. Rosie didn't make me uncomfortable. For me, she had become more vulnerable, and perhaps because of that, more approachable emotionally. I felt closer to Rosie. She was no longer super-human. Her Achilles' heel, it seemed, had been exposed. To what instinct of mine did she appeal, I wondered. Maternal? I wanted to take care of her, protect her from harm like I did my children. How peculiar, I thought, that I should think of myself as potential champion to such a powerful woman. Especially since I had no means of protecting her against the wave of hostility washing over her.

Ever since the news of Rosie's association with Catherine Gardiner had been revealed, I'd been looking for some of her poetry. The bookstores in town reported a run on the two volumes which were currently in print. I ended up driving into Sacramento to find them, and, after getting them home, sat alone in the family room reading, searching for something, I didn't know what, some essence of Rosie, perhaps. Most of the poems were unapproachable, too difficult for me, full of social criticism, subtle irony, harsh imagery. There was nothing sentimental about Gardiner's work. There was one poem, though, I read several times. It was called, simply, "Love Poem."

*Come home, ogress, claws bared*
*brown curls bouncing*
*rage in your veins*
*your blue-green veins*
*arms and legs thrashing crashing through walls*
*Come home,*
*scratch out my eyes*
*like a demon like a cat*
*I'll drive a stake through your heart, vampire girl*

*while you suck away my blood, my life*
*I'll drink it in again from your punctured breast.*

A curious sort of love poem, I thought. No, not a sentimental woman. Could this be about Rosie? A younger Rosie with "brown curls"? I tried to imagine Rosie in a rage and thought, yes, she could probably be ferocious "like a demon like a cat."

When Jerry got home and found me reading poetry, he seemed uneasy. "Since when have you been interested in poetry?" he asked. He read the author's name. "Catherine Gardiner? Where have I heard that name before?"

"She's Rosie's ex-lover."

He balked. "Oh, that crazy woman who wants to teach high school girls how to masturbate? Why are you reading her?"

"I'm curious," I said. "Just curious."

"Why?"

"I don't know." I examined my motives privately. I wanted to know more about Rosie, probably. She was still an enigma. I thought her poet lover would have some insight. Maybe I expected a poem entitled "What Rosie's Really Like," written just for me.

"What kind of poems does she write?" Jerry asked suspiciously.

"See for yourself." I handed him the books and went to the kitchen to make dinner, irritated by his questions.

I threw the vegetables into a hot wok with a little more vigor than was necessary, losing some of them on the floor in the process. What are you mad about, I asked myself. What's the problem? Jerry has a right to be suspicious. You've never read a whole book of poetry in your life, you've never written a letter to the editor, you've never shown any interest in learning Excel. If he was behaving in ways you didn't recognize, you'd be suspicious too. I breathed deeply and calmed myself. After disposing of the vegetables from the floor, I dumped a cup of rice into boiling water, covered the pan, and tossed the vegetables around the wok, more gently this time.

Jerry came into the kitchen with one of the books. "You know," he said, "she's good. Sophisticated and subtle. I especially like this one about the girl and the spinning wheel, how she's so careful and proud of her work, but she's oblivious to the thread that she's a part of, the rites of passage and all that, the matriarchal lineage that she's working herself into."

I looked up from my cutting board, startled. "Uh, yes," I said, "I did read that one, but I didn't think about it that much. I didn't even know you liked poetry."

"I used to like it a lot, but it's not the sort of pastime you continue after college, unless you're a teacher or something. I remember especially liking Gerard Manley Hopkins. Have you read him?"

"I don't know. Probably not. I don't think I've read anybody in the way you mean, if it wasn't some English class assignment."

Jerry had an associate's degree. I had no college at all. We had been married as soon as I graduated from high school, so my exposure to poetry did not extend much further than "Listen my children and you shall hear of the midnight ride of Paul Revere."

"Poets can do such clever things with just a few words," Jerry said. "They get just the right angle on a thing and it's like a revelation."

He looked thoughtful, then left the kitchen, reading on. Who was that man, I asked myself. An admirer of poetry? What disarmed me most was the idea that I could learn something new about my husband at this stage of the game. Is this what they meant when they said that if one partner brings something new into the relationship, the other will show new faces as well? They weren't talking about poetry, though. Or maybe they were. The only time in my memory that I could connect Jerry and poetry was when the children were toddlers and he did dramatic readings of poems like "Jabberwocky." I could see him in my mind pacing alongside Bradley's bed, his arms raised. "Beware the Jabberwock, my son! The jaws that bite, the claws that catch!" Then he'd swipe at the air above Bradley's head. Bradley would squeal with delight. I smiled to myself, remembering this.

Jerry had been the storyteller in our family, reading the fairy tales and Dr. Seuss books to Bradley and Amy from a very early age, which is where his nickname of princess came from for Amy. Jerry always changed the name of the princess in the stories to Amy, as in, "The witch grabbed Princess Amy and whisked her off to the deepest, darkest forests of North Umbria." No doubt Jerry was a much better dramatic reader of poetry than I was. That was probably where Amy got that from, after all.

When the vegetables were done, I turned off the stove and went into the living room. Jerry was lying on the couch, reading Gardiner, comfortable in his socks, shorts and T-shirt. I came up behind him and put my arms around his neck. He reached up and took my hand, then tilted his head back to look at me.

"Dinner's ready," I said.

The next day at the office, Faye and I went over the results of the latest e-mail poll conducted by the local news station. Rosie was holding at second place. Mike Garcia was third. Kiester now had a comfortable lead. "It looks like most of Rosie's backing has gone to Kiester," Faye said.

"Yeah, too bad it couldn't have gone to Garcia instead, if it had to go somewhere."

"This is just so damned disappointing. The only reason Rosie agreed to run in the first place was to get rid of Kiester. She had to be pushed into it, really. She didn't seem to want the limelight of public office. Well, now I think I understand that, but I didn't get it at the time. She's worked so hard behind the scenes all these years, I just figured she ought to be right out there, you know, hosting the show. I thought she was the perfect candidate to take him down. Everybody did."

"And she was," I said. "She is, actually, and if there was a little more time, I know we could recover from this setback. People are just reacting to the surprise of it. They would get over it and get back behind the issues. At least most of them would, enough of them would."

"But there isn't any time," Faye said. "They knew what they

were doing, Jean. They had this little firecracker in their pocket all along. They knew just when to light it for maximum impact. All this time we were so sure of ourselves and so cocky and they were sitting over there snickering to themselves, just waiting for the moment." Faye tossed the poll report on the table. "Oh, well, I imagine there's a part of Rosie that will be relieved to return to her comfort zone, although things are bound to be a little different for her after this."

Behind us, stacked into enormous piles, were the thousands of flyers that had yet to be mailed. Nothing much had happened in this office since the big revelation. Everyone seemed certain that there was no chance of winning the race now, so there wasn't much point in working at it.

When the door to the street swung open, Faye and I looked up in unison to see a strikingly beautiful woman stride in. She was elegant and exotic looking with long, thick eyelashes and black hair wound into a spiral on top of her head. She wore white silk pants and a feminine, navy blue Nehru-style jacket with huge gold buttons. She was a petite woman, but her bearing created an undeniable presence. She directed a sharp gaze directly at me as I stood to greet her.

"Where's Rosalind?" she asked authoritatively.

"Hello," I said, stepping out from the table. "I'm Jean, Rosie's campaign manager. Can I help you?"

"I am Dr. Patel," said the woman, her accent subtly English. "And I'm here to see Rosalind. Ah, I see she's in her office."

The woman brushed rapidly past us and let herself into Rosie's office, shutting the door immediately behind her. Faye looked at me, startled.

"Do you know who that is?" I asked.

"Yes," Faye replied, and with dramatic emphasis and a flourish of her arm, she said, "That is Dr. Patel!"

Faye then giggled at herself and I laughed obligingly.

"I only know her by reputation," I said. "She's a huge contributor to Rosie's campaign. I think she's a pediatrician. Has an office in that new medical building over by the hospital."

Faye nodded thoughtfully, then said, "I guess I won't be running into her at Wal-Mart anytime soon then. I'd better get to work, Jean. See you later."

After about fifteen minutes, Rosie and Dr. Patel emerged. "Nothing to worry about, dear," Dr. Patel was saying. "Let's get together as soon as this is over for dinner or something. Why does it always have to be business?"

"You're right, Chandra," Rosie said. The two of them hugged one another familiarly, and then Dr. Patel glanced briefly at me before walking out.

"What was that about?" I asked.

"She's just checking on her investment," Rosie said. "Wanted to see the bottomless pit that she threw all that money down, I guess. Of course, she knew the risk and agreed from the beginning that we shouldn't go public with my sexual orientation. Chandra's a good friend. She was concerned about me, actually, how I'm holding up. And she wanted to know how they found out. I wish I knew."

After Rosie returned to her office, I didn't really know what to do with myself. Tina was at her desk, silently doing something on her computer. No one else was there. Even the television was turned off. We no longer wanted to hear the news, apparently. I ate my lunch while working the newspaper crossword. Rosie came out of her office around noon, saying to Tina, "I'm going over to the printer's to pick up an order." This would be an order for her advertising business, as Rosie had shifted her attention away from the campaign now and back to her regular work.

"Do you want me to go?" Tina asked.

"No, that's okay. I'll get lunch on my way back." Rosie turned to me and glanced at the crossword puzzle, which was almost completed. "You're doing that in ink?"

"I always do."

"Wow!" She shook her head. "Those things are way beyond me. You've got to know far too many obscure words."

"I guess," I said. "But I'm sure you know a lot more obscure words than I do, with your knowledge of arts, literature, languages and all that."

Rosie smiled crookedly at me. "Bildungsroman," she said. It was a challenge.

"Coming-of-age story," I said calmly, pleased with myself.

Rosie laughed and nodded approvingly at me. "You want anything while I'm out, Jean?"

I shook my head. I finished the puzzle and my sandwich, my mind preoccupied with the disaster that this campaign had become. Clark had been right. The voters felt cheated. I had even spoken to a couple of gay men who were still undecided, citing Rosie's denial of her sexual identity as a disappointment. They were young men and their experience of living as homosexuals had to be vastly different than Rosie's had been at their age. But I was in no position to argue this case. I was unqualified and didn't pretend to fully understand either her rationale or theirs.

When Rosie returned with a box from the printer and a paper bag from Burger Barn, she walked straight over to me and said, "Trompe d'oeil."

Her pronunciation was so perfectly French that I hesitated because my knowledge of terms like this was strictly as they were written. "A trick of the eye," I said, after visualizing the phrase, "an optical illusion, like in a painting."

"Ha!" she said, gleefully. "So you don't know obscure words, huh?"

As though she had somehow tricked me, Rosie strode into her office in triumph. I smiled to myself as I opened the mail. And, then, quite suddenly, like one of those lightbulbs over a cartoon character's head, I had an idea. I jumped out of my chair and rushed into Rosie's office. She was eating her hamburger while watching a demo commercial on her DVD player. She pressed the pause button on the remote control as I entered.

"*Coup de main!*" I said.

Rosie looked puzzled, unsure how to play this game. "Okay," she said tentatively. "Surprise attack?"

I nodded, excited. "Mike Garcia."

Rosie put her hamburger down. "What about him?"

"Would he be a good mayor?"

Rosie shrugged. She seemed annoyed with me. She didn't want to think about the election. "I don't know. What difference does it make? He doesn't have a chance. He's farther behind than I am, even after all of this."

"But what's your opinion of him?"

"He seems okay. He's honest, smart. He doesn't have any experience, really, but with the right people around him, he'd be effective, I think. His political views are agreeable. At least he probably wouldn't run the city into the ground like Kiester is doing."

"Why's he doing so poorly, then?"

"He doesn't have a lot of money. He doesn't have the name recognition either Kiester or I have. In this kind of race, people focus on the two most popular candidates and don't pay any attention to the others. And, as far as politics goes, his stand on most of the issues is similar to mine, so he isn't offering a real alternative."

"Then why didn't the votes you lost go to him?"

Rosie sighed. "I assume the voters just didn't think of it. Like I said, it's been a two-person race. Kiester and I have spent all of our time and money attacking each other. We have completely neglected Mike, so nobody else has noticed him either." Rosie narrowed her eyes at me. "Jean, what are you thinking?"

"Let's get him elected," I said.

She stared. She said nothing. Then, seeming to understand what I was saying, she shook her head. "Oh, no, Jean, it's crazy. There's no time left."

"Your primary concern is getting Kiester out, isn't it?"

"Yes, sure, but…"

"Then let's put Garcia in. I know we can do it. People don't really like Kiester. They liked you. They have probably taken their votes to Kiester very reluctantly. Show them they have another choice."

"Are you suggesting I drop out of the race and endorse him?"

"No, no, that's not what I'm proposing. I don't think that would do it. I'm suggesting sucking Kiester's support away, to you where possible, to Garcia where possible. I'm suggesting a ferociously aggressive strike against him, a consolidated strike that will hit him so hard he'll be down for the count before he even knew he was in the ring."

"A cooperative effort?" A flicker of a smile came to Rosie's lips.

"Yes, exactly."

"Hmm. Now that is an intriguing idea. Oh, Jean, it's impossible. If we had more time, maybe."

"We can try. We don't have to just give up and play dead. There's a little fight left in you, isn't there, Rosie?"

She hesitated, then looked at me slyly. "You're really something," she said. "Okay, Jean, you've got it. Arrange a meeting with Garcia tonight. I want you there. And nobody else can know about this. Tell Foster we're back on for the interview as planned. We may still have a couple of tricks up our sleeve, after all."

Rosie was flushed, motivated, herself again. I was elated.

# Chapter Six

We met Mike Garcia and his manager, George Appleton, in my living room to avoid detection. Amy and Jerry went out to dinner at my bidding so we'd have the place to ourselves. This was the first time Rosie had been to my house, and it was all very exciting because it was clandestine and because it was my own plan they were going to discuss. Everyone was there on time at seven. Garcia was a handsome young man with dark eyes and a firm, clean-shaven chin.

"So what's this about?" Appleton asked Rosie once we were all settled. He was clearly on guard.

"We want to join forces with you against Kiester," Rosie said bluntly. "I want to help Mike win the election."

The two men did not hide their amazement. "Why?" Garcia asked.

"Because I've lost my chance at it. You haven't."

"But I'm way behind," he said. "I'm behind you, Rosie."

"I know. But we can change that. At least Jean thinks we can, and I trust her instincts." Rosie glanced at me and the look she gave me washed over me like a warm bath. She looked back at the two men and leaned toward them. "Tomorrow I'm going to tape an interview with David Foster. In it, I'm going to confirm the rumor, give them what they want to hear and the only thing they care about now. I expect that to prompt the gay community to come out on my side. Right now, they're lukewarm about me because I haven't come out in public."

Garcia and Appleton sat transfixed. Rosie had them in her spell. "They'll swing instantly behind me," Rosie continued. "Gays and lesbians are more politically active than many groups, unlike, for instance, Latinos. That's another issue we need to address. You've got to get the Hispanic community to the voting booths. Only fifteen percent turned out in the last local election. When you consider that we have a forty-three percent minority population here, their potential strength, if they vote, is enormous. We've got to get them to the polls. If we can do that, you win. It's as simple as that."

"Rosie," Garcia said, looking suddenly boyish, "I don't have any money."

"I know that, Mike. That's why I'm going to be campaigning for you too. My staff is your staff. In the interview tomorrow, we'll get David Foster to ask me something about you. I'll say you're a decent fellow. I can't exactly appear to endorse you, but it will have the same effect. It will get people looking at you. And then we both attack Kiester. I'll draw back some of my support in the time that's left. You'll draw the rest, and together we'll bury him."

Garcia and Appleton looked at each other wordlessly.

"You do want the job, don't you?" Rosie asked.

"Yes, yes, I do. I just never thought I had a chance."

"You do, Mike. You're the long shot who's going to come from behind and sweep the race." Rosie shook his hand warmly.

She was beautiful—buoyant and vibrant. She flashed me a brilliant smile.

The following day we went to the television studio. I was nervous. So was she. The set was furnished with a chair for the guest, a chair for Foster, a coffee table containing a water pitcher and glasses, and an artificial plant. Rosie went in for makeup before the show and came out a few minutes before airtime, looking splendid in black slacks, a conservative tan jacket and a print blouse. Before taking her chair, she winked in my direction. There was no audience, just the crew. The interview would be taped and aired later, before the local news. I had already spoken to Foster and prepared him. It had been no problem getting Rosie's cancelled time slot back once I explained what we wanted to do. Foster promised to take it easy on Rosie. He could afford to, as he was getting such a scoop—Rosie would be coming out on his show.

As the cameras hummed, he introduced her and began to chat about the course of the election. She sat with her legs crossed, looking relaxed. How did she do it? I was so nervous that I'd pushed my thumb through my Styrofoam coffee cup without even being aware of it until the coffee started running across my hand.

"Your popularity has declined dramatically," Foster said, "since speculation about your sexual orientation surfaced. In the only public statement you've made on the subject, you refused to address it. That has led, predictably, to further speculation that by not denying the rumor, you're confirming it. Would you like to comment?"

Rosie turned to face the camera. "Unfortunately for me and unfortunately for the citizens of Weberstown, that issue has taken precedence over the real issues in this campaign. I haven't changed my opinion that it's irrelevant, but a lot of people disagree. They seem to think that my reticence to discuss my sex life is a form of deceit."

"So you're seeing this as a matter of trust between you and the voters?"

"Yes. I believe people understand what's important for our city, that they'll vote fairly and intelligently if they feel trust. Because I need and want that trust, I'm now prepared to address the issue of my sexual orientation."

David Foster looked into the camera and raised his eyebrows, a rather comical expression meant to lock the listeners' attention. Then he turned back to Rosie. "So you admit that you're gay," he said.

"'Admit' is a poor choice of words. I'm not ashamed. Yes, I'm a lesbian. It happens to be one fact about me. I regret very much that it has become the focal point of my campaign because it really has nothing to do with being mayor."

"Some people would disagree with that statement, Rosie. They point to your association with such people as Catherine Gardiner, whose politics are extreme and unpopular."

"My friendship with Catherine occurred many years ago and I never shared her politics. I know that some people equate homosexuality with a certain set of political views, but my politics are strictly my own. They're no one else's agenda. My values are the same as other Weberstown residents." Rosie was insistent and sincere. "I want safe neighborhoods for our children. I want education to be available and effective. I want the arts to flourish. I want to reduce crime and homelessness and poverty. I've always wanted these things. I've always worked hard to achieve them, and my long record of community service proves what I'm about."

"So, are you saying that you wouldn't take a stand on the side of homosexual rights if such an issue arose?"

"No, I'm not saying that. Obviously, I would be sympathetic to the rights of homosexuals in our community and uphold those rights as the law proscribes, the same way I would anyone's rights. I do believe in civil liberties and I am very much opposed to any type of discrimination against any of our citizens on the basis of gender, race, national origin, age, disability or anything else. And I believe that most people in this town would agree with that. However, the hot-button issues that get people really concerned, like gay marriage or gays in the military, are not issues that we would ever deal with at this level of government. When it comes right down to it, as mayor of Weberstown, there's not much I could do to help the gay rights movement even if that was my only objective for getting voted into office." She glanced at me and smiled, then turned back to Foster. "Which it isn't."

"But wasn't it a city mayor who defied state law in two thousand and four and opened his City Hall to gay marriage, allowing over three thousand same-sex couples to wed?"

Oh, great, I thought. We didn't see that one coming. I could barely remember any details about that incident myself. I waited to see what Rosie would say.

"You're referring to Gavin Newsom, Mayor of San Francisco."

"Right," Foster said. "Practically the first thing he did after being elected was order the county clerk to issue marriage licenses to gay couples."

"I suppose a mayor can try to do something like that, something that he believes is right, especially if his constituency is going to rally behind him. But, in reality, a mayor doesn't have the authority to take that kind of action. Same-sex marriage legislation is not a city government issue. All of those marriages were declared invalid by the California Supreme Court in August, two thousand and four, which proves my point that, as mayor, I wouldn't have that sort of power. I would uphold the law as it stands, whether I agree with it or not. At the moment, California doesn't allow same-sex couples to marry. I'm not going to pretend that I'm neutral on this subject, but my personal opinion has no bearing on my responsibility under the law."

Okay, Rosie, I thought. That was good. She was on top of this subject after all.

"Just for fun," Foster asked, "if you were mayor of Weberstown and gay marriage was legal and you were in a committed relationship yourself, would you get married?"

Rosie's smile was wide and close-lipped. "That's a lot of ifs," she answered, obviously amused. "Hard to imagine all of those ifs coming together, in fact. No, I wouldn't. It's not for me. But I understand completely how important it is for many other people and hope that they someday get their chance."

He went on to another subject, for which I was grateful. Rosie handled the remainder of his questions with ease, jabbing at Kiester with every opportunity. She made several points about his neglect of the problems faced by minorities in Weberstown, particularly Asians and Hispanics.

"Your own loss of popularity," Foster said, asking the question I'd given him, "seems to have done little to help Mike Garcia rise in the polls. Are you surprised at that, since you and Garcia share similar stands on the issues?"

"No, I'm not surprised. I don't think people have taken a good look at Mike Garcia. This has always been a two-person race. It's been fortunate for me, I suppose, because Mike is a man with a lot to offer and if people were paying attention to him, they'd probably be the same people who have supported me."

When the interview was over, she thanked Foster and joined me, heaving a tremendous sigh. "How was it?" she asked.

"Fantastic!"

"It's a very scary thing to do." Rosie shuddered.

"You're a brave woman."

We left the studio together, landing ourselves in front of three reporters with microphones aimed our way, cameras rolling. "Rosie," one of them called, "what did you discuss with David Foster?"

Then another reporter asked, more pointedly, "Did you talk about being a lesbian?"

I took hold of Rosie's arm and pulled her toward the side steps.

"Watch the show," Rosie called to them. Once we were safely in the car and on our way, Rosie said, "In some ways, it's a tremendous relief, everybody knowing. Now I won't have to wonder who suspects."

"Sorry about that whole gay marriage thing," I said. "I had no idea he was going to ask you about that."

"He was bound to throw in something unexpected."

"You handled it perfectly. I guess that's a topic you didn't need to review. I mean, you have an established position on this sort of issue."

"Right. It would be hard to be a lesbian without a position on same-sex marriage."

"So you're for it, even though you don't want to get married yourself."

"Yes. It's a civil rights issue, Jean. It's not just about marriage. It's about equal rights under the law. As long as this ban exists, society is saying that our relationships are not as valid as yours."

I was sure that Rosie's statement wasn't meant to put me on the other side, but that's what it felt like. There were so many ways in which she was living in a different world from mine. One of the biggest differences between us was that she was always aware of that, aware of the subculture she belonged to and how it was marginalized. I had always taken my privileges of normalcy for granted. I had never even seen them as privileges, in fact.

Rosie laid her head against the headrest and closed her eyes, her expression serene. "I'm so glad this is over."

On the teaser for the evening news, Rosie and I appeared on the studio steps while an announcer said, "Rosie Monroe taped an interview with David Foster this afternoon in which she reportedly made a major announcement regarding the sexual orientation question that has been buzzing around her all week. That story, and others, tonight at six."

"I don't think you ought to touch her like that," Jerry said, referring to my nabbing of Rosie by the arm. "Not on television. People might get ideas."

It had been a natural gesture to take Rosie's arm, to get her away from the reporters. If she weren't a lesbian, Jerry wouldn't have even noticed. Nobody would. "Who cares what ideas people get?" I asked.

"I care. I don't want people to think my wife's gay. And I'm not too happy about how closely you've become associated with her. I'm frankly surprised that knowing she's a lesbian hasn't put you off some. Saying it's not a political issue is very different from saying it doesn't matter to you."

I didn't know how to answer him. Faye was of the same opinion. It should matter to me that Rosie was a lesbian. It should at least make me feel a little differently toward her, shouldn't it?

I wasn't having the normal reaction, the reaction that everybody else was having. All I could conclude from that was that I wasn't prejudiced after all. I was more open-minded than even I had known. Although some people I knew were gay, I had never interacted this closely with them before, and this issue had never really had anything to do with me before. It wasn't that I was unaware of it. It was just that I didn't concern myself too much with it, one way or another. Because of that, a lot of new thoughts were now going on in my mind about what it meant to be gay in this town or in this world.

Things happened fast after Rosie's interview aired. Mike Garcia, using his new slogan, "You've Got Another Choice," sent out mail to nearly every home in Weberstown. We held neighborhood barbecues in parks where the population was largely Latino, ostensibly to promote Rosie, but more importantly, to bring out the voters against Kiester. At Rosie's suggestion, Garcia distributed information in Spanish, Chinese and Vietnamese, the largest of the minority groups in town. I designed the flyers and produced them in our office after hours to insure that no one knew about our collusion with Garcia. I had thought the pace was tough before, but it had been nothing compared to this. If this was going to work, we had to use every minute we had left. I was more exhausted than ever, but more enthusiastic as well. I felt that I had a bigger stake now in the outcome of the campaign.

Rosie had been right about the gays rallying behind her. Local chapters of three gay and lesbian groups endorsed Rosie and became outspoken advocates against Kiester. They also became a rich source of volunteers for us, so we soon had a small army of people working the streets and phones. It was a good thing, too, because there were no more funds to pay for anything. I didn't know how Rosie was doing it, but donations to Garcia came pouring in while ours dried up, as though she had diverted a canal.

"What's happening?" Faye asked on the second day of the blitz. "Why is Rosie back in?"

"Maybe she thinks she can win," I said noncommittally. And

for a while there, I almost thought so myself. Once Rosie came out openly as a lesbian, the media simply dropped the subject. It wasn't a story anymore. There were still, of course, many voters lost over that issue. Those were the people we were pushing hardest toward Garcia.

"What a team we are!" Rosie said one evening, her eyes aglitter. I loved to see her on the high-energy platform again. And I was ecstatic to be there with her.

Somehow, despite all of the extra hours going toward campaigning, she was still tending to her other commitments. I marveled at her energy and tried to emulate it.

"Jean, are you free Thursday night?" Rosie asked me on Tuesday.

"Sure," I said with just a minor guilty thought about my family.

"I'm having a meeting with the Vision Partnership. Our secretary quit a couple weeks ago to take another job. Do you think you could take the minutes for us? You'll be paid, of course."

"I'd love to do it. It would be a pleasant change to work for money." Even if she didn't pay me, I'd have done it. I adored watching Rosie in action. I was learning from watching her, learning how to motivate people, how to solve problems, how to turn pressure into an advantage.

At the meeting, which was held in a conference room at the Weberstown Inn, I sat with a laptop computer to Rosie's left at a table of seven other people. She sat at the head of the table. The other members of the Partnership were, like Rosie, local business owners. Tonight they were discussing the impending closure of a Chevrolet dealership, the only one in town, which would put twenty-two people out of work. Before this meeting, I had no idea that anybody did anything about problems like this.

"He says he can't make a profit without an aggressive advertising campaign," a local restaurateur was saying, "and he keeps getting slapped by the DA's office with fines for illegal advertising. The competition is so tough right now that he's stretching the limits of fair practices."

"So it's the fines that are the problem?" Rosie asked.

"Well, it's the economy that's the ultimate problem, but, yes, the profit margin is so small for these guys that if he has to pay these fines, he says he won't have a profit, so he may as well go out of business. He claims he's being harassed by the DA. He currently has three outstanding fines."

"Does he really want to stay in business?" asked a woman on the other side of the table.

"I think so," said the man who spoke before. "He's owned that dealership for ten years. He says if he could just hold on a couple more years, he would, because he thinks the present slump is temporary."

Rosie looked around the table, then said, "Okay, so how do we save this guy and twenty-two people's jobs?"

"The DA's office can't turn a blind eye to the violations," pointed out the man to Rosie's right. "The advertising methods he's been using have to be changed."

"Agreed," Rosie said. "There's no reason why an advertising campaign has to be illegal to work. How about if we ask the DA's office to revoke the outstanding fines if we guarantee there will be no further violations? Then I'll take over the advertising for the dealership at the same cost he's currently paying the other ad company. If he gives me three months to bring him a profit, I think we can avert disaster. However, I'm not on the best of terms right now with the DA's office." One of the men laughed involuntarily. Rosie continued, "So, let's have Ken deal with those folks to get the fees dropped and I'll focus on the advertising angle."

Everyone agreed with the plan and Rosie reminded me that I was there not merely as an observer. "Ken Sturtevant," she said, pointing at the man to her right. I quickly made notes about what she'd just proposed. I'd gotten caught up in the discussion and forgotten.

"Okay, what's the next issue?" Rosie asked.

"We've made some headway with Sunco," Ken said. "But Sacramento is after them too. And with the city's regulations, I'm afraid we'll lose this one. As soon as they find out about the red tape, they may just stay in San Diego."

"How can we compete against other cities," someone said, "when our government refuses to implement pro-business policies?"

"We go over and over this," someone else said. "Two months ago we lost that plastic pipe manufacturing plant to Fresno because the city government was, as usual, in slo' mo'."

Rosie nodded, thoughtfully.

"Excuse me," I said, tentatively. Everybody looked at me. I hope you're not out of line, I thought to myself. "It seems rather shortsighted to be focusing so heavily on attracting businesses from other California cities. I mean, we win one away from San Diego, and Fresno wins one from us, and you just keep circling about like that. How is that, ultimately, benefiting the economy of the state?"

Nobody said anything for a moment, then Rosie addressed me without a trace of condescension, as though I were one of them. "What would you recommend, Jean?" she asked.

Then I was sorry I'd spoken. I was being asked to give an opinion on a subject I knew nothing about. It would be okay, Rosie, I thought, to treat me like the rest of you if I *was* like the rest of you. Why are you putting me on the spot?

"Well, I don't know that much about it," I began. "But just from an outsider's viewpoint, it seems that stealing business from other California cities is a short-term fix. We can't be a thriving community in a dying state. We have to consider the health of the larger structure. I would think you'd be putting more emphasis on creating new businesses, new areas of business, high-tech, for instance. Why not try to attract out-of-state companies, even foreign markets to expand to California, Weberstown in particular, which may have a small-town mentality, but hasn't been a small town for a long, long time. There's no reason we can't compete on a large scale."

I waited to see if they would laugh at me or simply ignore me. But they didn't. It was Ken who said, "She's right. That's exactly right. That's what we were supposed to be doing here, and we haven't done it. Most of our recent successes are simply the luring of companies away from our neighbors. You're perfectly on the mark, uh, what was your name?"

"Jean Davis," I said.

"Well, Jean, you're perfectly right. Aren't you the one handling Rosie's campaign for mayor?" I nodded. "Well, you've done a remarkable job. Since Clark left, Rosie's skyrocketed back."

"Jean's indispensable to me," Rosie said. She was smiling at me proudly with just a trace of amusement. I knew I was blushing.

"Yes, we've lost sight of our original vision," Rosie said, back on the subject, "because it's easier to steal businesses looking for a place to relocate than to open up new business opportunities."

"That sort of thing takes a lot of work and a lot of time," someone said. "And I just don't have it."

"None of us has been able to devote enough time to this organization," someone else said. "It's a full-time job. It takes a lot more than good intentions and ready money."

"Money I got," one of them said, "time I don't got."

"Maybe we should consider hiring someone," Rosie suggested. "If we've got money, as you say, Gordon, then let's pay somebody to do it right."

They took a vote. It was unanimous. They were all in favor of getting someone else to do the legwork for the Partnership.

After the meeting, Rosie drove me home. "I'm very proud of you, Jean," she said, not taking her eyes off the road. "You've got an instinctive grasp of how things work. And Ken was right, you've turned around a campaign that anyone would have labeled hopeless." She turned the car down my street. "I think you need to reassess your view of yourself and define some more challenging goals for your future. You have a lot more potential than you seem to know. I don't think you know yourself very well."

No, I thought, I don't. Not anymore.

Rosie pulled up to the curb in front of my house and stopped. She turned and looked at me in the dark. "As you heard, we voted to hire a full-time administrator tonight. In a couple of weeks, you're going to be out of work. So, if you don't have any other prospects, I want you to take the job. I'll have to talk to the others about it, of course, but before I make my case for you, I'd like to know if you're interested."

I was stunned. About to protest, about to point out my lack of qualifications, I stopped myself. Rosie didn't want to hear that. She wanted to hear something positive. She was pushing me into new realms. She thought I could handle it.

"Discuss it with your husband," Rosie said. "Let me know as soon as you can."

I discussed it with Jerry. He was less than overjoyed. "If Rosie ever retires from public life," he said resentfully, "you'll be unemployed. Why would she hire you for such an important position anyway? You have no qualifications. What's going on?" He was jealous. I was confused. A few months ago I would have had the same reaction as Jerry. What insanity would cause anyone to hire me for such a job? But things had changed. I had changed. I was running a successful campaign for mayor.

"I guess she thinks I can do it," I said lamely.

"I don't want you to take it," he said with finality.

"Why not?"

"It's not for you. It's ridiculous to think so." And then Jerry got angry and blew up at me. "I've been putting up with a lot of shit since you've been working for Rosie. The only reason I've kept quiet about it is that it was going to be over soon. You're never home. You never talk to me anymore, and when you do grace us with your presence, all you can talk about is poll results, fund-raising dinners, Rosie, Rosie, Rosie. I'm sick to death of Rosie! And now, on the brink of getting my wife back, you tell me you want to take another job working for Rosie. I don't want you working for Rosie any more. I want you to stay away from her. After election day, you're no longer one of Rosie's minions. Rosie is out of our lives and things will get back to normal. Take a class next semester. Get a job if you want to. But not this one."

I didn't really have an argument for Jerry. I understood what he was saying and what he was feeling. But, for some reason, it just didn't matter as much as it should have.

The next day I told Rosie I'd take the job. Jerry was already apologetic because he'd lost his temper and it was stupid to turn down a full-time job with this much promise. What else could I get? Just more of the same flunky office jobs? No, this was a real opportunity that couldn't be dismissed.

"Good girl!" Rosie said. "We'll rent you an office and do this properly. It's about time the Partnership had its own office anyway."

Jerry's objections, though, did make an impression on me. I tried not to talk about Rosie or her campaign at home at all anymore. I'd seen clearly enough how jealous Jerry was of the time I was devoting to Rosie. But I resented it that he felt entitled to my rapt attention without reciprocation. I was enthusiastic about what I was doing and felt cheated keeping it to myself.

The hour or two after Jerry fell asleep while I lay awake, which happened almost every night now, my mind raced through the events of the day and my plans for tomorrow. Relaxing my thoughts had become quite a challenge. I stared at the luminous red numbers on the alarm clock. It was midnight. I recalled Rosie laughing in her relaxed fashion into the phone, and wondered what she was doing, and with whom, as I gradually fought my way into sleep.

# Chapter Seven

"The next thing we have to think seriously about is the election night party," Rosie said. "It has to be planned—food and drinks have to be ordered. I expect we'll have a couple hundred people."

"Do you want me to hire someone to organize it?" I asked.

"I was sort of hoping you'd be able to do it. I know I've heaped a lot on you, Jean, but the money's getting tight. This campaign has cost me."

"Okay," I said uncertainly.

"Super. Tina has already sent out the invitations and rented the building. All you have to do is take care of decorating, hiring a caterer and servers, and whatever else you think we need."

I was way out of my comfort zone again. I'd never done anything like this before, had never even invited more than two other couples over to the house, and the only parties I had organized were my kids' birthday parties. Rosie's guests would not be interested in pin the tail on the donkey or Neapolitan ice cream. It seemed like every day was stretching me to the limit of my capabilities.

When I tried to get Rosie's help, she waved me off, saying, "It's up to you, Jean. Whatever you think."

For the next several days, my energies were split between running the campaign and planning a party for two hundred people.

"Don't serve caviar, Mother," Amy said in an affected voice. "Too snooty. In politics, you must avoid ostentation." Why does your daughter sound like Julie Andrews, I asked myself?

"To drink, I thought probably we should have champagne, since it's a sort of celebration."

"Sort of?" Amy said. She opened her mouth wide and mouthed "Oh, my God!" silently at me. "Mom, it's the highlight of your career! It's your shining hour."

"Okay. Champagne it is, then."

"Mom, what about music?"

"Oh, I hadn't considered that. Do we need music?"

Amy's mouth fell open again. She stared at me as if I was a major freakazoid.

"I don't know," I said. "There's so much to do. Maybe we can just have the sound system tuned into a classical radio station or something."

From Amy's expression, I gathered "major freakazoid" again.

"Let me do it!" she said. "Who better? How many hours do you need? I'll get Wendy and Tommy and we'll make some CDs."

I shook my head. "No. The people at this reception are not going to want to listen to Smashing Mouth or whatever."

"Mom, do you even know what decade this is?" I didn't answer. "I know a lot about music, Mom. I know how to do this. You get some loud, upbeat pop music that doesn't scream the seventies or something bizarre like that. Something modern that nobody's gonna notice that much."

The fact that she wasn't doing an impression made me realize she was serious. "Okay, Amy, give me three hours. We can repeat it once. That should be enough. I'll listen beforehand, of course, and I have veto power."

Amy was off in an instant with her MP3 collection to round up her friends.

Reporters from all over the country were following our little election for mayor, turning it into a curiosity. It was odd hearing about it on network news. Would a mid-sized California city elect a lesbian for mayor? Rosie had become a symbol after all, despite herself. To the rest of the country, it was probably not much of a story. They wouldn't think it remarkable because they didn't understand that California was not just one homogenous, liberal haven for nuts and fruits. For Weberstown, being in California notwithstanding, electing a lesbian mayor was not something to take in stride. If we had ever doubted that, the last few weeks would have put those doubts to rest.

The atmosphere around the office had now taken another dramatic turn. There were more people around, for one thing, with the influx of the gay contingent. Suddenly I was surrounded by gay men and lesbians who, because they were all together in a group, didn't worry much about how their behavior would impact the few straight people around. There were a lot of off-color remarks and sexual innuendos flying about. Someone had hung an eight-foot long rainbow flag across one wall. I think Rosie was more uncomfortable than I was with these changes. This wasn't normally the way she ran things in the office, so loosely, so casually, but she appreciated the support and said nothing to discourage the exuberance.

Ginny, who it was now clear to me was also a lesbian, always showed up to volunteer now with her girlfriend Aura. One evening while they were there stuffing envelopes, I approached her, saying, "You knew about Rosie all along, right?"

Ginny nodded matter-of-factly. "Sure."

It was like that, then, I guessed. There was some secret lesbian society that the rest of us knew nothing about where they all got together and did...whatever they did, and Rosie was a part of that.

"So you and Rosie have known each other for a long time?"

"Yep."

Aura was looking at me suspiciously, I saw, distrusting. She's scary, I thought, looking at the tattoo on her neck and the rows of silver jewelry on her ears. Maybe if Ginny had been there by herself, I could have questioned her more about Rosie's secret life. She wasn't going to offer up anything, apparently. I was frustrated. Here was someone who knew the other Rosie, the one that none of the rest of us had even known existed, and I didn't know how to pry anything loose from her.

"You're straight, right?" Aura asked me in a challenging tone.

I nodded.

"Thought so," she said dismissively.

Ginny smiled a little apologetically at me, but said nothing more. So the campaign went gay in the last week and I found myself on the outside looking in.

One of the female volunteers, Tracy, who joined us during the final week, developed an immediate and severe crush on Rosie. She was about twenty, cute, with a thin, boyish figure. She went all pie-eyed every time she saw Rosie. The second morning after Tracy arrived, as Rosie breezed through, Tracy asked, hopefully, "Can I get you a cup of coffee, Rosie?"

"No, thank you," Rosie said, then glared in my direction. "Jean, I need to see you, please." I followed her into her office and shut the door. "That girl, Tracy, she's making me nervous."

"She adores you."

"I know she does. That's what's making me nervous. Did you just see what happened here? I *do* want a cup of coffee, but now I can't get one because I just told her I didn't. I don't want her to bring me coffee because she'll hang around in here and look at me like she does and I'll get irritated and snap at her and she'll be hurt and probably cry and I'll feel guilty and try to comfort her and she'll start apologizing and saying how she can't help it, how she's in love with me, and then we'll have to have a God-awful heart-to-heart talk about her feelings and how she ought to handle it and…well, do you understand?"

I nodded. "Sounds like this isn't the first time somebody's had a crush on you." I was amused at Rosie's ruffled feathers. "I'll assign her non-office duties for the rest of the week and keep her out of your hair."

"Good. I don't mean to be insensitive, but I'm too busy to deal with this now."

"I understand." I opened the door. "I'll bring you a cup of coffee."

I sent Tracy out canvassing.

On the Sunday before the election, with two days to go, all indications were that Garcia had pulled into the lead. We had done it. We had done the impossible. And, surprising to all of us, Rosie was securely in second place. As we predicted, the electorate was returning to her. Wow, I thought. If I had just one more week, I could put her in the mayor's office. Kiester, still reeling from our one-two knock-out punch, didn't have a chance of regaining consciousness in time.

When I told Rosie the news, she just stood there, lips pursed, eyes shining, looking at me with gratitude. She shook her head, unbelieving. It was a very happy day.

On election day, I spent the afternoon at the rented hall supervising the last-minute decorating, the placement of the flowers, the arrival of food, the setting up of the sound system. Amy had surprised me with her musical contribution. She did know what she was doing after all. I had expected "Who Let the Dogs Out?" and, instead, I got some really nice music like the kind they play on JCPenney commercials, songs that don't really penetrate your consciousness usually, but make you want to buy towels.

It was all coming together splendidly, and I was high on adrenaline. After assuring myself of the arrangements, I went home to change clothes. Jerry fussed with his tuxedo, complained about his hair, but ended up looking as handsome as he ever had. Before we left the house, he put his arms around me and said, "I love you. And I'm proud of you."

Touched, I said, "Aren't you going to tell me how beautiful I look too?"

"You'll be the most beautiful girl at the ball."

That may have been Jerry's opinion, but when I saw Rosie, I had to concede that honor to her. She was jubilant when we located her in the crowd, a glowing beacon.

I introduced her to Jerry. "I don't know what my wife will do now," he said. "Our lives will be much duller."

"You'll probably enjoy that," Rosie observed, good-humoredly. "I want to thank you, Jerry, for being so generous with her. Without Jean, this election would have been a disaster. And this party—just look at this place. What a marvelous job you've done, Jean. And all the pink roses, they're perfect. They just fill the air with perfume."

"I'm glad you like it, Rosie."

"I love it! A brilliant touch. My financial advisor will probably not love it, though."

"You might be surprised," I said. "After all, I've been budgeting for a family of four for a while now. You learn a few things."

Jerry put his arm around my waist possessively. "Oh, yes," he said, "Jeannie's very clever. You should see what she can do with a can of tuna."

I slapped him playfully, then we went to the refreshment table for a glass of champagne. I inspected the table's contents—snacks, utensils, napkins, glasses, punch bowl and ladle. Everything seemed to be in order, but I still felt nervous. I drank two glasses of champagne in a row, then sampled some snacks—marinated shrimp, bruschetta with goat cheese and olive tapenade, crab-stuffed new potatoes. The food was good, high-class and fresh-tasting. Yes, I had done a fine job, a fabulous job, in fact. I met Rosie's challenge with style. Congratulations, Jean! I said to myself, raising my champagne glass.

The room was jammed with men in tuxedos, women in evening gowns, the clinking of glasses, laughter and music. A ROSIE FOR MAYOR banner hung over a platform at one end of the room. Bud vases holding miniature pink roses adorned the tables. Large sprays of pink roses on stands were strategically placed around the room. A man and a woman in black inconspicuously worked their way among the guests, retrieving abandoned glasses and plates, replenishing hors d'oeuvre trays.

"She looks very feminine tonight," Jerry said, as we observed Rosie from some distance. It seemed an idiotic thing to say, so I didn't respond. Rosie, dressed in a low-cut aqua evening gown with a sheer over-jacket covering her shoulders, looked ravishing. My eyes searched her out all evening, watched her talking to people, laughing, touching their arms, shaking their hands, her diamonds sparkling, her eyes glittering. She was never alone for a moment. Everyone wanted to be in her sphere of radiance.

People came and went, congratulating me and telling me what a valiant effort I'd made, how close we'd come. I smiled and chatted with the city's elite: government officials, business executives, members of the Arts Commission and the Vision Partnership and various other community-service organizations, rich and influential citizens who had financed Rosie's bid for mayor. One of these was Dr. Chandra Patel, of course, who looked incredible in a colorful sari and magnificent diamonds covering her ears and fingers. Her black hair was pulled up off of her thin neck into a French twist.

"Jean," she said, taking both my hands in hers. "I'm so happy that we won!"

"Well," I said, "I'm afraid we didn't win."

Dr. Patel tilted her head to one side, a crooked smile on her lips, and said, with certainty, "Oh, but we did! And I understand you are responsible for that. Rosalind has told me all about you, and I'm very impressed." She glanced somewhat dismissively at Jerry, and then smiled serenely at me before leaving us.

"That woman is worth millions, maybe even more," I told Jerry after she was out of earshot. "She bankrolled the portrait gallery at the museum almost single-handedly."

Poor Jerry was feeling intimidated. As was I, but not as badly. I'd met some of these people already and was beginning to know some names and faces, and, although their watches cost as much as my car, I knew there were good-hearted people among them and they had only wished Rosie the best. They had recognized her potential, and that was good enough for me. And I had learned too that the best of them saw their fortunes as a lucky happenstance and an opportunity to contribute to the welfare of the community that supported them. This was all new for me, this point of view, and I was sure that Jerry was still in that frame of mind that resents all of these lucky bastards.

Not everyone at the party was rich, though. There were the regular folks, too, who had given time instead of money, like Faye. And there was Ginny and her girlfriend Aura, who showed up in matching rented white and lavender tuxedos. When I saw them, I felt my face stretch into a wide smile. They were adorable and seemed very pleased with themselves. I thought I could read Rosie's lips as she gripped Ginny by the shoulders and said, "Aren't you two the cutest things!" I saw Ginny hand her camera to someone so that she and Aura could stand on either side of Rosie to get their picture taken between sprays of pink roses. She was their hero too. And they had a special connection with her that I envied.

In one corner, we'd mounted a chalkboard. Periodically, one of the volunteers wrote in the latest figures from the election returns coming out of the county courthouse. Consistently, Garcia was ahead, Kiester was last. The polls had been accurate. Rosie's position fluctuated slightly up and down, but maintained second place, and by ten o'clock, she was far enough behind Garcia to concede.

Rosie climbed onto the stage and took a microphone, motioning to someone to turn the music down. "Listen up," Rosie said. "This is the official announcement. I would like to congratulate Mike Garcia for his resounding win." Boos and cries of protest arose from the crowd. "To those of you who stuck with me, I want to thank you for your dedication. I know it wasn't easy and I know you took a lot of abuse. I'm sorry I couldn't pull it off for you." Rosie's gaze scanned the crowd. "Jean, where are you?" I raised my glass and she caught my eye. "Ah, there she is. My deepest gratitude goes to Jean Davis for her heroic performance as my campaign manager. When I was ready to give up, Jean knocked me upside the head and back into the race. Because of her remarkable efforts, we have achieved the most important victory of this campaign—we've kept Kiester from being reelected." The crowd cheered. "That was my aim from the beginning, so I'm counting this election a success. To Mike, I give my heartiest congratulations, as well as all the help I can give him in his new position." She offered a toast to Garcia, then said, "As of this moment, I am retired from politics forever! Drink up, everybody!" She raised her champagne glass to her lips and drained it in one swallow.

I, too, drank some more champagne, feeling overwhelmed with emotion.

"Congratulations, Jean," Faye said, running into me in the kitchen where I was stacking some trays. I felt restless and wanted to occupy myself. Faye, looking flushed and sexy in a revealing gown, said, "Rosie told me about your idea to oust Kiester. Very clever. And you did it, too. I knew something was up. I just didn't guess that was it. A victory after all."

"It might have been my idea, but it was Rosie who did it."

"All the same, Jean, you should be proud of yourself. I was there, remember? I've seen you in action and I'm proud of you." Faye took hold of me and gave me a warm hug. "Rosie's right, you two make a great team. She really can't say enough about you."

Well, that was good to know. Rosie was always so willing to share credit with someone else, one of her most agreeable traits.

As the evening wore on, my mood gradually deteriorated. The momentum was wearing off and I found myself forcing smiles.

"What's the matter with you?" Jerry asked me in a quiet corner. "Why aren't you enjoying yourself?"

"I don't feel festive," I said. "I'm just sad, I guess, that it's over. It's been a hell of a ride."

He nodded his head agreeably, but I knew what he was thinking. Thank God, it's over!

I was the only one who was gloomy. Rosie clearly wasn't. She was overjoyed. She would soon be on to other projects and wouldn't look back. This was one adventure in her life among many. For me, it was singular. The best I could hope for is that I didn't revolve around this spot for the rest of my life, that I could do something else of interest. The experience was valuable, however brief it had been. I felt like crying.

Late in the evening, after several of the guests had gone, Jerry and I got separated. When I was ready to leave, I went looking for him. I hoped he had kept his promise about not drinking so he'd be able to drive safely. I was in no condition to do it myself. I looked through the main room and the kitchen, then went through a sliding glass door out onto an unlit sundeck. No one else was there. I went over to the railing and leaned against it, looking out across the lake. Down by the water, two shadowy figures stood with hands clasped between them. They kissed briefly, then leaned against one another, watching the sky.

Toward the south I easily picked out Orion, the three bright stars of his belt prominent. There was no moon, no breeze. The air was chilly, but tolerable, a fine November evening. I stood for a while listening to a flock of Canada geese far overhead, out of sight, meandering south, and to the sound of loud music from within, feeling sick to my stomach and unsteady.

"There you are," said a low voice close to me. It was Rosie's voice. I turned to see her standing just behind me. I hadn't heard her approach, didn't know if she'd been there for a while. "Your husband is looking for you."

I stared into her eyes. "Yes, it's time for us to go."

"Sit down for a minute, Jean," Rosie said, indicating a redwood bench placed beside the doors. I sat beside her. Someone had put one of the pink rosebuds behind her ear and she looked, well, rosy. This was the first time all evening I had a chance to get a really good look at her. The diamond earrings and matching necklace were dazzling clusters of teardrops. Ostentatious for Rosie, but this was a big night, appropriate for big statements. The straps of her aqua gown were thin on her shoulders, a gauzy film of the same color covering her arms. The neckline dropped across her chest to meet in a V over the plump curve of her breasts. The dark, mysterious groove of her cleavage disappeared beneath the silky material. Soft, everything about her was so soft.

"Jean, I have something for you," she said, producing a bulky rectangular object with a big red bow on it. "To thank you, though this will hardly suffice."

I took the gift. It was a roan-colored leather accordion-style briefcase. The lining and edge stitching told me that it was finely made and undoubtedly expensive.

"For your new job," Rosie said. "I guessed that you didn't have one."

"No, of course I don't," I said, near tears. "Oh, Rosie—"

"You really threw yourself into this campaign," Rosie said, seeming uncomfortable. "I expect you'll suffer a bit of post-election depression. Not surprisingly."

"This has been one of the happiest times of my life. I'm going to miss it. I'm going to miss you."

"Don't start bawling, for God's sake." She attempted a laugh. "Look, Jean, just because the election's over, it doesn't mean good-bye. There's the Partnership. We'll be working together often, I expect. I'm counting on you to throw yourself into that with as much enthusiasm as you did this."

Yes, I thought, but it won't be the same. I won't see you every day. She patted my hand, holding it between both of hers briefly. There was nothing I could say because everything I thought of to say sounded so ridiculous, so childish, so pathetic.

"It'll be okay," she said tenderly, looking directly into my eyes. "You'll get over it." And, then, with an unconvincing smile of reassurance, she touched my cheek lightly before standing and leaving me.

I sat where I was for a few minutes. Rosie was right. I had the new job to occupy me. It would be a challenge. And it would be important work. As she said, I would get over it. Over this sadness, over the post-election blues. Is that what she meant?

I could hear the song playing inside. Second time around

now.

*I think I'm falling in love with you. There's a universe in your eyes. That's where I want to live.*

Jerry and I drove home in silence. After we'd gotten into bed, Jerry said, "It was a pretty good shindig."

"Uh-huh," I said, already half asleep.

"That briefcase Rosie gave you is really nice."

Jerry was talkative in his joy, the joy of averted disaster, perhaps, for, whether he could articulate it or not, the end of this election was cause for hope and celebration for him. He no doubt hoped that it meant the return to all that he cherished in our lives.

"And Faye's date, Bob, wasn't he good-looking?" he was saying.

"Yes, extremely. We'll probably never see him again, though."

"You're right. Faye doesn't let any mold grow."

No, I thought, Faye wouldn't let herself get moldy. I snuggled into the bed, curling up on my side.

"That Bob said he saw two women kissing out back," Jerry said. "Wouldn't you know there'd be some of that going on."

Two women? I recalled the couple by the lake. Yes, they had been women. I had known it at the time, but it hadn't registered. How peculiar.

"Do you hate them?" I asked Jerry.

"Queers? No, I don't hate them. As long as they keep quiet about it and keep away from me. I'm so glad Brad and Amy turned out normal."

"They're a little young to know for sure," I said.

"No, they're not," Jerry said emphatically. "Brad's had half a dozen girlfriends. And Amy, you know she lives for boys."

And what about me, I thought. I've been married to this man for twenty-two years.

"No, our kids are normal," Jerry concluded.

"Yes, probably," I said, then fell asleep.

# Chapter Eight

We usually got a lengthy e-mail once a month from Bradley. He would take a couple of hours out of his schedule to write us from an Internet café in some exotic locale. On November 22, Thanksgiving Day, this month's message arrived from Paris, and Amy printed it out for all of us to read.

*Last night we went to see the Follies. Ooh la la! I had a huge dinner, lots of wine, and then the show kept us out until the wee hours. People dine very late here. I'm getting used to sitting in a restaurant for three hours in conversation, as though it's someone's living room. We drink beer and watch the people and talk about life and art and politics. I feel like Hemingway. You would love it here, Mom. I can just see you waltzing carefree along the bank of the Seine at midnight. It's all so liberating.*

*One of the things that overwhelms me about Europe is the omnipresent sense of the past, the great weight of it. Memories are long here, identities stabilized, and people don't get excited about everything like Americans do. I saw a man doing an oil painting of Notre Dame and thought that probably a lot of people had sat just there doing just that for hundreds of years. It made me happy, and I had to stop and think about that before I recognized it as happiness. You know, you don't know what can make you happy. You don't know it until it happens, and then you don't understand it. But I think it has something to do with finding your place in the scheme of things. It's hard to know where you belong in a world this complex, but I think you can feel it when it happens. It's like how fish know the place where they go to spawn, even when they've never been there before. They know it's the right place, though. I don't think people are so different, on some level.*

I read several pages of Bradley's upbeat letter, glad that he was happy, wanting to be there with him, although my imagination wasn't wild enough to place me in that picture. I've never been to Paris, I thought wistfully. Probably never would be.

Funny that Bradley saw me waltzing carefree along the Seine. He was remembering when Jerry and I had taken ballroom dancing classes. I'd really enjoyed that, and Bradley, who was six at the time, had clamored to be my practice partner on weekdays after school when his little sister was napping. He always insisted on clipping on his little red bow tie to practice, just the two of us in the front room, music playing, waltzing awkwardly and giggling, my little gentleman and me. Those happy interludes, something I'd nearly forgotten, were obviously some of his fond early memories.

Bradley's letter left me sad, pretty much my mood all the time now. The election had been over nearly three weeks. I hadn't seen Rosie. She called once to tell me that the Partnership members had approved me as their administrator. They were still in the process of looking for an office space. Meanwhile, they would send me information at home so that I could prepare.

Rosie's call was brief and professional. I was hurt by her impersonal tone. She was friendly, but in the same way she always was when speaking on the phone with anyone. After nearly three months of being swept along by the winds of a hurricane, I'd been dropped into a calm so complete that my senses seemed atrophied. There was nothing on the horizon. I was adrift on a monotonous ocean.

I called Faye at work the Monday after Thanksgiving and asked her to meet me for lunch. She came from her office, smartly dressed and madeup. I must have looked dowdy in comparison. "I'm glad you called, Jean," she said, glancing over the menu. "I needed to take a break from that place. How are you? You look tired."

I just shrugged.

"I think I'll have the salad bar," Faye told the waitress. I ordered the same and we headed toward it to pile chilled plates with baby lettuces, spinach and radicchio.

"So, are you seeing anyone?" I asked Faye, once we were settled at our table.

"Yes. Bob," she said.

"Bob? The same Bob as three weeks ago, Bob?"

She nodded. "He could be around for a while, Jean."

I raised an eyebrow. "Good. It's about time."

I wasn't really hungry and ate without much interest. Faye told me a little more about Bob. She seemed genuinely fond of him. I was glad for her.

"You're in a funk, aren't you?" Faye said after a few minutes of silence.

"I don't know what's the matter with me. It's like everything was great and then suddenly nothing is. Nothing is right. Nothing." I was frustrated, unable to articulate how I felt.

"Nobody sick? Kids okay?"

"The kids are wonderful."

"Your parents are okay?"

"Yes, they're fine."

Faye shrugged. "So what's wrong?"

"I'm not happy."

"Well, I've got to tell you that 'happy' is not a word I would have used to describe you for years. Which is strange to see, for me, anyway, because I knew you in high school."

"It's a long time since high school, Faye."

"Sure, but you weren't the serious type, not even close. I mean, you can tell by your GPA that you weren't. You were smart, but you didn't have much interest in school. Too busy having fun. That's why we were friends, remember? You and me, we were the same. Don't you remember all the fun we had, all the trouble we got into?"

"Sure I do." I smiled.

"Oh, my God," Faye continued, "all the boys! You were such a tease! They were all ga-ga over you, Jean. You were so cute. Oh, how I used to envy you that, but, if I couldn't be as cute as you, I could at least run around with you and reap the benefit."

"You were cute, too, Faye," I said. "We made a pretty irresistible pair. But you can't just have fun all the time once you grow up."

Faye's lip curled up on one side, as if she wanted to contradict that, but she didn't. "No, of course not. That's not really what I meant. I know you have to be a responsible person. But you were so carefree, Jean, and it was great to be around."

Carefree? That was the word Bradley had used in his letter, "waltzing carefree." When, then, had I lost that capacity?

"I suppose I'm no fun to be around any more."

"Don't get defensive. You're fine, but I've got to say that I was just thrilled watching you running Rosie's campaign. It was a glimmer of that lively girl that I remember. And that's why I think you'll be okay once you're working again. There's no doubt that Rosie is going to kick you into gear. As soon as you get into that new office and the phone's ringing, you'll be right back in action. That's all you need. Hard work is a terrific high, when it's work you enjoy, of course."

"Have you seen Rosie lately?" I asked, clinging to the mention of her name.

"I saw her yesterday, actually. She came into the office. She was making plans to go to Phoenix. A business trip. She asked me about you."

"Did she?"

"Yeah, how you were, if I'd seen you."

Rosie's thinking about me, I thought, and my pulse quickened.

Faye went on. "She seemed well, keeping busy as usual. I booked her flight and her hotel, rental car, you know. Not everybody does it all on the Internet yet, thank God." Faye took a sip of her iced tea. "She made me promise never to get her involved in a city election again. She was so glad that was over with. I feel a little badly about all that, about how it turned out for her. But we had a nice visit and I guess she isn't holding any grudges against me. No, I don't think she spends much time on regrets."

"Did she say anything else about me?" I asked stupidly.

Faye looked puzzled. "No, Jean, she didn't. She was sort of preoccupied with getting ready for this trip. Apparently she normally has a neighbor boy take care of her place when she's gone, feed the horses and cats, you know, watch the place, and he is not available. Gone off to college or something, so she's gotta find somebody else."

"I could do that," I said impulsively. "I'd be happy to do it."

"So call her and tell her," Faye said matter-of-factly.

By the time Faye and I said good-bye, I was obsessed with the idea that I could house-sit for Rosie. It took me several hours, however, of agonizing over it to actually make the call.

"Hi, Jean, good to hear from you," she said when I announced my name. "What's up?"

"Rosie, Faye was telling me at lunch today that you need a housesitter for next weekend."

"Yes, that's right. Mainly for the animals. Would your daughter like to do it?"

"Well, I was thinking of me, actually. I could do it."

"Oh." There was a long pause which I couldn't interpret. "Well, I liked having the boy do it because he lived next door. I appreciate the offer, but I should probably get someone in the neighborhood. It would make me feel more secure. Also, the horses need to be fed first thing in the morning and again in the evening."

"I could stay overnight," I said. "Not a problem. I could come over in the afternoon, stay over, and then tend to the horses in the morning before going about my day. I'd do that. It would be like a vacation for me. I need a vacation, believe me." I attempted a casual laugh, but it didn't sound very casual, nor even much like a laugh.

Another long pause before she said, "Great."

"Great," I repeated.

"You'll need to come over before I leave so I can show you what to do. I'm leaving early Thursday morning, so how about some time on Wednesday, after I get home from work? Come over for dinner, then. How's that?"

After hanging up, I danced into the kitchen. I was excited, too excited. By the time Amy came home, I was calmer. When Jerry came home, I told him the plan. He didn't look pleased.

"So I guess this will take up your entire weekend, then?" he asked.

"Yes, I guess it will. Did we have plans?" I realized that I'd forgotten to check the calendar.

"Well, not really, no. I guess not. That woman sure does get a lot of free service from you." I recognized the tinge of bitterness in his voice.

"She's got horses?" Amy asked. "Would she let me ride them?"

"I'll ask her."

"That would be cool." Amy swaggered out of the kitchen, saying, "You'd better watch yer step, pardner, heh, heh, or my horse Polka Dot is gonna clobber you."

"How does she know Walter Brennan?" I asked Jerry.

"She gets it off The Comedy Channel," Jerry said. "It's recycled through an older generation of impressionists. She's probably never even seen Walter Brennan. Just like when she does Katherine Hepburn. I'm sure she's never seen the real Hepburn in a movie or anything."

"Do you think she's having an identity crisis?"

"No, she's just exuberant, Jeannie. And I think she's very good at it."

I shrugged. "Yes, you're right. It's just healthy, youthful

exuberance."

I suddenly realized that when I was Amy's age, I was married and had a newborn baby. Looking at her, I saw a child. I had been too young to have a clue, too young to know what choices there were, what life might offer if given the chance. I hoped for Amy's sake that she would have more time to learn about herself than I did.

Each day after Jerry and Amy had left the house, I sat with the jumble of paperwork sent to me by my new employers. Sorting it all out was a massive chore. It was easy to see that the partners hadn't had a handle on these things for months. Among the papers sent to me by the Partnership was a Xeroxed copy of a letter from a man looking for a permanent site for his Dolls of the World Museum, a remarkable collection of eight thousand dolls, some of them centuries old. The letter was addressed to the Weberstown Chamber of Commerce asking about available redevelopment property. It was dated October 4.

"He wants to turn his collection into a tourist attraction," I told Jerry.

"Sounds interesting. Bring in some tourist business, something we could desperately use."

"I wonder if the city answered his letter. I haven't found a reply."

"Isn't it your job to follow up on such things?" Jerry asked.

I liked the sound of that. "Yes," I said.

The next morning I made some phone calls, eventually getting someone who told me, sounding embarrassed, that the letter had not been answered. It had been overlooked.

"It's been nearly two months," I said. "Don't you think this is important enough to deserve top priority?"

"Yes," said the young man on the other end of the phone. "I'm sorry, Mrs. Davis. I'll get on it right away."

"I hope he hasn't gotten an answer from some other town," I said, "while we've been sitting around picking our noses." Amy, who sat at the kitchen table listening, giggled. I frowned at her, anxious to maintain the dignity of my side of the conversation.

After all, the city worker I was talking to couldn't know he was making excuses to a mom in her bathrobe at the kitchen phone.

"I think I'd better take care of this myself," I said. "Have all of the information faxed to me first thing tomorrow morning. I'll call Mr. Madison and see if I can persuade him to bring his museum to our town after all."

"Okay, Mrs. Davis. I'll make sure we get you what you need. We'll need a transcript of your call for the record, also."

"Fine. Thank you." I hung up, grinning at Amy. "Well," I said, "I've got him running scared."

"He doesn't have any idea who you are, does he?"

"No. It's a good thing, right?"

Amy nodded. "My mother the business executive. Do you want me to show you how to set up the computer to receive a fax?"

"I was hoping you would."

The next day, Wednesday, at eight o'clock, Amy stood by while the faxed documents came through as promised. I called Mr. Madison, who seemed surprised but pleased to hear from me. "I was wondering if they ever got my letter," he said.

"I'm very sorry about that, but we've just gone through a city election and city government is a little confused. That's why I've gotten involved in your project. Believe me, Mr. Madison, the city is very interested in your fascinating collection." I talked to him for a half hour, at the end of which I felt secure about his interest. I told him I was sending him the information he requested and would be in touch with him again in a few days after he'd had a chance to look it over.

"I've got to go to school now, Mom," Amy said, slipping on her backpack. "Have a good time at Rosie's tonight. Dad and I are going to watch a movie."

"Oh? What movie?"

"Dad's choice. A classic from back in the day. *Casablanca*."

I nodded. "That's perfect. You'll enjoy that, especially since I've heard you quoting lines from it on several occasions."

"Really?" She looked smug, as though it was a superior

accomplishment to be able to quote from a movie she had never seen.

"What about dinner? I can give you a couple of suggestions if you want to try."

"Mother, why can't you just admit that I'm a failure as a domestic? I'm a modern woman. I don't cook. I shove frozen things into the microwave and, presto, dinner. Just like on *Star Trek*. None of this tending to a fire with a hunk of raw meat on a spit. We have evolved!"

I kissed her good-bye, prepared a package for Mr. Madison, which I went out and mailed, and then changed my clothes several times until finally settling on jeans, a long-sleeved cotton shirt and leather jacket. Casual, simple, uncontrived. I looked good, I thought. Would Rosie agree? As I fussed with my hair, I felt my anxiety level soaring. I hadn't seen Rosie in a month, but I had thought of her every day, savoring memories of the campaign, the excitement and tension that had made me feel more alive than I ever had. I wanted desperately to recapture that feeling and I felt that it wasn't possible except in her presence. She was the catalyst to my newfound vitality. I couldn't wait to see her.

# Chapter Nine

Late in the afternoon I drove off into a downpour of cold rain feeling like someone else. I thought of Bradley's description. Yes, I felt like a woman waltzing carefree along the bank of the Seine at midnight. Just driving by myself, anonymously, felt good. I felt free and happy and I didn't understand it. I passed familiar landmarks—the Pak 'n' Save, the waterslides, Costco, Wal-Mart—and felt like I was exploring a new world. I turned onto the highway and drove a couple of miles north to Rosie's exit.

By the time I drove through the shaded seclusion of her neighborhood, I felt I had gone a long distance, though it had been a mere twenty-minute drive. I wasn't familiar with this area, knew it only as an upscale section of town, almost out in the country, where the lots were several acres apiece. Obviously, this area had all been farmland once before the city expanded to engulf it. I drove slowly, checking road signs and my map. I remembered when Faye had told me that she'd never been to Rosie's house. I felt like I was driving into the inner sanctum, a magical kingdom that few mortals had ever glimpsed. I was feeling silly, giddy.

A couple of miles from the highway, I turned into a long gravel driveway lined by old walnut trees left over from an orchard. Some of the walnuts had fallen and were lying along the edges of the roadway, crunching under my tires. The house came into view, a sprawling ranch house, white with forest green shutters. Rosie's hybrid sedan was parked in front. I pulled in behind it. The rain had turned into a light drizzle. The air smelled musty, sort of green like torn leaves.

Rosie greeted me on the front doorstep wearing jeans and a flannel shirt with the sleeves rolled up to her elbows. I'd never seen her dressed informally before, and the difference was a little shocking, especially since the last time I saw her, she was wearing a low-cut evening gown and dripping in diamonds. She looks good in jeans, I thought, comfortable and approachable. She hugged me warmly, a friend's greeting, and then gave me rubber boots to wear out back. We sloshed out to the barn where her two horses stood, both of them walking toward us expectantly.

"Jean," she said, "meet Violet and Vita." Rosie showed me how to give them water and food. She went to the corner of the barn and pulled a bale of hay off of a stack, then cut the wires holding it together. I stood in place, astonished. I had never touched a bale of hay, but I had a feeling they were heavy.

"This one bale will be enough while I'm gone," she said, "to supplement the feed."

She showed me how to operate the gates and the security system on the house. She showed me what and where to feed the two cats and how a cranky kitchen faucet could be made to behave. She showed me where the keys were to the doors and the pickup. She gave me the relevant phone numbers and the name of her hotel in Phoenix.

"I'll be leaving Phoenix Saturday morning," she said, "and flying to Sacramento. I'll stay with a friend overnight and drive back Sunday. Here's her phone number if you need to get in touch with me, if there's a problem with my cell phone. I'm notorious for letting the battery run down."

I read the name and number on the note. Grace Carpenter. Who is she? I wondered. Another lover? But I didn't ask any questions. I just said, "Okay."

At last my training was complete. Rosie made dinner. I sat at the kitchen table observing, feeling comfortable in this old-fashioned kitchen, seated at the simple square oak table on a hard wooden chair. The house was appointed in rustic country fashion except that it wasn't decorated. It came that way. It was authentic, an old farmhouse. There weren't antiques on the walls, but some of the implements in the kitchen looked like antiques, still in use as functional items, like a metal colander that reminded me vaguely of something from my childhood.

I told Rosie about the doll museum.

"Jean, I'm so glad you noticed that. So you've already earned your keep and we haven't even gotten you a desk yet. Good job! Oh, that reminds me, I have some paperwork for you to fill out. Basically, your employment contract." She took a sheaf of papers from the edge of the kitchen counter and brought it to me at the table. "Look this over and let me know if you have any questions. You can drop it off at the office or mail it when you're ready."

I folded the papers and put them away to take home with me. Rosie had stuffed Cornish game hens with wild rice and mushrooms. They were baking. "Living alone," Rosie said, "I seldom cook real meals. That's why I especially enjoy company at dinnertime. Do you like to cook, Jean?"

"More so now than in the past, now that the children are grown. Cooking for kids is a thankless job. If you try to serve them real food, they just make faces and say 'ycchh!', and so you pretty much go with fish sticks and tater tots. Fighting over vegetables is such a drag."

"I can imagine." Rosie poured me a glass of chardonnay and then turned back to her kitchen counter. "Your husband didn't mind your staying here?" she asked. I shook my head. "He seems like a nice guy. Nice-looking too. How long have you been married?"

99

"Twenty-two years."

Rosie turned to me and raised an eyebrow. "That's a long time. I guess you're older than I thought."

She could have estimated me as young as thirty-four without knowing about Bradley, I realized. "I'm forty, actually."

Rosie sliced radishes without regard for uniformity. "Married very young, weren't you? Would you say you were happily married?"

"Yes. Jerry and I have never had any serious problems." And that was true. Ours was an ideal marriage in many respects, an ideal family. "We've been lucky."

"So it's one of those, then," she said. "In it for the long haul?"

"I suppose so." She glanced at me with a wistful smile. Was she envying me my conventional life, I wondered. Or was there something else? "Tell me about *your* marriage, Rosie."

"Oh, my marriage. That was a long time ago." She opened the oven to check the Cornish hens, the door springs squeaking, then came over to the table, wiping her hands on a dish towel. "I got married when I was in college to David Lamont. He had big, waggly ears and impossible hair, but I thought he was perfect. For a while. It was one of those relationships, you know, founded on nothing. You get all googly over somebody and it gradually wears off and there's nothing there, underneath. Except, perhaps, cordiality, if you're lucky."

"How long did it last?"

"Just two years, the last one of which we were like brother and sister. I'd fallen in love with someone else by then."

"A woman?"

Rosie nodded, looking slightly embarrassed. She returned to the stove. I decided against pursuing the subject, though I wanted to. I also wanted to ask her about Grace Carpenter. But Rosie had made it emphatically clear that her romantic life was private. And I had learned, from people like Ginny and Aura, that I was not welcome into the confidences of these women and their loves. They had a closed society. I didn't blame them for that.

Theirs was a much-maligned lifestyle. It was natural for them to be insular.

The music drifting in from the front room had an appealing Latin sound.

"What kind of music is that?" I asked.

"Brazilian jazz," Rosie said, suddenly doing a quick-quick-slow step on the kitchen tile in time to the music. "This is a samba."

"Oh, right. That's what it reminds me of. We did samba when I took ballroom dance classes years ago."

She delivered the food to the table and sat across from me. "Ballroom dancing? Did you enjoy that?"

"Oh, yes, I did. My favorite was the waltz. Old-fashioned, I know, but so elegant."

"Yes, extremely. I'm partial to it as well. The ultimate romantic dance, don't you think?"

"Absolutely. Jazz is your specialty, though, isn't it?"

Rosie nodded, filling my wineglass. "I guess my main style to play is cool jazz. Like Miles Davis and Dave Brubeck."

"I've only heard you play that one time, but I thought you were fantastic. Faye mentioned something about a band?"

"Yes, just a few friends. We've played the Sacramento Jazz Jubilee a couple of times and a few gigs around the area. Just for fun. Actually, one of the women is someone you know, Ginny."

"UPS Ginny?"

Rosie nodded. "She plays string bass."

The meal was elegant but simple, the Cornish hens, wild rice stuffing and a green salad. Simple seemed to be Rosie's style in many respects. Her house was simply furnished, uncluttered and unpretentious. She didn't have doodads, and the art which hung on her walls was tasteful and modern, lots of artistic photographs, the occasional museum poster.

I tasted the Cornish hen. It was perfectly cooked. As we ate, watching each other, the conversation lagged, and I could feel a curious tension build between us. Rosie was uncharacteristically quiet during the meal and I found it disconcerting. I was so used to her lively personality dominating every situation. Other than a few comments about the food, we were unable to start a conversation.

I watched her eyes, deep brown and luxurious, focus on mine and then look away, almost shyly, it seemed. How beautiful she is, I thought, admiring the streak of gray hair above her ear, the delicate neck in the open collar of her flannel shirt, her bare forearms with their fine covering of light-colored hair, her long fingers resting on the base of her wineglass. As I admired her features, I allowed myself to admit what I had been pushing out of my mind for some time—I wanted to touch her. I knew what that meant and how frightening it was, but it had been there for a long time, suppressed, growing more insistent and more impossible to rationalize away.

I looked away from her captivating gaze. "The wine is very good," I said nonchalantly, my voice sounding strangely unlike me.

"Yes, it's one of my favorites. I have a friend with a vineyard. He always comes through with a few bottles of this one for me. He's got the most fantastic cabernet too. Maybe next time, we can…" She stopped and looked embarrassed. "Well, perhaps I'll snag a bottle for you sometime if you'd like."

I was grateful to hear the phone ring. Rosie went into the living room to answer it, while I sat immobile at the kitchen table, nearly frantic on the inside, afraid to examine the jumble of thoughts and feelings erupting toward the surface.

When Rosie returned, she was frowning. "That woman is such an idiot," she said, sitting down.

"Who's that?"

"Tanya Lockhart."

"I don't know her, do I?"

Rosie shook her head. "Arts Commission charter member. The wife of a doctor with lots of time to devote to humanitarianism. She's been plaguing me for years. She wants to be part of everything, and people tolerate her because she has money and she's generous with it. But you can always count on her for inanity.

This time she was worried about one of the entrants in the art scholarship contest. She said he was Yugoslavian and didn't speak English." Rosie used her fork for emphasis. "So, I said, what's the problem? She said it would be disastrous if he won."

"Why?"

"My question too. She said because he wouldn't be able to deliver a thank you speech to the commission." Rosie laughed. "Imagine that. That tells you a lot about this woman. Is she concerned about art, really? Does she even know anything about art? No. She wants to make sure the Commission—she—gets the gratitude of the little people it helps…in English."

"He could have a translator."

"Exactly. She said it wouldn't be the same. And then I got mad at her and threatened her with a charge of xenophobia if she did anything at all to bias the judges. Of course she didn't know what it meant, but she's too insecure to ask for a definition. Probably she's looking it up now in her dictionary, probably under 'z'."

Rosie grinned and swallowed a large bite of rice. "Oh, Jean, that reminds me of a funny story about Tanya. You've got to hear this one."

I was glad we'd found something to talk about, something to overcome the tension.

Rosie talked excitedly with her mouth full. "It's been years ago now, when the Hmong people first arrived in California. I guess that was early eighties? Tanya was the director of the Women's Action League of the county, and she was looking for a project. I was a new member at the time. Someone mentioned that San Jose had started an Adopt-A-Hmong-Family program which had been very successful. We'd heard of all of the difficulties facing the Hmongs in our society. They were obviously in need of help in assimilating, more so perhaps than the other Asian groups who had already arrived after Vietnam. Well, Tanya took off after that idea like a squirrel up a pine tree. She promoted the program with flyers and posters and held fund-raising activities." Rosie started giggling. "'Adopt A Hmong Family' was an omnipresent slogan around town. The response was tremendous, really. They had educational lectures at the college about the Hmongs to raise public awareness. There was even a five-page report distributed at various service agencies explaining the Hmong language and listing the most common words. It was an impressive campaign, and Tanya was responsible for everything, except, of course, that she borrowed most of her material from San Jose. Well, the result was that we raised a lot of money. Then came the day when we would identify the Hmong families deserving of our goodwill. You can't really appreciate the humor of this unless you were there, but I'll just say that's when we found out that there were no Hmongs in our county."

I laughed.

"Not one," Rosie added. "Tanya panicked. She sent out pleas to Sacramento, to the Bay Area, to Bakersfield to please send us some Hmongs! None came. She couldn't stall indefinitely, of course. People were waiting. Finally, Tanya found a group of Laotians who were willing to accept our help. They were photographed and passed off as Hmong."

"That's a good story," I said.

"Tanya wasn't daunted. She never is. But the next year, when the Hmongs came, nobody paid any attention to them. Unfortunately, as they've had a hard time of it. Tanya is concerned primarily about image, her image. That woman grates on me so, I can't tell you."

We finished our meal and Rosie poured the last of the wine into both of our glasses equally. "I'm going to turn off the ringer for the phone while I'm gone," Rosie said. "My phone rings a lot. I'll let voice mail take the calls, then I can check them from Phoenix and not bother you. You'll have your cell phone with you, right?"

Of course she wouldn't want me taking her calls. That was one area where her personal and professional personas would mingle, and she wanted to keep me away from that. I finished my wine, feeling hot.

I saw that Rosie was looking at me as if she had something to say, but then she said nothing. Instead, she just stood, saying,

104

"Are we done here?"

I nodded.

"I'll be leaving obscenely early in the morning," she said. "I'll feed the horses before I go, though, so you can just come out tomorrow afternoon." Rosie put the dishes in the dishwasher, then said, "Come into the living room, Jean. I have something for you."

While Rosie rummaged through a pile of papers on a counter in the living room, I sat on the couch, taking in my surroundings. This room was simply and comfortably furnished with a mix of old and new like the rest of the house. It was a little disheveled too, a little neglected. One bookshelf contained a puzzling assortment of objects. There were books, but they were shoved in haphazardly, some upright, some lying flat in stacks, some even with the bindings facing in, and then there were papers and photos interspersed among them. There was very little order in the room, but it wasn't especially cluttered. It had the look of a room that hadn't received much attention over the years other than the obligatory cleaning.

After a few moments, Rosie said, "Oh, here it is," and produced a five by seven photo in a frame. She sat beside me on the couch as I took it from her. It was a picture of the two of us, taken in Valencia Park at one of our last neighborhood barbecues, me in a Rosie for Mayor T-shirt and wearing one of those white straw hats, serving spoon in hand. She was standing beside me, her arm around my waist, her smile large, showing teeth. My smile, I noticed, was joyful, and I was looking at Rosie. Her head was slightly inclined toward me, as if she'd been listening to something I said. It was a great picture of us both. Looking at the expression on my face in that photo, I recognized something that I hadn't actually seen with my eyes before, but had only felt.

"Somebody took that at one of the barbecues," Rosie said. "I made this copy for you. I thought you'd like to have a memento."

"Yes," I said. "Thank you. I'm very happy to have it."

"It captures the moment well, I thought. The crazy fun of the thing, you know."

"Yes, it was fun."

"Excellent likeness of you."

So this is what Rosie saw when I looked at her, I realized—eyes full of joy, expression almost childlike in admiration.

When I looked up from the photo, I saw that she was looking at me with a slight, affectionate smile. The gray shock of hair above her ear stuck out whimsically at an odd angle. I reached over with my free hand and tucked it in, my fingers lingering for a moment on her exquisite ear, my thumb resting on the blue vein in her temple. I had to struggle to remove my hand. As I looked back to her face, I saw that her smile had faded.

"I'm falling in love with you," I said, so quietly I barely heard it, and then wasn't sure I had said it aloud after all.

She was just looking at me, no expression, eyes unblinking. "I know," she said at last.

So I had said it aloud. "When did you know?"

"I've suspected for quite a while. But I didn't think you'd recognize it. I knew, finally, that you knew it too on election night, at the party. When I found you on the deck, you were clearly lost in thought, watching Valerie and Carol down by the lake. When you turned and saw me, you looked like you expected me to be there. It was as though you had projected yourself, and me, out there. The way you looked at me that night, just like you're looking at me now, it's become painfully obvious."

"Painfully?"

She nodded.

"And you've been avoiding me ever since that night," I said.

She nodded again. "I've tried. But here you are." She laughed nervously.

I put my hand to her cheek. Or rather, it went there of its own accord. Her skin, covered with fine, invisible hairs, was silky. Her eyes closed. My hand slid down to her pale neck. I felt a crawling sensation in the pit of my stomach, spreading upward to my breasts, downward to my thighs. I sensed a relaxing of her body, an inclination of her head, as if she were giving herself over

106

to the touch of my hand. I moved my fingers along the line of her jaw and up to her lips. They were warm, soft, velvety soft, and between them, where I placed my index finger, they were moist. I was burning up. Rosie opened her eyes, reached up and gently took my hand away.

"No," she said softly. "Don't." She gripped my hand tightly between us, as though afraid of letting it go. "Stop yourself, Jean. I don't want this. I won't let it happen."

I was being rejected, I realized. "Why?" I asked, hurt and confused. "Is there someone else?"

"Yes," she said sharply. "There's a guy named Jerry. Remember him? Twenty-two years of marital bliss."

Oh, I thought, seeing her point. I had never cheated on Jerry, had never considered it. And here I was forgetting him altogether, because this wasn't me at all, this wasn't his wife sitting here wanting this woman.

"There are lots of other reasons too," Rosie said. "You're much better off not complicating your life."

She's right. What was I thinking? The problem was that I wasn't thinking, of course.

"I shouldn't have let you come here," Rosie said, appearing distraught. She released my hand. "I should have stopped this when I first realized."

She didn't want trouble. Her life was in order. Rosie's not available, I thought, and neither are you. Thank God she at least has some sense.

"Please don't allow yourself to do this," she said. "It's only going to cause trouble."

A minute later she was giving me a house key and I was walking to my car. Where will I go, what will I do, I thought, feeling like a person with no home. Somehow I did manage to drive myself home, though, because I eventually found myself lying in my bed, unable to sleep.

I lay awake through the night, the image of myself in that photo blistering my brain. My emotions were volcanoes, my thoughts jungles as I relived in my mind all of the moments of my association with Rosie, trying to understand how I had arrived at this place. I replayed every second, from the day Faye had asked me to volunteer and I'd said, "Who's Rosie Monroe?" to this evening when I told her that I was in love with her. How did that happen? When exactly did it happen? It happened long before tonight, that was evident. That woman in the photo was already so obviously in love. The curious thing was that the other woman in the photo also looked as though she could be in love.

# Chapter Ten

Thursday afternoon I went back to Rosie's with my suitcase. She was gone, of course. Her house was chilly and quiet. I turned up the heat, put my things in the guest room and went out to feed and water the horses. They were standing in the barn calmly with softly blinking eyes. I stroked their sleek noses and gave them some feed. I went over to the stack of hay and grabbed hold of the end of one of the bales, giving it a hard tug. It moved, but not much. Yes, they were heavy. Very impressive, Rosie, I thought.

As night descended, I wandered through the house, trying to feel Rosie's presence, trying to imagine being her, living here. On her bedroom dresser were a few photographs. I recognized the subjects of only one. She and Catherine, arms locked, smiling fondly at one another. Rosie was younger, her hair longer, thicker, curled. "Brown curls bouncing," I remembered.

In the lower corner of a picture of a young woman, about twenty, Chinese ancestry, was the inked inscription, "Your Doting One, Sue." She matched the voice on the phone—shy eyes, a small mouth turned into a tentative, appealing smile. Her hair was long, straight and black. She was standing on bare granite wearing a backpack, an expansive vista behind her, obviously Yosemite. Too young for you, Rosie, I thought, but there was no date, so this photo could have been taken long ago. There was a photograph that could have been her family, mom and dad, a brother, a sister, and Rosie between them, about thirty years old, her smile quite recognizable, though her features were leaner. I realized that I had never even asked if she had living parents or siblings. There were several photos of Rosie at various ages with women who could have been lovers. No matter how long I stared at these photographs, they kept their secrets from me.

In the study, one bookcase was filled with awards—statues, plaques—testimonials to Rosie's work. There was the City of Weberstown Citizenship Award, the Businesswoman of the Year Athena Award, the Chamber of Commerce Lifetime Achievement Award. Wow, what an overachiever! Seeing all the honors given to Rosie renewed my anger against the small-minded public who had failed to elect her mayor.

On all of these tributes, Rosie's name appeared as Rosalind. The only person I had ever heard call her that, though, was Dr. Patel. It was a rich, romantic sort of name. Rosalind Monroe was a complicated woman, an ogress and a vampire girl crashing through walls, an ardent lover of women whose eyes said yes, whose voice said no, the tormented heroine in a historical romance.

The other bookshelves were a mix of fiction, non-fiction, cooking, gardening, plumbing, art, history and music. Then there were rows of nineteenth century novels, sixteenth century plays, modern mysteries, reference books on ancient Greek civilization. They were only loosely organized so that every shelf was a trove of discovery. The selections were so varied that they said almost nothing about Rosie's interests or tastes except that she had many.

About nine, I called Jerry. "How are things at home?"

"Just fine. Amy wants to go to a rock concert next week. I thought I'd check with you."

"Who's she going with?"

"Tommy. Or as she puts it, Tommy, of course!"

"Of course. Where's the concert?"

"I think she said Lincoln Park."

Okay, I thought, so I am not the only one who's out of touch. "Jerry, I think that's probably who she's going to see. Should be no problem."

"She's at this point now, Jeannie, where she doesn't ask anyway. She just tells you so you won't be alarmed when she comes in at two in the morning."

"I know. Well, she's nineteen, a college girl. She's an adult, Jerry."

"Scary, isn't it?"

"Very scary."

"What's it like out there in the boondocks?"

"Peaceful. Why don't you bring Amy over Saturday? She can ride the horses. We can have a barbecue."

"Are you lonely, hon?"

"A little."

"I'll ask her if she has any plans. Oh, the neighbor's dog broke through the fence again. He dug up your chrysanthemums, the lavender ones. I've replanted them, but I don't know if they'll make it."

My response to this "news" was apathy. It didn't seem to matter, and it also didn't seem to have anything to do with me, yet I had picked out those mum plants two months ago with precision and had lovingly put them into the ground. "Did you talk to the neighbors?" I asked.

"Yes, when I hauled the dog back. Like it will do any good. I'll let you know tomorrow about Saturday. Remember to lock the doors and windows."

"There's a security system."

"Good. Good night, Jeannie. I love you."

"Good night, Jerry." I hung up, feeling inexplicably forlorn.

As I lay in bed before sleep, I thought of Rosie, of her liquid eyes and her alluring mouth. I felt the touch of her fingers in my palm, and my gut ached with longing. I envisioned myself kissing her, and my thighs and arms and hands were alive with yearning. "Oh, God," I said in the dark. "How is this happening to me?" I rolled onto my stomach and buried my face in the pillow, forcing Rosie out of my mind. I replaced her with an image of uprooted mums.

Friday morning after taking care of the cats and horses, I went home and tried to do some work for the Partnership, managing to accomplish almost nothing, but I did end up sorting some things into folders so it felt a little better organized. While working, I made a pot of vegetable soup for Jerry and Amy's dinner.

Remembering the contract Rosie had given me, I pulled it out to take a look at it. There was no reason to question the legalese of the thing. I trusted her absolutely regarding the details of my employment. The thing that stunned me, however, was the figure of my salary. My God, I thought, staring at it. I had never made anything close to this. Of course, I had never had a job with this kind of responsibility before, either. Seeing that figure scared me. They'd be expecting a lot in return. I can do this, I thought, trying to bolster my confidence. I was determined not to let Rosie down.

While I was waiting for the soup to finish cooking, I decided to do a little research into the names of Rosie's pets. Her cats were Sappho and Meg. I knew who Sappho was, of course, if for no other reason than her frequent appearance in crossword puzzles with the clue, "ancient Greek poetess." There was only one of those, so that was always an easy one. Meg, however, was more difficult, since it didn't sound like a name that would have any association with Sappho or ancient Greece. Might have just been a name Rosie liked, of course. In a few minutes on the Internet, though, I discovered that Megara was one of several known female lovers of Sappho. I tried the horses' names next and discovered that Violet and Vita were also named for lesbian lovers, writers Violet Trefusis and Vita Sackville-West. Their tempestuous affair was apparently notorious and the subject of a PBS miniseries entitled *Portrait of a Marriage*. There were plenty of clues that Rosie was gay, if a person was paying attention.

Intrigued, I called some video stores asking for *Portrait of a Marriage*, and finally found a copy at an independent store. I had a bowl of soup before leaving the house, stopping at the video store on the way to Rosie's place. I arrived earlier than necessary, about three in the afternoon.

Bundling up in a thick sweater, I took a sack out to pick up walnuts in the driveway. Then I set to work cracking them on the stones of her rear patio, an exercise which left my mind free to wander. A bird called nearby and I jumped. My nerves were on edge. I hit my forefinger with the hammer and cursed. Hearing myself curse, I did it again just for effect. "Shit!"

You're not used to being alone, I told myself. The sound of your own voice startles you. "Shit!" I said again, gauging how unfamiliar my voice sounded. When I'd finished with the walnuts, I went inside and examined Rosie's extensive CD collection. Preponderance of jazz, some classical, but there was popular music as well, even some of the music Amy listened to. Yes, there was even a Linkin Park CD, some oldies from practically every decade from the fifties onward, and big names like Melissa Etheridge, Billy Joel and Norah Jones. And there were names I didn't recognize: Joan Armatrading, Chris Williamson and Ferron.

I opened the player to read the label of the Brazilian jazz CD that Rosie had played for us Wednesday night. I liked it and thought I might get one for myself, but I found a different CD inside, a disc with a homemade label that said "Helen, 1995." Rosie must have put this on after I left, I realized, trying not to think about the fact that it represented yet another mystery woman from her past. I decided to play it. From the first couple of words, the song gripped me, so I just stood there in front of the stereo, listening to the plaintive female voice and accompanying acoustic guitar.

*Here you are, looking so much like someone I should love.*
*I wish I could touch you*
*but the world stands between us...like a wall.*

113

*You think you've come to steal my heart, but you've only come to break it.*

The song, from beginning to end, was evocative, full of yearning, and extremely melancholy. I had a hard time picturing Rosie sitting here in her house listening to this. But, obviously, she had. Was it possible that she had listened to this melancholy song with its message of hopelessness and thought of me?

*I wish I could hold you*
*but the world stands between us…like a wall.*

With that, the song finished. I found myself near tears and wondered if Rosie had reacted that way. But I was projecting. Rosie would not be sitting here listening to this song and crying her eyes out. That was not her. It was a beautiful song. A person could just enjoy it, a person like Rosie. What would she be doing sitting here pining like that about me anyway? If she was pining, it wasn't for me. I had to assume that Rosie had been through her share of loves and losses and had probably learned at some point to take it on the chin and move on when it didn't work out. As Faye had noted, Rosie wasn't someone who lived with regrets. Her relationship with life was extremely healthy. Still, I thought, perhaps she had wanted me a little, had wished it were possible. Since it wasn't, she would have given up the idea. Just as she had told me to do.

The next song was also a love song, though not a sad one, sung to a woman identified only as "she." The voice of the singer was clear and true, emotionally candid. The lyrics on these songs were too evocative for me in my vulnerable emotional state. I turned the music off and poked through Rosie's mail for reading material. People claim to be able to tell a lot about a person by what magazines they subscribe to. I didn't subscribe to any magazines and had only been reading the newspaper since August when I began working on the election. Prior to that, the newspaper represented little more to me than the daily crossword puzzle. I was hopelessly out of touch. Rosie subscribed to business, financial and news magazines. A large stack of them in the study suggested that she was behind in her reading.

She was such a stranger to me. I had thought I would be able to absorb her from her environment somehow. How could I feel so much yearning for someone I knew almost nothing about? The house, the case full of awards, the music, the books, the magazines, they revealed almost nothing. All this told me was what I already knew—Rosie was serious about her business and public life. I knew nothing more about her private life. Don't you mean sex life, I asked myself? Isn't that what you're really interested in, what kind of sex life she has?

They say that high-energy achievers like Rosie also have high-energy sex drives. She had claimed that she wasn't seeing anyone, I recalled, when her sexuality had become an issue, but what did she really mean by that? She obviously wasn't living with anyone. Maybe all she meant by it was that she had no special someone, no exclusive lover. It didn't mean she was celibate. And she admitted to Clark that she had led a "full life," implying that there were secrets, a colorful past, probably, full of excitement. She was a woman of profound passions, it seemed to me. Did that mean that when she went on a business trip to Phoenix, she'd never spend the night alone? She'd rejected me because I was nothing but trouble, but perhaps she would accept a stranger, a sultry, dark-eyed advertising executive met at the evening social where they would discuss the latest in computer-generated animation, and then they would ride an elevator to Rosie's room, staring seductively at one another, and do all the mysterious things that women do together. I tried to shake these tormenting thoughts from my mind.

It was peaceful at Rosie's house, so quiet you could hear the hum of the refrigerator or, if you were sitting still, the purring of a cat. I'd never lived alone. It would be a different sort of life, being in charge of your time and your activities, being free to make your own choices, to be driven by your own needs? To be lonely too. But I wasn't lonely just then. I was content. Who are you, I asked myself, when there's no one else in your world? When there's no parent, spouse, child, boss, doorbell, phone or television defining you? Maybe you're nobody at all. Or maybe you're someone you wouldn't even recognize. Or maybe you'll recognize her when you see her, recognize bits of her when you see bits of her, over time.

By six thirty, I decided to watch my video. I loaded the DVD into Rosie's player, then curled up on the sofa with a big cup of decaf for a three-and-a-half-hour diversion. Both cats joined me, one on the arm of the sofa and one on the other chair. My expectations, knowing that this series appeared on *Masterpiece Theatre* over a decade ago, left me unprepared for the tempestuous drama that unfolded as Vita and Violet pursued their love and lust for one another. I had never seen anything like this before. It was gorgeous, intelligent, stormy and sexy. I was completely transfixed as darkness descended around me and the only light in the house was the glow of the television.

When my cell phone rang, it took me several seconds to comprehend it. I paused the movie and grabbed my phone just in time before voice mail answered. It was Jerry calling to say thanks for the soup and to report that he and Amy would come over tomorrow. The chrysanthemums were wilting slightly, but he had flooded them with water and was optimistic. Anxious to get off the phone, I didn't encourage any further conversation and told him goodnight. I returned to Vita and Violet as their love affair took them through the nightclubs of Paris.

Later, when my cell phone rang again, it was Rosie. I was still sitting in the dark, the cats on their armchair perches. I checked the time on my phone. It was nine thirty. Was the dark-eyed beauty already gone from Rosie's hotel room, I wondered. Had they completed their passionate, no-strings liaison or was the seductress lying there beside her still, waiting impatiently for this phone call to be over?

"How are things?" Rosie asked.

"Everything's fine. How are things with you?"

"I'm having a good trip. After meetings last night, one of the guys took me out on the town. We went to a great Cuban restaurant, and then to a club where I danced so much I got blisters. I haven't been dancing in years. It was a lot of fun."

"It sounds like it," I said, wondering if there was more to this story. What did she mean by "one of the guys"? What did she mean by "club"? I couldn't ask, especially after she had told me to get out of her life.

"Tomorrow Jerry and Amy are coming over for the day," I said.

"Glad to hear it. Are you finding everything?"

"Yes."

"I'll be back Sunday as planned. If you want to go home tomorrow evening, go ahead. You don't have to stay. Slip the key under the back door. I know you must be bored there."

"I'm not bored, Rosie. I'm enjoying myself."

"Well, it'd still be a good idea if you went home tomorrow or, if you want, early Sunday."

Yes, Rosie, I get the message, I thought. She didn't want me there when she came back.

After saying goodnight to her, I returned to the movie. When it finally ended, I just sat where I was, watching, but not seeing, the credits roll by. I had always assumed that *Masterpiece Theatre* was for fuddy-duddies. If this was typical, that was a big misconception. I was emotionally drained, but also highly aroused by the violent passions I had just witnessed. It was essentially a tragic story, but it was also a story about an all-consuming obsession that burned in two women their whole lives long. When Sappho came up and butted my arm, wanting to be petted, I roused myself and went to bed.

Tonight my fantasies were more intense than last night's. I imagined Rosie making love to me, with her fingers, with her tongue. I imagined myself as the sultry woman in her hotel room, the stranger whose name she didn't know, whose face she would always remember. Holding these images in my mind, I touched myself, imagining that my hand was Rosie's, that she lay beside me, that her hands and mouth were all over me, that her voice was in my ear telling me how beautiful I was and how much she wanted me. I fell asleep with a sated body and a mind in turmoil.

"Be careful," I called to Amy Saturday as she climbed onto Vita's back. She had brought her boyfriend Tommy who was pretending, with some success, that he knew all about horses, though it was Amy who saddled them both. She rode off into the field looking confident and lovely. Our children had both turned out better than anyone could have hoped. Bradley was smart and decent and responsible. Amy was lively and outgoing and relaxed. Jerry looked at me and smiled affectionately, slipping his arm around my waist. Was he too thinking about our children?

Under the circumstances, I couldn't help wondering if I still loved this man. Sure, I thought, I must love him. Things had been good between us. I remembered what Rosie said about her marriage, about how she and her husband had become like brother and sister. Brothers and sisters love each other too. I couldn't honestly say I was in love with Jerry, not anymore. Years ago we had apparently fallen out of love and didn't even notice. Oh, I wasn't so naive that I'd missed the natural cooling down over the years. But I'd always thought that we still loved each other, that the things we did that looked like love were exactly what they looked like. We were still traveling through space like a rocket after the fuel was exhausted, maintaining course and speed with nobody at the helm.

Am I deluding myself, I wondered, because of Rosie, into believing I don't love my husband?

We barbecued steaks and potatoes for dinner on Rosie's gas grill. In the kitchen, I made a salad, listening to a Madeleine Peyroux CD. Amy and Tommy brushed the horses. When Jerry brought the steak in, he asked, "What's that music?"

"Jazz," I answered.

"Do you like it?"

"Yes. It's growing on me."

Amy and Tommy teased and insulted each other good-naturedly, just like siblings. He called her "dude" a lot. She called him "dude" a lot. It was funny to watch them. I concluded that Tommy was not going to be around very much longer. Amy didn't love him. There was no desperation between them.

118

After dinner, the three of them left for home. I stayed. Rosie would arrive tomorrow hoping I was already gone. I wouldn't be gone at all. Somewhere in my muddled brain, I was plotting, but I didn't even know what. All I knew was what my body knew, that it wanted to see her again, that it wanted to touch her again, even if the result was the same. Even if she turned me away. Which she would, of course, because she was too shrewd to give in to me. What did she need me for anyway? She had just spent a passionate night with a sultry advertising executive in Phoenix, and tonight she was lying in the arms of the enigmatic Grace Carpenter in Sacramento. What the hell did I have to offer her after that?

# Chapter Eleven

By Sunday morning I was so excited about Rosie's return that I couldn't be still. I mopped the kitchen floor, raked leaves, baked brownies full of my freshly shelled walnuts, and avoided thinking too much about how I would greet her or how she would treat me. I had to will myself not to think about that or I would have spun off into the stratosphere.

By noon, I was panicking and began throwing my things into my suitcase. You've got to get out of here, I thought with alarm. Then, looking at the turbulent pile of clothing, I realized that I was acting ridiculous, certainly not my age. Calm down, I advised myself, be poised, be rational. I cut the brownies into squares and gave the cats a fresh bowl of water.

When Rosie arrived, I would say hi, ask about her trip, give her the accumulated mail, and go home. Yes, you'll go home in time to make dinner for Jerry and Amy. That's the plan, then. No more of this life in Fantasyland. It was an entertaining diversion, a swerve off the highway of life, and now we had to get back on the main road. Being alone for a few days can fill your head with the most bizarre thoughts. Yes, I was over it. I chuckled at myself and ate a brownie, perfectly composed. Then I sat down to read a magazine and got caught up in a story about global warming. I needed to pay more attention to what was happening in the world, develop some civic-mindedness. I should "go green," I thought.

It was a few minutes after two when I heard the crunch of gravel under the wheels of a car. Rosie! I sat up stiffly. She would see my car, would know I was still here. I went out to help her with her luggage. Pulling a suitcase out of the trunk, she smiled and said, "Hi."

So she wasn't unhappy about my being here, not enough to let it show. What a relief. She wore slim black slacks and a knit sweater of gray and red rectangles. Rosie carried the small bag and I carried the large one through the open front door.

"How was the trip?" I asked.

"Successful. But it always feels good to be home. How are things around here?"

"No problems."

She put the suitcase in the front room, sniffing the air. "Smells good. What is it? Chocolate cake?"

"Brownies."

"Oooh, I love brownies!"

Our eyes met for the first time since she'd arrived. Rosie's eager smile gradually faded as we stood for several moments looking at one another like statues, so quietly I could hear the ticking of a clock in another room. My nerves had gone taut. My plans, whatever they had been, had no hope of reclaiming me.

"So," she said, looking away from me, "where are my babies?" Her voice was unsteady. She could feel it too, the powerful urgency between us. She wanted me, I realized. There was no doubt about it now.

"In the kitchen, I think," I said. "I just fed them." I could feel the trembling in my body, growing worse each moment like the rumblings of a volcano before it erupts.

Rosie, stepping around me, said, "Go home, Jean." It was a command. She strode into the kitchen.

I stood where I was, my mind whirling. When we looked at each other, there was such power, such emotion in that link. I hadn't understood it before, hadn't been receptive to what had been there all along—sexual energy. If she'd been a man, I would have recognized it instantly. And no man would have tried to hide it from me like Rosie had. I had thought it was the exhilaration of the campaign, that it was all just the rush of the work we were doing. But it was the excitement of mutual attraction that had infected us both. Realizing that, I was overjoyed. Rosie felt it too!

I heard her talking to Sappho and Meg in the kitchen in an affectionate tone you use with small children. I bolted through the doorway to find her with her mouth full and a brownie in her hand. The two cats were rubbing against her legs.

"Very good," she said, indicating the brownie. Then she popped the rest of it into her mouth and frowned. "Jean, you've got a look on your face like you're going to eat me alive. Go home."

"I want you," I said, feeling explosive.

"Forget it." Her voice was stern. "It's not going to happen." She swallowed, glaring at me. "Jean, I'm not kidding. I want you to leave."

I felt myself collapsing on the inside. "Rosie," I said, hurt, "can you honestly say you aren't attracted to me?"

She looked at me sort of helplessly, the resolve on her face falling away. "You idiot," she said. "Of course I am. That's why I want you out of here. Because this is dangerous. You don't know what you're doing."

I stepped toward her. "All I know is that I want to touch you."

Rosie stood staring at me, her eyes tormented. She made no move, said nothing. I reached out and took hold of her arm, pulling her closer. She let herself be manipulated, like a mannequin. I put my arms around her waist, loosely, then ran my hands up her back, over her sweater, to her shoulder blades. She didn't move, just stared at me, her look almost angry. For the first

122

time, I felt her body touching mine, her stomach, her thighs, her breasts swelling against me through our clothes as she breathed, and, at last, there was the roundness, the warmth, the reality of her. There was no way I could stop touching her now.

"You've got a crumb," I said quietly, my voice concealing the hunger of my skin. I moved my face closer and, with the tip of my tongue, licked a brownie crumb away from the corner of her mouth, letting my tongue linger for just a second. I closed my eyes and felt a flood of heat gushing through my veins.

And then I felt her lips on mine, pressing softly. I felt her arms surround me and the pressure of her kiss deepening. Her lips were full and luxurious, a mouth alive with desire. I pressed myself against her, my insides surging. I felt her tongue glide over my lips. I opened my mouth and took it in, and my body responded intuitively, closing the gap between our hips and thighs. She kissed my mouth with such a need. I was melting, going weak in the knees. I felt them giving way, and then she pushed me back into the wall, pinning me against it. She filled my mouth with her tongue, pushed my legs apart with her knee, held me against the wall with the pressure of her body, my feet barely touching the floor. Her strength surprised me.

My body moved, encouraged by the force of her thigh against my pubic bone. I was already so aroused that I could feel the fabric of my clothes sliding easily between my legs. The way she held me, pressing me into the wall, my legs useless, I could no longer act. My body was a limp object at her command. I was startled by how completely she had possession of me, not just physically, but in my gut, in my nerves. She rocked me against her thigh, her breath hot in my ear, until I came, not localized as I was used to, but radiating over my entire body, all the way out to my fingertips. A low cry escaped my throat and then I heard myself sort of whimper with each exhaled breath until, gradually, I was just breathing again.

She slowly released her grip on me and held me gently against her, my head on her shoulder, my body spent, and all of this had happened, I realized, in about two minutes. She lowered me to a chair, then stood watching me, looking bewildered, even apologetic.

What would have happened next, I don't know because just then the doorbell rang and both of us started violently at the sound.

"Hey, Rosie," called a feminine voice through the house. "I saw your car. Are you home?"

Rosie turned back to me to say, "We left the front door open. I'll have to go."

She went to greet her visitor and I stood, tentatively, testing my legs. Who was this person barging in on us, I thought, indignantly. Some lover who'd been waiting for her return? Is that why she wanted me gone when she came home?

I stood more firmly and straightened my shirt, coaxing my breathing back to normal.

Rosie returned, followed by a boy of about eleven. "Jean, this is Daniel, a friend of mine."

I started to say something, but found I still couldn't speak.

"He came by to collect his money for mowing the lawn. Sorry I didn't think to pay you before I went out of town, Danny. I'll be right back with your money. Why don't you help yourself to a brownie there?"

She glanced at me before leaving, a look of entreaty and concern.

Daniel flashed me a broad grin before grabbing a brownie. I smiled, grimaced or nodded, I'm not sure what, and wordlessly left the kitchen. My suitcase was already mostly packed from earlier when I'd panicked and started to run away. I finished packing in a flustered rush and lugged my suitcase out to the car. I could hear Rosie and Daniel talking from the kitchen as I went out the front door.

Standing in the driveway in the afternoon sun, I felt stupid and absurd. I was running away and I didn't know why. I had gotten just what I wanted, what I'd practically forced her into. As I slammed my trunk, Rosie and Daniel came out the front door. Daniel ran off with a spare brownie in hand.

"So, you're off, then?" Rosie said.

I nodded. Since we were standing outside, my departure was awkward, but safe. I didn't want to go back in the house now that I had managed to get this far. I knew that if I went back in, I wouldn't be leaving soon. The attraction between us was too strong. I was overwhelmed, feeling detached from my body. I had to get away.

"Thanks for taking care of the place," Rosie said, kicking gravel with one foot.

"Oh, sure." I sounded nonchalant, breezy even. It seemed like I was in some bizarre, badly written movie. "See you soon," I called, sliding behind the wheel.

Rosie didn't look happy about this development, but she didn't say anything more. A moment later I was driving away.

On the drive home, I didn't see or hear anything. I was in a trance, a disembodied spirit, my body still with Rosie, still feeling her insistent lips on mine. I almost had a wreck in town when I nearly missed seeing a red light and shot out partway into the intersection. No one was home when I arrived. I was glad. I needed some time alone to adjust to my surroundings, which were familiar, but odd, somehow. I felt as though I'd been sleepwalking for eons and had just now awakened to a strange, alien universe where no one spoke my language.

I unpacked, then wandered out to the backyard and looked at the mums. One of them was hopelessly wilted, but the others looked perky enough. Most of the leaves had fallen from the peach and cherry trees. Their branches stood out bare against a crisp blue sky sporting a few wispy clouds.

"Hi," called a voice. I looked up, startled. My neighbor, Abby, was on tiptoes looking over the fence.

"Oh, hi," I said.

"Want to come over for a visit?"

"Not right now, Abby. I'll have to start dinner soon. Maybe tomorrow." After I'd returned to the house, I realized that Abby no longer knew who I was. I didn't even know who I was. Maneuvering the evening with Jerry and Amy was uncomfortable. They were glad to have me home, glad to have things back to normal. But things weren't normal at all. I was aching to be somewhere else. I did my best to be who they expected me to be.

At dinner we talked about Christmas trees. "I think we should get an artificial one," Jerry said. "They're getting too expensive. Last year we paid sixty dollars for the tree, and that was a bargain."

"But artificial trees are so…" Amy began, "artificial." They both looked at me.

"Well?" Jerry asked.

"Does it matter?"

Amy frowned. "Of course it matters, Mom. A Christmas tree is like the focal point of your home's holiday decor. It's where the presents go. It's what people see through the window when they drive by."

I was irritated that I was being called upon to participate in this discussion. "They *are* very expensive," I said.

"Yes," Jerry said. "And a fire hazard. And they shed. Besides, princess, they make the artificial ones so lifelike nowadays, you probably wouldn't know the difference. They even have a pine scent." So the subject was closed. We would buy an artificial tree this year. Jerry was making an investment in our future, in our future Christmases together, and my mind was questioning the practicality of that. The thought that our future together could be called into question terrified me.

Monday I stayed in bed until long after Jerry and Amy had gone. I wasn't asleep. I was reliving my few intimate moments with Rosie in my mind, the evening before she left for Phoenix, the frantic minutes in her kitchen when she returned. When I finally got up, I called her house. Voice mail answered. I made some coffee and then called her cell phone. Voice mail there too. Was she screening me? I decided not to leave a message because I didn't know what to say. Thank you for the orgasm? Sorry I had to leave so soon?

By the time afternoon descended, I had gotten dressed. When I checked my e-mail, I found a note from Rosie, sent out to the Vision Partnership members, reminding us of December's monthly meeting tomorrow night. The agenda was attached. I printed it, wondering how I was going to deal with this.

I thought Rosie might call me, but she didn't. Maybe she was disappointed at the way I'd left. Maybe she was angry at me for seducing her. Or maybe she hadn't noticed so much. Maybe it wasn't a big deal to her. Happened all the time.

Somehow I managed to make dinner so that, by six o'clock, the three of us were sitting at the dining room table eating.

"How was school, princess?" Jerry asked Amy.

"Okay. I got out of psychology today because we were doing our experiments. It's cool. We drive around town and whenever we're in the front of the line, like at a stoplight, when it turns green, we just sit there. Then we wait until something happens."

"Something like what?" Jerry asked, alarmed. "Like you get shot?"

"No, like somebody honks. We keep track with a stopwatch to see how long it takes, and we write down the sex, age and car model of the person who honks."

"So what'd you find out?" I asked, forcing myself to pay attention.

"Pretty much what you'd expect. Young people are impatient, boys are more aggressive than girls, people in red cars get pissed off faster, that kind of stuff."

"Sounds like a lame excuse for a psychology experiment," Jerry said.

Amy shrugged. "We had to think of our own."

Our evening proceeded like any other evening with Amy on the phone, Jerry in front of the television. I sat in my chair with the newspaper crossword puzzle on my lap, pen in hand, all of the little squares staring blankly up at me. Periodically I shut my eyes and tasted her mouth again in my mind while the crossword remained untouched.

Tuesday I tried to distract myself with work. I looked over the agenda for the meeting. They were going to discuss the office rental—my office, and my position. I suddenly had a frightening thought. Maybe Rosie was going to fire me tonight. Had I blown this opportunity by forcing myself into her private sphere and blurring the lines between the professional and personal?

I sent her an e-mail, asking if she wanted me to attend the meeting.

"Yes, Jean," she wrote me back. "Please attend."

That was all. She wasn't giving me any help to determine her state of mind or her intentions. If she did fire me, I couldn't blame her. As the day wore on, I was convinced that was exactly what she was going to do. She would come up with some excuse for the rest of the members. No doubt she could find plenty, including my lack of qualifications. I was to come to the meeting so she could hand me a check and thank me for my services.

When I arrived at the meeting room, Rosie and Ken Sturtevant were already there, comfortably conversing about Calder mobiles, which meant nothing to me. I realized again how little I had to offer someone like Rosie, even if I'd been an unattached gay woman. I knew almost nothing about the things she was interested in.

"They appear simple," Ken was saying. "But if you stop and look more carefully at the distribution of elements, the structure is not the least bit symmetrical. Still, it's perfectly balanced. That's what I like about them, the precise engineering."

"Exactly," said Rosie. "That's no accident, of course. Calder was a mechanical engineer before he became a sculptor." Rosie looked up to see me. "Hi, Jean," she said as naturally as could be.

I greeted them both as the rest of the members wandered in. The meeting began at seven, on time. I was so nervous that I could barely look at anyone. The subject of my office was the first item on the agenda. Terry reported that a space had been selected, and the figure of the rent was discussed. I took notes on my laptop as the members approved the office space.

"I thought we should talk about the roles and responsibilities of this new position," Rosie said. "We can't just throw Jean out there to figure out for herself what her job is."

She wasn't going to fire me, then? I looked up and caught Rosie's eye. The look of gratitude and relief on my face must have been obvious because she looked briefly confused and then smiled reassuringly at me. I listened, captivated, as they debated over my job duties, and this went on for quite a while with no real consensus reached.

"Well," said Rosie at last, "perhaps we should revisit this subject later on, after Jean has had an opportunity to get more involved and she can contribute her opinion. Sometimes these things determine themselves, and since this is a new role, a lot will depend on the individual. In my experience, Jean tends to go well beyond expectations anyway."

Rosie was speaking as though she still thought the world of me, as an employee, anyway. This ability of hers, to compartmentalize her life, still impressed and astonished me.

"Let's go on to the next topic," Rosie said. "The delegation from Beijing will be arriving on February fifth and departing on February eighth. There will be four businessmen and their interpreter. We need to draw up a plan for their tour and provide them an escort. Since we've been talking about our administrator's responsibilities, I'd like to propose that we assign these tasks to Jean."

"Great!" said Gordon. "Jean, you're going to get all of the dirty work. I love it!"

"I think I'm going to love it, too," I said, genuinely excited.

The meeting ended at eight thirty and everybody left except Rosie, who would be locking the room and returning the key. I waited until we were alone to approach her. I handed her my signed employment contract.

"Thanks," she said. "I guess you didn't find anything to object to?"

"No, not at all."

"Salary is acceptable?" Her voice and manner were a little cool, I noticed with dismay.

"More than acceptable," I said. "Very generous. I'll do my best to earn it."

"I have no doubt you will." She slid the papers into her briefcase.

"Rosie," I said, "I just want to say I'm sorry about last Sunday, about how I ran off like that. As my daughter would say, I freaked."

She looked at me more kindly. "It's okay, Jean. I know how confused you must be right now. I'm sorry too. I'm sorry that I let you get to me. I underestimated your determination. Let's just forget it, okay?"

I hesitated, looking at her mouth and wanting so much to kiss her. "I don't want to forget it," I said, realizing that I was about to put my job in jeopardy again. "There's no way I can forget it. What I meant was that I'm sorry I didn't stay."

"I don't see any point in pursuing this," she said quietly. "What do you think can come of it?"

"I don't know," I said, my voice breaking with despair. "I just know that I love you and I don't see how something like that can be ignored."

I saw her glance at the closed curtains across the window. She moved toward me and held me close. I put my head on her shoulder, choking back sobs. She stroked my head maternally and said nothing, and we stood like that for a few moments. When I lifted my head and looked into her eyes, I saw that there was nothing maternal about her gaze. She wiped a tear from my cheek and then kissed my mouth, gently. I closed my eyes and returned her kiss.

Her mouth became more insistent as she pulled my body tightly against her. We stood inside the meeting room kissing in a close embrace. She was ardent, but very much in control of herself tonight. She hadn't been taken off guard this time. I, on the other hand, allowed myself to go liquid in her arms. Her kisses alternated between tenderness and hard desire. I felt the heat rise between us and imagined myself turning into a molten puddle at her feet.

After a few moments, Rosie pulled away slightly. I opened my eyes, wondering why she had stopped kissing me. As far as I was concerned, I was prepared to spend the rest of my life standing here in this room with my mouth linked to hers.

She was breathing deeply and her eyes were dark and intense. "Come home with me," she said. It was a command, not a request.

Oh, yes! I thought, calculating how many minutes it would be before I was lying beside her in her bed. And then a horribly unwelcome reminder of who I was swept over me. My mind struggled. Rosie released me, seeing that I wasn't going to assent.

"I can't," I said, hating my life. "I'm expected home any minute."

Rosie nodded, clearly disappointed. "Yes," she said, turning away. "That's exactly my point."

She went to the table and packed her things into her briefcase. I did the same and stepped into the hallway, feeling defeated. Rosie turned off the light, locked the door and pulled it shut behind us. As she turned to look at me, I said, "I wish—"

"I know," she said. "Me too."

As the week continued, all I could think about was Rosie, all day long, no matter what I was doing. I resisted the urge to call her. I had nothing new to offer. But my preoccupation with her did not diminish. Washing my car in the driveway Thursday afternoon, I was overcome with daylight fantasies and found myself lying across the hood, my face in a wet rag, completely oblivious to what I was doing. I kept telling myself to resist my desire. Giving in to this thing, whatever it was—lust, love, insanity—would topple too many truths. Like a tsunami, it would come slamming into people's lives, laying waste.

Friday afternoon Amy coerced me into helping her rehearse her part in a school play, Sheridan's *The Rivals*. She was Mrs. Malaprop, a character, she explained, who gave us the term "malapropism." I had to ask what a malapropism was. "A word that's misused, used in an improper context," she said, handing me the book. "This is my first scene, Mom. You play Lydia, a young woman in love with a man I don't approve of."

Amy stood akimbo in front of me, puckered her lips, frowned, then pointed at me with a straight and accusing finger. "There, Sir Anthony," she said in a dowager voice, rolling her r's. "There sits the deliberate simpleton who wants to disgrace her family, and lavish herself on a fellow not worth a shilling!"

It was my turn. "Madam," I read, "I thought you once—"

"You thought, Miss! I don't know any business you have to think at all. Thought does not become a young woman. But the point we would request of you is that you will promise to forget this fellow—to illiterate him, I say, quite from your memory."

"Illiterate?" I asked.

"Mom," Amy objected. "It's a malapropism."

"Oh, yeah, I forgot."

Amy tossed her hair out of her face and began again. "But the point we would request of you is that you will promise to forget this fellow—to illiterate him, I say, quite from your memory."

"Ah! Madam!" I read, "our memories are independent of our wills. It is not so easy to forget."

I couldn't even help Amy with her play without taking everything personally. Having her point her finger at me and accuse me of wanting to disgrace my family was disconcerting. And, of course, thoughts of *illiterating* somebody from my mind made me think of Rosie. No, it is not easy. It is not possible.

I finally broke down and called her office Friday after Amy left for rehearsal. When she answered, I said, "Rosie, I can't stand it. I'm dying without you."

"Hey, love, this is a business phone."

"I have to see you. Please don't say no. Tell me where, when. Just ten minutes. Just let me look at you."

"Whoa!" she said. "Calm down. I'm going to San Francisco tomorrow, to an afternoon meeting. I've got a hotel for the night. Come with me."

"Yes!" I blurted into the phone.

"Meet me here at the office at ten tomorrow morning."

"I'll be there," I said, overwhelmed with relief that she would see me.

"By the way," Rosie said, "who is this?"

Oh, very funny, Rosie! Well, she did make me laugh, which was the point, as it was obvious that my mood needed lightening up.

"See you tomorrow, Jean," she said calmly.

After hanging up, I wondered how I would explain this to Jerry. By the time the three of us sat down to dinner, I was composed enough to lie my way through it, touting this as a business meeting for the Partnership. "I'm going with Rosie to San Francisco tomorrow," I said, "to meet with some people who've implemented a program to clean up the streets. Rosie thinks we might be able to use some of their ideas here."

"Tomorrow?" Jerry asked. "On a Saturday? Why do *you* have to go?"

"Well, I am the administrator. We'll be staying overnight, by the way."

Jerry looked frustrated. "Are you going to get overtime for this? Look at the work you've done already. You haven't gotten a single paycheck yet."

I realized that I had not shared any of the details of this job with Jerry, had not even told him what the salary was. And for some reason, I didn't want to.

"Why do you have to stay overnight?" Jerry asked.

"It's just the schedule. We're committed to dinner with these people. It's hard to know how late that will go." How many lies was he going to make me tell?

"Can I go, Mom?" Amy asked. "There's nowhere to shop in this hick town."

"Uh," I said, thinking fast. "No, I don't think so, Amy. It's a business trip. We're not going to be downtown anyway. The meeting is at the airport and the schedule is tight, so it'd be too much trouble to get to the shopping district."

Amy wrinkled her nose and stuck out her bottom lip. I realized that I had no idea where in San Francisco we were going. What did that matter to me? What did it even matter what city or state or planet as long as I was with Rosie?

# Chapter Twelve

I was up earlier than usual Saturday morning. To help assuage the guilt, I made Jerry breakfast, a real breakfast of eggs and sausage, fresh-squeezed orange juice. Not the usual bowl of cereal. He loved it. "Sorry about the weekend," I told him as he ate.

"It's okay," he said. "Sorry for bullying you. I guess I'm just having a hard time adjusting to you not always being here." He was being too nice to me. I kissed him, tasting sausage grease, then kissed him more deeply. I felt nothing. His mouth seemed thin and lifeless. Disappointed, I took my overnight bag and left.

Yes, I was disappointed that kissing Jerry was like kissing my grandmother. If only I was in love with him again, things would be so much easier. But the truth was that I had never felt the kind of physical desire for Jerry that I felt for Rosie. In fact, I had never felt this sort of desire for anyone.

Amy dropped me off at the office where Rosie was just locking the door. Rosie and Amy waved at each other and I kissed Amy on the cheek, then hopped out of the car. I watched her drive away. Turning back to Rosie, I saw that she was leaning against her car, grinning at me. She looked so beautiful standing there in blue jeans and sneakers, a self-satisfied look on her face. I knew that she was mine at last. I ran over and tossed my overnight bag into her open trunk. A minute later we were on our way.

"How do you feel?" she asked.

"Excited."

"Me too." Rosie glanced over at me with an easy smile. She merged onto the freeway and we headed out of Weberstown. I tried not to stare at her in profile as she drove. At one point, I reached over and put my fingers through the hair at the back of her neck. My stomach flipped. Wow, I thought, taking my hand back.

"I have a meeting this afternoon," she said. "But the evening is entirely free. I originally had plans for dinner with friends, which is why I was staying over, but I've cancelled them." She turned briefly to catch my eye. I smiled to let her know that this was welcome news. "How did you explain this to your husband, by the way?"

"I lied, sort of."

"Bad habit."

"What else could I do? And Amy wanted to come along."

"That would have thrown a wrench in the works," Rosie said. "Because you do know, I suppose, that I intend to make love to you every possible moment that we can find to be alone together."

Yes, I knew that. And now I was speechless, but there was an involuntary smile taking up most of my face. Rosie put on a soft jazz CD and I watched the cows lounging under the windmills as we climbed out of the valley and over the Altamont Pass.

"How is Amy, by the way?" Rosie asked.

"She's good. She's got a part in a play. Mrs. Malaprop."

"Oh, yes, Sheridan. What a terrific part."

Did everybody know everything but me, I wondered. If that wasn't bad enough, Rosie, in a dreadful British accent, quoted,

"Sure if I reprehend anything in this world, it is the use of my oracular tongue, and a nice derangement of epitaphs!"

I laughed. "Amy seemed to think I should be familiar with the play. I guess she was right."

"Well, don't feel badly about it, Jean. It's a well-known play, but not like *Macbeth* or something. And, remember, I've been going to the theater regularly for decades."

I didn't have the courage to tell her that I'd never seen *Macbeth* either. Why hadn't I been paying attention to anything all these years?

It seemed forever getting to San Francisco, driving across the Bay Bridge and through horrendous traffic to Union Square and the Blanchard Hotel where Rosie had requested early check-in. When we finally closed ourselves inside our hotel room, it was just after noon. The room was huge, a suite, actually, with a sitting room and a separate bedroom dominated by a single, king-sized bed. There was a whirlpool bath on a second level with its own window out to the world. I suspected that Rosie had upgraded the room, that this was not the room she'd originally booked for her own overnight stay.

"At last," breathed Rosie after closing the door. She held out her arms to me. I flew to her and we kissed for several minutes, our mouths learning each other with deliberate tenderness. She pulled away eventually, saying, "I have to change clothes. Not much time to get to where I'm going. What will you do while I'm gone?"

"Die."

She kissed the tip of my nose and released me. "Well, while you're doing that, you should have lunch. Once I return, we won't want to go out again."

Rosie changed into a pair of tan slacks and tweed jacket, a soft pink blouse, a necklace of white and gold beads, brown flats, simple gold earrings.

"How do I look?" she asked, emerging from the bedroom.

"Scrumptious. Good enough to eat."

She snorted. "Later, love."

136

Just look at her, I thought, so beautiful, so smart, so perfect. And tonight she would belong to me. That was as far ahead as I would allow myself to think, fearing to shatter the happiness that engulfed me.

For the next three hours, after seeing Rosie off in a taxi, I tried to amuse myself downtown while the sun made a brave attempt to break through the low coastal fog. I walked around Macy's, perusing the street-level windows where they'd set up displays with live puppies in them. That was a predictable draw, so each window had a nearly impenetrable crowd around it. Huge wreaths with red bows hung all around the upper story of the building facing Geary Street. I walked through the ground floors of Neiman Marcus and Saks, through the St. Francis Hotel, and then stood outside a gallery window where a large mobile hung, red metal triangles connected with wires. The whole sculpture moved slightly with the air currents. I read the card next to the piece. It was Calder, Alexander Calder. Oh, yes, I thought, remembering Rosie's conversation with Ken. I recognize this artist. The key to knowing about these things was just to pay attention, to foster an interest. I could do this, I thought.

I wandered back to Union Square and took an outdoor table at a café so I could have a good view of the decorated tree and the crowd. By this time the sun had won out over the fog and was shining brightly. Despite the time of year, it was warm enough to sit comfortably outside.

The city was resplendent in its holiday decor, and the artists in the Square were out in full force, for this was Saturday, one of the few precious shopping days before Christmas. I had a twinge of guilt thinking about Amy. There was no way I could have brought her along, of course. Here you go, girl, I thought, take my credit card and blaze through the stores while your mother gets initiated into the joys of lesbian sex.

I watched the people walking by, especially the women, wondering which of them knew what I knew about the velvety, full lips of another woman. There were those who looked like they might know, and, occasionally, two women walked by who were obviously a couple. I couldn't really imagine what their lives were like, but I envied them their easy affection with one another, the complicit glance, the simple gesture of familiarity. As I sat by myself with my coffee, I had that feeling again that I was a character in a movie, not Jean Davis at all, but some more interesting woman with dark desires and deep mysteries. I was the heroine in a forties detective story. I liked that. With that thought, I could hear Amy doing her Bogart impersonation. I smiled to myself.

A woman in her early forties, short hair, casual clothes, was admiring a painting nearby and turned to catch my eye as I was smiling. She smiled back at me and, after a meaningful hesitation, her eyes showing recognition in the subtlest way imaginable, she turned and walked off. And that's how it was communicated, I thought, awestruck. These women can recognize one another, somehow, and now they can recognize me too. Was I already one of them, before I had even touched the naked breasts of another woman?

A young man with shoulder-length hair, wearing a porkpie hat, was sitting not far from me on a low brick wall playing a dobro. It was an interesting sound. It appealed to me. On my way out, I dropped a five-dollar bill in his guitar case. Oh, how Jerry would have sputtered at that! Everything today seemed new and fascinating. Today I was someone else, a woman of the world, a patron of the arts, even. And my lover, my female lover, was about to meet me for a secret tryst.

On my way back to the hotel, I stopped at a corner grocery and bought a bar of Ghirardelli dark chocolate and a bottle of pinot noir. Then I went back to the room and took a shower, pulling on an oversized shirt that fell mid-thigh, nothing under it. I thought she would like the look, the simplicity of it.

I waited for Rosie, feeling slightly desperate, trying not to think about what was about to happen. I messed with the bedside radio until I found a jazz station and turned the volume down low. At last I heard her key card slide into the lock. She stepped inside, tossed her briefcase into a chair, then slipped off her jacket and tossed it there as well, not taking her eyes off of me.

"What've you been doing?" she asked.

"Waiting for you."

She approached me and took me in her arms. "You're a lovely sight to come home to." We kissed. As her hand slid down the back of my shirt to rest on my behind, I heard her suck in and hold her breath. "I can't wait to sink my teeth into that," she said. I opened my eyes and saw that she was smiling mischievously at me. She was enjoying my naiveté.

"I'll be back in a minute." She disappeared into the bathroom. I turned the blankets down on the bed, then bolted the door and shut the curtains, plunging the room into dimness.

When Rosie returned, she was wearing a silky royal blue robe loosely tied around the waist. She held me and we kissed. I slipped my arms inside her robe and felt her cool skin. I watched my fingers tentatively touch her waist, her hips. Her body was milky white and lush. She had long, muscular legs, luxurious breasts, a soft, rounded stomach. Her pubic hair was dark brown, barely concealing the creamy skin beneath it. I'd never looked at a woman's body this way.

"You look scared," she whispered. "Change your mind at any time, Jean."

I would have liked to have said something to tell her how far I was from changing my mind, but words failed me. I was raw emotion. I just shook my head.

She led me to the bed where we sat facing each other. She unbuttoned my shirt. I sat stiffly, stupidly, watching her undo the buttons. She slipped the shirt off my shoulders. My breasts stood out greenish in the dimness, much smaller than hers. Looking at my body, her eyes full of emotion, she said, "God, you're gorgeous!"

She pulled me close and kissed me again and our breasts enclosed each other in the softest of embraces. Then she slipped off her robe and drew me down to lie beside her. I slid my hands over her body, her back, her hips, then to her breasts with their pink nipples, pink like mine were as a girl. We touched and kissed and sucked each other hungrily. She was passionate, but patient, leading me slowly into intimacy.

No matter how many times I had imagined this, my imagination had been inadequate. Imagination could not have involved all of my senses the way the real thing did. I saw the curve of her shoulder, heard her soft moans, smelled her warm skin, tasted her mouth, and felt the heat and energy of her body as my fingers tried to take all of her at once in their grasp. Whatever doubts I'd had about loving a woman were gone instantly. It was easy, and it was so natural.

"You're very quiet," she said at last. "Are you okay?"

I nodded. "I'm incredibly okay."

Rosie played me like a musical instrument, her hands and mouth touching all the right notes. I looked down across my torso to see the top of her head, her freckled shoulders. I felt her fingers open me up and I closed my eyes and lay my head back. And then I felt her warm, wet mouth gripping me, her tongue running across and into me, probing, circling. As I became more and more excited, her hands found my hips, holding me in place under her mouth, her tongue moving expertly. My frantic body raced. She knew exactly how much pressure to apply, how fast to move, what stage I was in, when to take me over the edge. When at last the orgasm came, it was long and deep and drenching. Lying still, throbbing from temples to toes, I listened to Rosie's hard breathing and felt her moist breath on my thigh.

When she moved up beside me, I kissed her mouth, tasting and smelling myself.

"I want to do that to you," I said.

"Please do."

She was extremely aroused, her breathing erratic. From the moment my tongue found her clitoris and her body arched at the touch, I knew what to do and it felt like something I'd done all my life. I loved it. I loved the dark, wet earthiness of her filling my mouth. I loved the smell of her and the taste of her. I loved feeling her body respond to my slightest touch, and the way I could feel her gripping my fingers as I pushed them hard up inside her. I could almost feel it myself, what she was feeling.

Once I started, I didn't want to stop. She came and came as my tongue grew smarter, my fingers more adept. She knew how to teach me, wordlessly, where and how to touch her. I listened for the catch of breath in her throat, the gasp, the small cry, the deep moan. As had always been the case where Rosie was concerned, I learned from her effortlessly.

By the time it was dark outside, we were both exhausted and lay unmoving in each other's arms for a long time, just listening to one another breathing.

"Where have I been all my life?" I said at last.

She smiled. "An interesting question. You do seem to be a natural."

We ate the chocolate and drank wine from plastic water glasses without leaving the bed. I sat behind Rosie, my legs and arms wrapped around her, while she leaned back against me, her wineglass held loosely in her hand. I let my hands roam freely over her stomach and her breasts.

"You're so sweet," she said, her eyes closed, her mouth turned up slightly into a tranquil smile. "And so hot." She took a drink. "Are you sure you haven't done this before?"

I held her ear lobe between my lips, sucking gently, then said, "Maybe you're just a good teacher."

"Oh, no," she said. "I have nothing to teach you."

"Nothing?" I asked, amused. "So this is it, then? We've done everything that lesbians do?"

Rosie's lips curled into a grin, her eyes still closed.

I slid a hand down through her pubic hair, teasing her gently with my fingers. I kissed her ears and neck, feeling the hunger returning to my limbs. I had already learned that there was a spot behind her ear, on her neck just below the hairline, that drove her wild. I touched that spot with my tongue and saw her body tense. I reached around and took her glass, setting it on the side table, then moved from behind her and kissed her mouth deeply, tasting the wine and chocolate.

"You're insatiable," she whispered, lying back agreeably.

141

"I've been waiting a long time for this."

A lifetime, I thought, as we made love again. And then Rosie protested that she could take no more, so I relented and let her rest. The sensations I was feeling were unfamiliar. My body seemed to belong to itself, like a growing thing feeding and flourishing by instinct. It tingled, it glowed, it radiated energy.

We both slept on and off, fitfully, unfamiliar with one another's bed habits.

"Tell me about Catherine," I asked at some point in the night.

"Catherine? Why?"

"I don't know. Just curious. I bought two of her books, you know. I read every poem looking for you."

"Did you find me?"

"I think so, vampire girl."

Rosie kissed my neck and growled through her teeth. "You're quite the detective," she said. "I wouldn't think I'd be recognizable in that poem. She wrote it after one of our many fights. A not too flattering view of our relationship."

"She was in love with you?"

"I suppose so."

"And you?"

Rosie nodded. "I met her at Berkeley. We were both graduate students. It was a fantastic time to be a lesbian poet, then, because those women were riding on the momentum established by the feminist movement. They had inherited the right to defiance. She was one of a group of them, and they took themselves oh so seriously. Well, didn't we all? They called themselves 'The Third Wave' because they fancied themselves the third wave of feminism, and they defined themselves as the most radical." Rosie stroked my shoulder gently as she spoke. "And it could have happened, perhaps, because they were right there at the locus of social change, but, as it turned out, there wouldn't be a third wave of feminism. Well, I believe some more modern feminists have now adopted that term. But for Catherine, the time was past. Still, they did stir the hearts of some young coeds.

I was impressed, at the time, with their conviction, and Catherine emerged as the most angry and outspoken of all, and therefore the most appealing to me."

"I can certainly see that," I said, imagining this young, impressionable Rosie caught up in the excitement of activism.

"She and I were on and off for years after that, but I changed more than she did, and we were left with almost nothing to agree about. Catherine is a terrific ego, impossible to get along with. And we were both younger, so both of us were impossible to get along with. A rocky relationship."

"It's over, then?"

"Yes, absolutely. I love her dearly, but not that way, not for a long time."

"Is there anyone else, now?" I asked with trepidation.

"No, sweetie, nobody."

"Grace Carpenter?"

Rosie laughed loudly. "I can see you've been driving yourself insane with jealousy. Grace is eighty-seven years old. She was a friend of my mother's, and, no, we were not having a romantic interlude last weekend. At the moment, I'm all yours."

At the moment, I repeated in my mind. Not the most comforting of thoughts. And I couldn't even say that much in return. After a few minutes of silence, I asked, "Rosie, when you first suspected that I was falling for you, before I knew it myself, why didn't you send me away?"

"Oh, that's a complicated question. The simple answer is that I didn't want to. I convinced myself that it was safe. I figured you'd never acknowledge it for one thing. People don't. They need to protect themselves. You were just so adorable with your tremendous enthusiasm, the way your eyes lit up when you looked at me. I was enjoying watching you discovering yourself, and I really wanted to be a part of that." She stroked my face, pushing my hair back. "But the truth is that I could tell almost from the beginning that the two of us were connecting on a sexual level. I've no idea what *you* were thinking, and it's always a sort of mystery to me how you straight women can't see that enormous pink elephant in the room. Do you have any idea how hard it is to talk about campaign finances to a beautiful woman with lust in her eyes?"

When I woke in the morning, Rosie was still asleep. I glanced at the clock—seven thirty. I slipped out of bed, pulled on my jeans and shirt, my shoes without socks, and silently left the room. As I rode down in the elevator, I was hit with the sobering realization that I would soon be going home.

In the breakfast room, I filled two cups with coffee, and then realized I didn't know how the woman I loved took hers. No, wait, I'd gotten her coffee once, at the office. Black, I think, same as me. I took the coffee back up to our room, along with a couple of blueberry muffins.

Rosie was awake, watching me, her eyes puffy, her hair standing on end, holding a sheet over her chest. "I thought maybe you'd run away again," she said.

"No, not this time." I came over, kissed her on the cheek and handed her a coffee cup, crawling into bed with mine.

"Thanks. Just what I needed." She swallowed a few gulps before asking, "So how does it feel in the light of a new day?"

I fed her a piece of a muffin with my fingers. "Beautiful. I can't believe how perfect this feels."

"Uh oh," Rosie said with mock alarm. "Look out, ladies, there's a new girl in town."

I was so happy, I knew that it wasn't me. Someone else had possessed my body. "Rosie," I said as she sucked the sugar off my fingers, "how do you feel about me?"

She took my finger out of her mouth and looked puzzled. "What do you mean? I'm sitting naked in bed with you, sucking your fingers."

"Seriously, Rosie. Tell me." I wanted something to hold on to.

She was reluctant. "Well, I enjoy being with you. Right now, I'd rather be with you than anybody else. I try not to think beyond that because what's the point? This is a complicated situation and I don't feel like I'm in control. I'm worried about you, about how you'll handle this."

"I don't want to leave. I want to stay here with you forever."

"Forever?" she said, amused. "Forever only happens in fairy tales." Rosie took a swallow of coffee, then smiled at me. "I want you to know that I've enjoyed this very much. But I don't make any claims on you, Jean. You're a married woman and you've got a life that has no place for me."

Was this was just a passing bit of fun for her? I wondered. Was she done with me now? I didn't want to think about any of that, not now, not yet. "I love you so much," I said. "I can't keep my hands off you." I threw my arms around her.

"Lust," she said. "It's called lust."

I buried my face in her neck, smelling sex, sweat and the faint odor of her skin, mingling together into an intoxicating elixir that stirred my most basic instincts. I kissed her, not caring what she called it, and as our lips closed in on each other, I felt my body filling with desire. I kissed her more deeply.

"Again?" Rosie said, setting her coffee aside. "I haven't had a night like that since, well, since I was young enough to take it. I guess we have time, but then we really need to get going."

"How am I going to tear myself away?" I asked.

"Ruthlessly, my darling."

We lingered for a while in our room and then took a bath together before dressing to go back to the world. While we drove home, both of us were mostly silent. The nearer we got to Weberstown, the more bereft I became. I didn't want to go back. As we exited the freeway, Rosie turned to me and said, "You're going to have to make a decision, Jean, eventually. If you decide that you want to be with women, keep in mind that it means a lot more than that your lover is female."

Women? What did she mean "women"? There was only one woman on my mind.

"You mean like how to know who leads when you go dancing?" I asked, trying to lighten the mood.

She smiled briefly. "It will change you. It will change your politics and your religion and your entire way of interacting with

145

the world. It has to. It will shift your center of gravity."

"I don't know that I'm being given a choice."

"Perhaps you're not," she said sympathetically. "Perhaps you've come too far already."

# Chapter Thirteen

Overnight, the world had changed. Though the buses still ran in the streets and the radio stations were still playing the same songs, everything appeared distorted to me, as if reflected in a carnival mirror. Arriving home Sunday, I stood on the front porch staring at the birch sign engraved "The Davises" as though I'd never seen it before. This is your home, I told myself. You're Mrs. Davis. I turned to look down the street where Rosie's car was just turning the corner. I should be going with her, I thought. But for some reason, I had come here instead.

I went inside. In front of the living room window was a Christmas tree, an artificial Christmas tree that stood seven feet tall. The box it had come in lay on the floor. Apparently, Jerry had gone ahead with this purchase. The room smelled of a soapy, astringent aroma, the tree manufacturer's idea of "a fresh pine scent." The house was quiet. Jerry's car was gone and, since there was no music playing anywhere, I assumed Amy was also out.

Bradley's Christmas letter, posted from Madrid, was taped to the refrigerator.

147

*Merry Christmas to everyone. I've just arrived here from Barcelona. I miss you all very much, especially because it's this time of year and we've never been apart before. But Spain is going to be an interesting place to spend Christmas. I'm going to a Catholic Mass tomorrow. I'm excited about that. Don't worry. I'm not converting. I'm just trying to immerse myself in everything. It will be a Latin Mass, you know, which will be moving, I expect.*

*My landlady has made wreaths for all of the doors, so there's a pine scent that greets me every time I come in and swing the door open, which is sort of homey. I understand from Amy that you're getting an artificial tree this year. I'm sure it's practical and an economically-sound choice, but perhaps a couple of boughs from the tree in the McCord's yard would be worth bringing inside. There's nothing like a scent to evoke a whole flood of good feelings. At least it's doing that for me. In particular, it frequently reminds me of that one winter we drove up to the mountains to cut a fresh tree, and while we were carrying it back to the car and tying it on, Amy was playing with the sappy stump. By the time Mom noticed, she had covered her face and hair with it and pine needles were stuck all over her head. She looked like a porcupine. I wish I had that photo right now. It would give me a laugh, I know.*

Amy had dug the photo out of a family album and taped it on the refrigerator next to the letter, as if any of us could forget it. She was only four years old at the time, sitting on the ground in a dense forest in a bright pink jacket, covered with pine needles, just as Bradley remembered. All you could see of her was a round pink blob topped with green and straw-colored needles, jutting out at all angles, her eyes peering out and her mouth open because she was crying in earnest by the time the photo was taken. I was in the picture too, kneeling beside that screaming child, lifting pine needles one by one off her sappy face. I smiled at the photo and then returned to the letter.

*Even though I'm missing you guys, I'm so thankful I've made this trip. I've become a different person since I've been traveling. It's helped me know myself. I think it has to do with getting out of the environment you're used to, off where no one knows you and everything you see is unfamiliar. You don't have a context for anything so you respond to it naturally, with your real senses. You begin to understand what you like and don't like, what you're afraid of, what things matter to you.*

*The other day I was walking through Barcelona by myself. I didn't have a destination, was just soaking in the atmosphere. I couldn't communicate with the people, at least the ones who didn't speak English, but I pretended none of them did. I pretended I was isolated. Every face I saw was a stranger, every word I heard was meaningless, every sight was new. That morning walk was the most incredibly free experience I think I've ever had. I know I'm not making much sense. But I'm having a good time. I wonder if you will recognize me. I think I've matured tremendously on this trip. Thanks so much, Mom and Dad, for helping me out with this.*

I read Bradley's letter twice. His experiences in Europe seemed remotely like my own at home, new and evocative experiences with the power to liberate. He was discovering himself in foreign territory. So was I. But I'd been on the planet forty years, almost twice as long as he had, and I still didn't know what I liked and didn't like, what I was afraid of, what mattered to me. It had all been too easy for me up until now. There had been no challenges.

I'd been home only a few minutes before Jerry arrived, and I was still feeling out of synch with my environment.

"Hi, hon," he said, giving me a peck on the cheek. "How was your trip?"

"Okay," I said. "There's a new letter from Bradley. I don't know if you've seen it."

"No, I haven't. Amy must have printed it while I was out. I just ran down to the hardware store to get a couple of PVC fittings." He held up a small plastic bag. "Got a broken pipe. I was hoping it would rain again, but I think I'm going to have to water the lawn after all, so I guess I need to fix it."

He was looking right at me, but didn't seem to notice anything unusual. The change, as dramatic as it felt, was not visible, apparently. Perhaps things would be easier if it was visible, I thought, a flashing neon sign over my head or a scarlet letter on my chest, an "L," of course. Or maybe an "A" would be just as appropriate.

Jerry chuckled at the photo of Amy as he approached the refrigerator to read the letter.

"Well," Jerry said when he had finished, "no one can complain that Bradley writes 'How are you, I am fine' postcards."

That was true. And it worried me a little that my extremely serious young son reported that he had "matured tremendously." At this rate, he would come home to me an old man. It would have been a sort of relief to get one of those "How are you, I am fine" postcards from him. He should be having fun, but fun wasn't something that just descended on you. It had to come out of you. Perhaps he was experiencing his particular brand of fun after all.

My longing to be with Rosie gradually gave way to an overwhelming sense of grief as I tried to step back into my life. That first day was nearly intolerable. The ornaments Amy laid out on the dining room table were enough all by themselves to annihilate any thoughts I had of breaking with my past. They represented a steady twenty-two year timeline of my life, a string of Hallmark moments. There was the orb proclaiming Bradley's first Christmas and the black Scotty dog with its red collar that Amy had made for me in first grade. These objects marched forward through time with the certainty of perpetuity.

And then Amy insisted on the three of us watching *A Christmas Story* together Sunday night.

"I don't really feel like it," I said.

"But we have to watch it," she said. "We always watch it."

"That's not a very good reason."

"Sure it is," Jerry said, grabbing Amy around the waist, twirling her right off her feet. Both of them fell onto the sofa.

"Right," Amy said, sitting up and grabbing the remote. "It's tradition."

Jerry smiled at her as she turned on the TV. "Come on, Jeannie. Humor us."

I sat with them to watch, for about the twelfth time, how Ralphie longs for a Red Ryder BB gun for Christmas. As usual, when appropriate, we all three joined in with the movie to chant, "You'll shoot your eye out." And every time, Amy and Jerry laughed in joyful collusion.

When the movie was over, I went to my room, laid down with my face on a pillow, and sobbed quietly into it, listening to Amy and Jerry laughing in the other room. While under Rosie's spell, I hadn't realized how hard this was going to be. All I knew while I was with her was that it was absolutely blissful to be with her. But to really be with her, I would have to give up everything I knew and everything I had been for the last twenty years. I would have to become something that was a total mystery to me. I had no idea how to do that.

Monday afternoon, she called and asked, "How are you?"

"Torn," I said, and thought to myself that the word was too mild. I was feeling shattered, shredded. "I'm actually pretty messed up. I don't know who I am anymore."

"Did you know who you were before, Jean?"

I didn't need to answer that. I knew her opinion of that, and she was probably right, but at least I had words for who I was before. I was Jerry's wife, Amy and Bradley's mother, my parents' daughter. I realized as I thought this that the only way I had to describe myself were through my relationships with other people. I didn't know if this was a bad thing. If I left this life for Rosie, then I would be her lover, and maybe still Amy and Bradley's mother, and I didn't see how that was any different. There had to be some other way to describe myself.

"You're feeling confused right now," Rosie said. "It's probably the worst possible time for this dilemma to come at you because of the holidays."

"Yes, probably. But I don't regret it. It was absolutely wonderful. No doubt about that, Rosie. I loved every second of it."

"So did I." Her voice was sincere.

She was, perhaps, thinking of asking to see me again. After the last forty-eight hours, I knew I couldn't face that. The huge emotional see-saw I was on was breaking my heart.

"I need to think things through," I said. "This is just too hard. I can't describe to you what it's like here."

"Yes," she said. "I understand."

"I want to see you, of course. I just can't. Not now. Do you really understand?"

"Yes, I do. You're right. You need to be alone to work it out. It's a complicated situation."

"Thank you," I said. "I do love you, Rosie. And I'm incredibly grateful."

"Try not to beat yourself up too much, Jean."

I didn't talk to Rosie again before Christmas, but she did e-mail me to tell me that she was going to Portland to visit her sister. She said I could call her on her cell phone while she was gone if I wanted to.

I did want to, but I didn't. I lapsed into a paralyzing depression instead. Bradley's absence wounded me deeply. It would have been so much better if we had all been together this year as a family. Jerry and Amy both noticed that my state of mind was troubled and my behavior was unpredictable. Jerry asked me what was wrong more than once. I found myself snapping at him, frequently, in irritation, because I was blaming him for my unhappiness, for standing in the way of what I wanted. Even though he didn't understand it, he had started snapping back. It was a natural response.

We spent Christmas Day with my parents, eating turkey and wobbly, can-shaped cranberry sauce and sweet potatoes with marshmallows melted on top, the same thing we ate every Christmas Day since I can remember anything. "It's too bad Bradley isn't here," my mother said more than once. "Where is he now?"

"He's in Madrid," Jerry said. "Boy, is he going to have some great memories from this trip. I wish I'd done something like that when I was young."

"You could have gone to Europe later," I said. "Maybe not for six months, but for a couple of weeks. We could have done it together."

Jerry glared at me. Must be my tone of voice, I reasoned. Maybe that was a resentful statement.

"We went to England once," Dad said. "I've got a little silver spoon with a Union Jack on the handle to prove it."

I saw my mother watching me, looking concerned. What, I thought. Everybody looks at me like I'm giving them the heebie-jeebies. Amy was mostly silent throughout the ordeal. She was sulking because she didn't get to bring Norman, her current boyfriend. He was with his own parents, and I had refused to allow her to spend the day with them. I had no idea what had happened to Tommy. One day she was saying, "I'm going to the mall with Tommy," and the next day, "I'm going to the mall with Norman," without the slightest indication that anything had happened or that she had suffered in any way.

When the kids get married, I thought, holidays will become terribly complicated, what with the in-laws wanting their fair share of children and grandchildren. And then I remembered my own complicated situation and became disconsolate. It would be so easy, wouldn't it, just to resign myself to the life I'd made, to make a rule that you had to live with your original choices, even if you weren't happy. Happiness was selfish, anyway.

But happiness wasn't such a neat package that could be accepted or rejected intact. Since falling in love with Rosie, I'd become less and less content with Jerry, and had been seeing him, unfairly, as the source of all of my unhappiness. It came out... often, in a lot of little ways. Our marriage was falling apart. Even if I recommitted myself to him now, I didn't think I could repair the damage. You can't go back to the time before enlightenment, to innocence. So, really, turning away from your own happiness was almost a guarantee of misery for the people around you.

I felt so completely alone. There was no one I could talk to. I had nothing to counsel me but clichés. You made your bed, girl, now lie in it. Or maybe poetry, and the only poem I had ever bothered to memorize, Robert Frost's "The Road Not Taken," was startlingly apt.

That poem had seemed quaint to me in high school, a nice

little observation about life's choices. But it was my youth that had reduced it to that, I realized. It seemed so much more now. I was standing at an ominous crossroad. One direction was well-worn and safe. The other was a total mystery. That path beyond the bend, that void of the unknown, no matter how hard I kept peering down it, its potential dangers and delights remained impenetrable.

And like the poem said, it was extremely unlikely that I would ever be here again, facing this same choice. There would be no second chance to take that road less traveled. Looked at in a certain light, in the light of my quandary, it was a dark and oppressive poem after all. There was no signpost. There was no guide. You just had to have the guts to do it, to venture forth, not look back, and take whatever came your way.

"What's wrong with you today?" my mother asked as we stood side by side in the kitchen washing dishes.

"What do you mean?" I knew absolutely what was wrong with me. I was standing at that damned crossroad in a yellow wood, trying to peer around that damned bend into that damned unknown that I had to choose that would make all the damned difference. Damned Robert Frost!

"You're testy. And you and Jerry seem ready to cut each other's throats. Did you have a fight?"

"Not especially." I dried a large white platter with a turkey shape molded into it. "It's nothing, really, Mom, nothing to worry about." What could I say? What could I possibly say to my mother about damned Robert Frost?

During the week between Christmas and New Year's Day, I didn't hear from Rosie. I knew she'd come home and was back to work as planned, as there were e-mails. Not to me, but to the business, to groups of people of which I was merely another group member on the cc list.

I walked through my days like a woman in a trance, doing all the things I had learned to do out of habit, but living elsewhere. My unoccupied body continued to function, remarkably, without my presence, its atrophied heart and lungs still forcing through enough oxygen to sustain itself. I had lived all of my life without her and it had been okay. Why did I now feel like I was drowning every minute that I wasn't with her?

On New Year's Eve, at midnight, as the firecrackers popped all around the neighborhood, Amy declared, "Two thousand eight is the year I'm going to become engaged to be married."

"No!" I shrieked.

Jerry and Amy both stared at me through the zeroes in their red plastic 2-0-0-8 glasses. "That bad, is it?" Jerry asked calmly.

"No, it's not that. It's just that she's too young. Amy, it takes longer than nineteen years to find out who you are and what you want. Besides, it doesn't even make sense to plan to get married when there's nobody around you want to marry."

I wasn't in the mood to make any resolutions myself. I didn't dare think about the year ahead. I knew that whatever happened this year, there were changes coming, formidable changes that seemed too large to grapple with. I had never in my life looked with such dread into the future.

When Jerry came to bed shortly after midnight, instead of sliding in beside me in the dark, he switched on the light and sat up on the bed in his shorts and T-shirt. I rolled over and looked up at him, seeing that he was full of purpose. We were going to have a confrontation, I realized. I shoved another pillow behind me and sat up. "What?" I asked.

"I've had enough, Jean. It's time you explained why you're behaving the way you are, why you act as though you no longer want to be here. Don't you?"

I avoided his eyes, and looked instead at the stubbled depression between his nose and mouth. I hesitated, not wanting to answer. Then, deciding a lie would only make things worse, that I had lied enough, I said, "I don't think I do."

His lips quivered. "You don't?" he asked, unbelieving. That wasn't what he'd expected. He had expected the opposite, obviously, had expected that we could find out what little thing was wrong and fix it and things would be good again. Something fixable, that's what he'd expected. Forcing the issue hadn't been a risk for him, so he had thought.

"I don't think so," I repeated.

"Since when?"

"I don't know since when. Maybe a long time. I was in the habit of loving you for a long time. I don't know when it became just habit. I'm just not in love with you anymore."

He looked confused. Why are you making me tell you this, I thought. It's going to hurt. If you knew how much, you wouldn't ask. "I'm so sorry, Jerry." I started to cry silently. Saying it aloud had made it seem more true. And now I had made a move forward, had taken a step that couldn't be reversed.

After a silent moment, he bravely asked, "What do you want to do about it?"

"I don't know what to do about it. Please give me a little more time."

He sat staring at me for a minute, probably trying to think of something to say, but in the end, he gave up. He turned off the light and lay on his side of the bed silent but, I knew, awake. We lay there in the dark, back to back, not touching, more distant from one another than we had ever been.

# Chapter Fourteen

Two weeks into the new year, Rosie left me a courteous voice mail asking me to meet her at my new office. It was ready to be occupied. She was there when I arrived, sorting through paperwork. It seemed like a lifetime since I'd seen her, but it was really just a month. When she turned and looked at me over her reading glasses, I felt the strength drain out of my limbs. The softness of her cheek and the curve of her lip beckoned me on some primeval level. It all rushed back at me in an instant, all the need and overwhelming singleness of purpose, as if I was nothing more than a fish in a stream or a turtle on a beach.

She was dressed simply today in black slacks, a tan jacket and an unadorned print blouse open at the neck, revealing nothing. I wanted to dive into that blouse.

"Good morning, Jean," she said cheerfully, but with no indication that she shared my feelings.

"I've missed you, Rosie." There was no cheer in my voice.

"I've missed you too. How were the holidays?"

"Miserable."

"You look tired. There are dark circles under your eyes."

"I've had some rough nights." I put my new briefcase on the desk and looked around the office. It was small, covered in a fresh coat of off-white, still smelling slightly of paint. There was a computer, fax machine, copier, all the modern necessities of operating a business. On the door window, "Vision Partnership," was stenciled in block lettering.

"This is really nice," I said. "Good location, too."

"Jean," Rosie said, enthusiastically, "look what I got for us." She showed me a four-foot wide framed sepia print leaning against the wall. "This is a photo of downtown Weberstown, 1877. It's taken from the bank of the Deep Water Channel, you see, looking east at the heart of the city when that's all there was of the city. The waterway is about the only thing you can recognize, but if you look here, right here where Main Street comes in, you can see the little red church, St. Mary's, where it still is today, and the original Weberstown Hotel. You've got to admire the job they've done restoring that, don't you think? I mean, it's spot-on except that there are no horses out front at the moment."

I don't know why, but I loved Rosie for loving her town. Her face was alive as it had been when I first met her, sparkling with optimism and innocent joy.

"It's perfect," I said.

"Well, it ties things together, I think, the past and the future of the town, and that's what this organization is about. We can hang it up later."

"Thank you, Rosie," I said. "I'm really grateful for all of this."

"Well, you're going to have to earn your keep. This is not going to be an easy job. But I'll help you as much as I can. The others will too, of course. Why don't we start right away? Let's go over the outstanding business."

Rosie was strictly professional. I wanted to know what she was feeling. Was I already something in her past? Had the holidays, with their huge emotional demands, stolen her away from me? Had she found someone else? After all, it looked as though all I was offering her at this point was misery. Who could blame her for leaving me behind?

We sat together at a work table where she had arranged some folders.

"The first thing I want to see is the itinerary for the Beijing delegation," she said. "Who are you going to meet with, where are you going to take them? It's important to plan everything for these people, right down to where they take meals."

"I have a tentative schedule," I said. "I'll e-mail it to you later today."

"Okay, great. I've made you this list of contacts," she was saying. "These are the people you call when you have questions—government officials, community leaders, etcetera." She handed me the list. "I'll try to introduce you to some of these people personally, as circumstances permit. We'll be asking for a financial report once a month, of course, so keep track of your expenses. You'll be reimbursed for anything out of pocket, but it's always better to use the company credit card or the petty cash account. Gordon has set all of that up for you."

I nodded.

"Jean, are you paying attention? You don't seem to be with it." She sounded irritated.

"Sorry," I said. I felt like crying, but somehow managed to avoid it. "Yes, I understand. I've been keeping up. I set up a filing system at home."

"Good. Then you know about the Career Day we're planning. We've got two months to organize it. Send out invitations to county businesses and send flyers to all the high schools and the college, of course. You'll have to design the flyers yourself. Can you handle it?"

"Yes," I said emphatically.

"That's the first smile I've seen since you got here, Jean. You'll be surprised what hard work can do for you, to distract you from your problems."

So that's what she wanted, to distract me from my problems, namely, my preoccupation with her? She wanted to move on, then? I knew that I couldn't ask her, not then. I would have broken down, and I knew she wouldn't want to see that. I was too weak, too vulnerable. And, Rosie, I couldn't read her today. She was all business and there was no affection in her voice, as if she had never held me in her arms and tasted my body with her brilliant tongue.

After leaving the office, Rosie took me to meet the Superintendent of Schools, where we discussed Career Day specifics. I was feeling better by the time we left. Rosie wanted to stop at her office to check her calls, so we went there next, to the place where this had all begun. It was an emotional homecoming for me, walking into that office again.

The posters were gone. The rainbow flag was gone. The big-screen TV was gone. There was nothing, in fact, to be seen from that riotous, euphoric episode in my life. It would not have taken much to persuade me that it had never happened. Tina was sitting quietly at her desk and everything was back to normal for Rosie. Her life seemed undisturbed by all that had happened between us.

"Hi, Jean," Tina called as if there was nothing remarkable about seeing me walking about on the planet. "Nice to see you again." It seemed odd to me that she even recognized me.

I stood in the doorway of Rosie's office while she checked her messages. One of them was a male voice saying, "Rosie, there's a meeting of the Arts Commission this afternoon at two at the Ramada. I think you should be there." I glanced at my watch. It was almost exactly two o'clock right then.

"Arts Commission meeting?" Rosie said to nobody in particular. She looked at the calendar on her Blackberry. "Why wasn't I invited?"

"Who was that?" I asked.

"A friend." There was a strangely sinister look on Rosie's face. "A good friend. I think the time has come for a showdown, Jean. Strap on your six-shooters."

I'd never seen Rosie really pissed off. I didn't know what to expect. I also didn't understand what was happening. Was I now going to see Catherine's "ogress"? It was clear that Rosie's mood today was harsh. I felt that it was somehow my fault. Perhaps she was looking for a fight.

In the lobby of the Ramada Hotel, I said, "I'll wait for you here."

"No, Jean, I want you to come with me."

A woman at the information desk directed us to the conference room where the Arts Commission meeting was already underway. Rosie had said almost nothing to me since we left her office. She stood outside the closed door of the conference room for a moment as though gathering strength, then turned the knob and threw the door open. A group of men and women seated at a long oval table turned to look in unison. Up in front of the group stood a well-dressed woman of about sixty-five in a teased and bleached bouffant reminiscent of a long-gone era. She looked absolutely terrified when her eyes landed on Rosie. My guess— Tanya Lockhart of Adopt-A-Hmong fame.

I shut the door and stood leaning against it, trying to be inconspicuous. "Rosie," said one of the men at the table. "Tanya said you couldn't make it."

"Oh, really?" Rosie said.

"Oh, it's good you—" Tanya started. Rosie gave her a stare that shut her up instantly.

"I couldn't make it because Tanya, who called this meeting, neglected to invite me," Rosie said, her voice wavering on the edge of restraint. All heads turned to an uncomfortable looking Tanya. Rosie stood at one end of the table, Tanya at the other.

"Oh, no," Tanya said. "You're mistaken, Rosie."

"I'm not mistaken. And I'm not surprised." Rosie paused, looking at the faces around the table. She was in command. "Suppose somebody tell us what Tanya said to this group two weeks ago after I left the room to attend another meeting. What she said about me, I mean. Robert, you were there. Why don't you remind us?"

A young man, uncomfortably put on the spot, hesitated, looked embarrassed, then said, "Uh, Tanya said something like, didn't we all agree that you weren't the best influence for young artists, that your special interests might lead us in an undesirable direction."

Rosie let the room grow silent and glared at Tanya. I didn't envy her. "What special interests were you referring to, Tanya?" Rosie asked sweetly.

"Well, I don't think I said that, that way. That's not what I said."

"What did you say, then?"

Tanya blushed. She stuttered.

"Well, what she meant was—" began an older man.

"I know exactly what she meant!" Rosie cut him off. He raised an eyebrow but settled back into his chair. She turned her attention back to Tanya. "Instead of sneaking around behind my back and making insinuations, let's get this thing out in the open. Let's see if you have the balls to tell me to my face what you think of me."

Tanya looked around the room with a look of self-satisfaction on her face. "Well, Rosie, you may have balls, but I most certainly do not." She thought she was pretty clever, but nobody laughed, so she continued. "You made it clear to all of us during the election that your values are not necessarily compatible with ours. I mean, you brought in all of those 'people' to help you. It demonstrated your true colors, and I was just reminding the commission of that."

"Rosie," interjected one of the women nearest our end of the room, "Tanya is not speaking for the rest of the commission. I want you to know that."

"Thank you, Kathy. I'm well aware of that. Tanya has almost never spoken for the rest of the commission. Tanya has always spoken for herself. She has, in fact, been a constant source of embarrassment for this commission. I can't say how many times I've had to apologize for her or fix something she's bungled."

"You don't run this commission," Tanya said defiantly.

"And neither do you. And you never will because there's no one in this room who respects you."

Tanya puckered her lips in an attempt to appear unruffled.

I was afraid she would fight back, would hurl insults at Rosie. I didn't want to hear it. But she was silent.

Rosie, taking a deep breath, said, "I can't work with Tanya any longer. She doesn't want to work with me, and the fact that she called this meeting and expressly excluded me is reason enough to think that we've come to an impasse. Everyone here is familiar with our work. I'm going down to the lounge for a drink. You all just stay here and let me know when you reach a decision."

"You're giving us an ultimatum?" the elderly man asked gruffly.

"I'm telling you to face reality. One of us has to go. We can't do the work we're here to do if we can't get along with one another. If you agree with Tanya that I'm an undesirable element, I'll graciously resign, on the spot." With that, Rosie turned, I opened the door for her, and we left. She glanced at me outside in the hallway, her fierceness dissipating. Then she shrugged and led the way downstairs.

"How was I?" she asked, sliding up to the bar.

"Formidable." She ordered a cognac. I ordered a Diet Pepsi.

"What if they choose her?"

Rosie laughed. "That won't happen, Jean. That lot has been bellyaching about Tanya for years. If it comes down to a choice, what can they do? They're going to choose me. I'm doing this to teach Tanya a lesson, to teach her that money, ultimately, can't compensate for lack of ability."

I hoped her confidence wasn't misplaced. I didn't want to see her beaten down again. The first time I'd seen that, I'd fallen in love with her. The second time, who knew? I might throw myself on the tracks in front of a train.

We'd been at the bar ten minutes before Robert came down and sat beside Rosie. "So they've chosen you to be the soother of feathers," Rosie surmised.

"Look, Rosie, Tanya's very upset. This is her favorite cause, you know that. And she's been with the commission for over thirty years. She's a founding member, for God's sake. You can't just chuck her out."

"If you're all that sorry for her, let her stay."

"But we can't lose you. There's nobody up there who would choose that."

Rosie shrugged. "Robert, I've neglected to introduce you to Jean Davis, administrator of the Vision Partnership. Jean, this is Robert Boch, an art professor at the junior college."

I reached around Rosie to shake his hand. He seemed annoyed to be momentarily derailed, but I was thrilled to hear myself being introduced that way. It sounded so authentic. It sounded important. And Rosie said it so nonchalantly, as though it had always been true.

"So what about it, Rosie?" Robert continued. "Don't make us do this." Rosie sipped her cognac, deliberating. I'd never seen Rosie wielding power this way before. I knew she had it. Obviously, she never would have been able to run for mayor if she didn't. She had enough power in Weberstown to destroy some important people if she was inclined to do so. I waited with as much apprehension for her decision as Robert did.

"Do this for me, Robert," she said at last. "Go back and tell them I'm intractable, that I'm furious and unreasonable."

"Oh, come on, Rosie."

"Now, wait. Tell them that you recommend putting the decision off until next month. That way I'll have a chance to cool off."

He grinned. "You want her to suffer."

"I didn't say that. I said I was too angry to be reasoned with. And with a month's reprieve, that will give Tanya a chance to apologize and perhaps placate me."

"Okay, Rosie. Thanks."

After he'd gone, I asked, "What are you going to do?"

"Let her stew for a while." Rosie was still angry, I could tell. She sipped on her drink and didn't look at me. I still had the feeling that I, more than Tanya, was the cause of her unpleasant mood.

"Why did you want me to come with you?" I asked after several minutes.

She turned to look at me coolly. "Because you need to understand what it's like in this world of mine, where you never know when you're going to be called upon to defend yourself because somebody wants to use your difference against you."

So, in her mind at least, we were still in this thing together. Or maybe she was trying to turn me away by showing me that it wasn't all fun and games. Maybe she didn't think I knew how serious it was, that I hadn't been paying attention for the last three months.

Rosie continued. "People won't be direct about it. They'll attack you behind your back. Tanya's not the only bigot in that room, just the dumbest. There are people much harder to defend yourself against. And you don't even know who they are because in our modern world, it's no longer acceptable to be anti-gay. Well, I'm grateful for that, but it does make it a little harder to recognize them. In the old days, they were the ones bashing your head in with a baseball bat. Now, the homophobes have had to go underground. Even Tanya knows that she can't come out and say, I don't want Rosie on the Commission because she's gay. In fact, I doubt if Tanya cares about that one way or another. Her real beef with me is that I'm not afraid to point out her failings and she's intimidated by me. But she can't use that, so she thinks she can use the other against me, that she will be able to rally a few people to her side with that. And she's probably right. I have to put a stop to it before she has a chance."

I remembered her asking me the day she was outed whether or not it mattered to me. I remembered her being relieved it hadn't. She was vulnerable to the disapproval of others, even her inferiors. It was a brave front, the face she'd shown to Tanya. Thank God Tanya didn't realize the power she had. At that moment, I felt a deep affection for Rosie. I loved her, her strengths and her weaknesses, and I didn't give a damn about the Tanya Lockharts of the world.

I looked around and saw that the bartender was still some distance away. "I love you so much, Rosie," I said.

She stared, her eyes wide and moist, but said nothing. The

look on her face was complicated, conveying a range of emotions which were hard to interpret, but which certainly included ambivalence, maybe even fear. I was dismayed to see this. What did it mean exactly, I wondered. Did she want me to stop loving her? Or was she afraid that it wasn't enough, not real enough or strong enough or pure enough? Why did she never tell me what was on her mind? There was obviously plenty to say, from the look in her eyes.

I wanted to put my arms around her. I wanted to kiss her eyelids and her lips and drive all the fear and doubt out of her mind. As I gazed at her, I felt an uneasiness in my fingers and my mouth. I remembered acutely what it felt like to touch her bare skin. Her lovely ear and a tantalizing glimpse of her collarbone beckoned me.

Ever since I had first felt the renegade urge of my body to possess this woman, I had been both amazed and alarmed by this awful splintering of myself. My nerves and muscles were driven by some force that I neither recognized nor controlled. They had their own agenda and left me with the cognitive ability of an infant or an imbecile.

No doubt this agony of my body had become apparent on my face because Rosie looked even more alarmed and then slowly shook her head.

My hand covered hers where it lay on the bar, gripping her fingers. There was nothing in my head or my heart at that moment but this woman, a woman who may as well have been a hurricane gripping me and sweeping me up into its raging currents.

"I want to be alone with you," I said urgently. "Can we go to your place?"

"No," she said, pulling her hand away. "You said you wanted to cool it while you sort this out. And I agree. So cool it."

I closed my eyes and tried to shake myself free of my desire. "I can't think straight when I'm near you," I said.

"That's the best argument I can think of, then, against being with you. You need to think this through rationally. You need to make well-considered decisions. Besides that, how can you even ask me?" Her voice was low but insistent. "You've been carrying on as though you're the only one involved in this thing. Did it ever even occur to you that I might want you as much as you want me? You can't just turn me on and off at will. I do have feelings, Jean."

"I'm sorry," I said, taken aback by her accusatory tone. She was right. I hadn't been considering her feelings at all. I was too overwhelmed by my own. "But, to be fair, Rosie, you haven't been expressing your feelings. You haven't said anything at all about how you feel about us, other than you had a good time in bed with me, I mean, and that isn't very helpful."

"I'm trying to let you work it out on your own. I'm trying not to put pressure on you."

"Maybe I can't work it out on my own. Maybe I need your help." In the lobby of the Ramada Hotel, we spoke quietly at an unoccupied bar. Could anyone guess, I wondered, from our gestures and expressions, that we were lovers?

Rosie looked tormented. She threw up her hands in exasperation. "Of all the ironies in my life, this has got to be one of the biggest. At the exact moment that I'm so far out of the closet that at last I can do what I want with whomever I want wherever I want, I get involved with a married woman." I saw her glance at my ring finger and the wedding band that represented my unavailability.

"If I leave Jerry…" I began.

"Jean, I know you want some kind of guarantee from me. You want this process to be easier than it is. You want to know what you're going to get if you give up what you have. How can I possibly tell you that? I don't want you to give up your life for me. I want you to give it up for yourself. I can't promise you that there's a fairy story ending for us. And, to be brutally frank about it, if you can't reconcile yourself to being a lesbian, there's no chance at all for us. That's the real issue, not my feelings, and that's why I'm trying not to pressure you. No matter how much I want you in my bed, in my home, and in my life, I have no influence over your ability to find and embrace your ultimate identity. That's something everyone has to work through on her own. Only you know what you can live with."

I had never seen Rosie this out of sorts, not even when she was brought down by Holloway's public proclamation. Now, she seemed to be splintered, even wrecked. And I had done this to her. Perhaps her heart was more vulnerable than I had imagined.

"I wish to hell that I'd met you two years from now!" Rosie said, swallowing the last of her cognac.

Well, I thought, the woman can't be accused of keeping her feelings to herself today. But, in the midst of all of that, she did actually say that she wanted me. As much as I wanted to hear something about that fairy story ending, I knew she was right, and that was the best I was going to get. I sat staring at my wedding ring, the sparkle of diamonds diffused through the tears that had begun to accumulate. That ring, I thought, doesn't just represent my tie to my husband. It represents legitimacy and a connection with my children, my parents, society at large.

When she dropped me off back at my office, her mood was less harsh, more compassionate. "I know this is hard for you," she said, "but I have a lot of faith in you. I know you can do whatever needs to be done. You're in a fight for your life here, and I don't think you fully understand that yet, but I know you're strong enough to face it. And, believe me, I'm on your side."

Although I was left feeling forlorn, the events of the day had revealed something new and important to me. I wasn't the only one suffering. Rosie, too, was in a state of painful limbo, waiting to see if I would, if I could, choose to embark on this new life. I was ashamed of myself for being so self-involved that I hadn't even considered that this could be true. Why had I assumed she was indifferent, that her emotions were somehow more superficial than mine? She was more stoical than I was, but maybe, inside, she was just as devastated. Certainly, today she had shown me that emotional side of herself in a way I hadn't seen before.

As always when I saw that Rosie was unhappy, I had an overwhelming desire to fix it. I'd do almost anything to see her smile at me again.

# Chapter Fifteen

That first week at the new office, I threw myself into the work as if it were a life raft. By the end of the week, the Partnership had no unanswered correspondence and no outstanding business to attend to. I had designed what I thought was a professional-looking flyer for Career Day. I e-mailed it to Rosie and her reply came back within the hour.

"Perfect. Send it out."

Like everything else she had ever said to me, and like every e-mail that passed between us, I reread that message over and over looking for the hidden meaning. There was no "I love you" lurking there, obviously.

At home, Amy and her friends came and went. Jerry alternated between hurt and angry silence and doting attentiveness. There was no middle ground, and both of those extremes were intolerable. He had moved into Bradley's room at my request, so I was sleeping alone for the first time since high school, though I was not sleeping much.

The new semester had begun at the junior college and Amy

had a full class load. On Wednesday nights I went to economics class. On a whim, I also signed up for Art History, Rosie's major, on Thursdays. Amy thought it was cool to be going to the same school as her mother. Between the job and school, I kept busy as my mind swirled around the unresolved situation at home.

I'd been on the job less than two weeks when Faye stopped by to see my new setup and ask me out to lunch. Her agency was only a couple of blocks away. "Nice," she said. "Very nice. I don't know how you pulled this off, Jean, but congratulations. Is it hard, what you're doing?"

"Well, it's interesting, that's for sure. For the most part, I've just been writing letters and making phone calls. Relaying information. I've been thinking, though, about how to get more involved in the negotiations aspect. The partners want me to. At least Rosie does. She expects me to make things happen."

"Rosie sure has a lot of confidence in you." Faye, who was admiring the photo of 1877 Weberstown which now hung on the wall, laughed suddenly, a nervous laugh, and turned to face me. "You'll never guess what I heard the other day, Jean. An incredible bit of gossip. It's just too wild. That you and Rosie have a thing going. Can you believe it? Someone's probably jealous of what she's done for you."

I looked away, alarmed. A rumor was circulating? How could anyone know? People make assumptions. They didn't actually have to have any real information. For all I knew, it was that horrible Tanya Lockhart who was spreading rumors. Or anyone with a little imagination who had ever seen me looking at Rosie.

I slid into my chair in shock. I opened my mouth and said nothing. Faye was looking at me, waiting for me to laugh, waiting for me to agree with her about how absurd it was.

"Jean," Faye said, "it's nothing to get upset about. It's just a stupid rumor."

I was sure I looked like a fish out of water, gulping vainly at air.

"It is just a stupid rumor, right?" Faye knelt in front of me. The longer I said nothing, the more alarmed she became. "Oh,

God!" she said at last, comprehending.

I choked up and began to cry. Faye put an arm around my shoulder and handed me a Kleenex from the box on the desk. "I can't believe it," she said. "And you haven't said a word? Why haven't you said anything?"

"Would you?" I asked, wiping my eyes.

"Uh, no, probably not." Gradually, the complexity of this scene was dawning on Faye. "What are you going to do?"

"Decide how to live the rest of my life."

"It's that serious?"

I nodded. Faye stood gazing at me, her expression a sort of frown. "I can't believe it," she said again. She sat with me for an hour as I poured everything out, relieved to finally have someone to tell. She appeared sympathetic, but I hadn't forgotten what she'd said about Rosie, about feeling uncomfortable around her. In Faye's mind, as I spoke about love and happiness, she undoubtedly saw images of lesbian sex. I realized that I might well lose Faye's friendship. This is the kind of thing Rosie had been trying to warn me about. If I left Jerry, I'd lose more than a husband and the shared experiences of twenty-two years. So far I'd only had a glimpse of what I would lose. And what would I gain? How could these things be measured? How could this decision be made?

"I know that if I give up this chance at happiness," I said, "I'll always regret it. I'll wonder what my life could have been if I had had the courage to follow my heart. I don't want to live my life wondering what could have been."

"I see what you mean," Faye said. "But if you leave Jerry, you might regret that too."

"I know. If it turned out to be the wrong decision. But, you know, Faye, even if it didn't work out with Rosie, I don't think I can ever be content living the way I've been living. That's not what I'm meant for."

"How do you know that? You're infatuated right now. I mean, Rosie's a fabulous woman. How do you know it isn't just her, a one-time thing? How can you know what you're meant for?"

"You just know," I said. "When you find it, you just know. What kind of wife can I be to Jerry or any man knowing this about myself?"

Faye shook her head. "It sounds like you've already made the decision."

Yes, I realized, it did sound like that. When Faye left, she was still, I think, in shock. She wished me luck. I would need more than luck, though. I needed courage and the ability to believe in myself in a way I had never done before.

Saturday evening I sat at my kitchen table doing my economics homework. My art history book was nearby, but was less urgent, since we were still covering antiquities in class and I had already read ahead to the Italian Renaissance. I was thoroughly enjoying both classes and was finding the assignments extremely easy. A lot had changed since high school, I realized, when I had spent more time resenting the assignments than doing them. School two nights a week, and the homework associated with it, provided a welcome distraction for me in the evenings. It allowed me to avoid Jerry, for one thing. He spent most evenings in the front room watching television. I worked in the kitchen or at the computer in the den. But I was aware that I was avoiding more than just being in the same room with him, that I was avoiding something much more threatening than that, and that it wouldn't wait any longer. It had been two days since Faye's visit to my office. She had sent me a cute electronic greeting card on Friday, trying to cheer me up and, I'm sure, letting me know that we were still friends.

Amy came home about eight thirty and raided the refrigerator, having missed dinner. With a great commotion, she made a cheese sandwich, and then, eating it, stood behind me looking over my shoulder. "Looks boring," she said.

"I thought so too, at first." I turned around to face her. "But when you consider that economics is the driving factor on which our society, even our morality, is based, well, then it becomes fascinating to observe how it operates in the real world. I mean, economics are central to pretty much everything we do, now and throughout history. It's how you can explain public acceptance of a morally reprehensible convention like slavery, for instance."

"Whatever." She frowned. "You're over my head, Mom."

"You're not stupid, Amy," I said. "Why do you pretend to be?"

She shrugged. "I don't know. I guess I just don't know how to deal with this."

I looked at her, concerned. "With what?"

"With you. I mean, did you just hear yourself? It's weird, you know."

"No, I don't know. What's weird?"

She sighed. "It's a good weird. I'm glad you're excited about school and about your job." There was an implied qualification in her voice. She tore a paper towel off the roll and wiped her mouth.

Maybe you're too self-absorbed, I thought. Maybe that's what Amy is having a hard time dealing with.

"How are the play rehearsals going?" I asked.

"Good. I think I've got my part down flat. Mr. Meredith loves my gesture of grandeur. Like this." She demonstrated, her eyes wide, her head tilted back, her arm sweeping dramatically in a wide arc.

"I bet it will look great in costume."

"We're having our first dress rehearsal next week." Amy sat across the table with her sandwich. "Where's Dad?"

"In the garage changing the oil in his car," I said. "Don't you have any homework?"

"Sure. But I'm not in the mood. Just chilaxin' with my mom." She fluttered her eyelashes at me. They were caked with mascara, as usual.

"Well, I appreciate that, honey, but I *am* trying to do my homework."

Sighing dramatically, Amy took her snack and went into the living room to watch television. Jerry came in from the garage, wiping his hands on a rag. He washed them in the kitchen sink.

"Is that grease?" I asked.

"Yeah."

"I've asked you a hundred times not to wash off grease in the kitchen. Use the sink outside."

He picked up the dishtowel, one of my good ones, and wiped his hands on it, wiped greasy soap on my good dishtowel, scowling at me. "It's freezing cold outside," he said. "This is my house and I can wash my hands anywhere I want to."

"Why did you do that?" I asked calmly.

"Why did I do what?"

"Use my good dishtowel to wipe your hands when you've got a rag right there."

He dropped the dishtowel on the counter. "To make you mad." He left the room.

Amy came back in for a soda. "Are you fighting again?" she asked.

"Again? I don't think we've stopped for weeks."

"Things are sure fucked up around here," she muttered.

"Amy!"

"Sorry." She stuck her glass under the ice maker in the refrigerator door.

"What do you mean?" I asked, overlooking the expletive.

"You and Dad. It's depressing. And, Mom, you're so touchy all the time. Like the other day when you yelled at Wendy. She wasn't doing anything. She'll probably never come over again. A dude's gotta walk on tiptoes around here. Dad too. He just sits around looking miserable. I don't know what's going on between you two, but you have got to deal with it."

Amy went back to the living room, leaving me incapable of completing my reading assignment. She was right. I had to deal with it. I went over what I would say, tried to imagine how Jerry would react. I had been through this in my mind hundreds of times already. When I went into the living room, I found Amy and Jerry watching television, enjoying themselves and each other's company. I don't want to interrupt that, I thought. I can wait until bedtime. Then I almost laughed out loud remembering a scene from Hamlet—yes, I had seen a few plays. Or was it a movie

I'd seen? Hamlet approaches his stepfather to murder him, finds him praying, and rationalizes that it isn't a good time to do it.

"Jerry," I said, "I want to talk to you."

"Now?"

"Yes, please." They were both looking at me curiously. Jerry must have sensed the urgency in my voice. He got up and followed me to my bedroom. We sat on the edge of the bed, facing each other. "I have something to tell you," I said fatalistically.

He looked resigned. "There's someone else, isn't there?"

"Yes," I said quietly.

"I knew it," he said, his voice breaking. "I knew you were seeing another man. That was the only explanation."

"It's not a man."

He looked confused, then, gradually, his expression turned to horror. "A woman?" he breathed, his eyes wide. Then, more emphatically, he asked, "A woman?"

I nodded.

"No, no," he said. "My God!" He stood, strode back and forth for a few moments, then came to the bed, sat and faced me again. He took my chin firmly in his hand and made me look at him. "It's a fluke," he said. "You're not a lesbian. You can't be. It's just one of those things." Then he put his arms around me, holding me tightly to his chest. "I'll help you through it, darling. We'll get through it together. Some pervert has taken advantage of your affectionate nature, that's all. Tried to brainwash you. I understand. These things happen. Don't worry, Jeannie. We'll make it through." He released me and started patting my hand hysterically.

"Jerry, try to listen," I said calmly. "I don't want to get over it. This is what will make me happy at this point in my life. I'm in love with a woman. I want to be with her. I want to get groceries with her and take her cats to the vet and feed her chicken soup when she has a cold."

His face was pale. "You've slept with her?" he asked. I saw that he was trembling.

"Yes."

175

His Adam's apple jumped up as he swallowed. "How did this happen? I don't understand."

"It just happened. I didn't know myself what was happening until it was out of my control. You remember, Jerry, what you said about me being miserable before I started working on Rosie's campaign?" He nodded. "You were right. I didn't realize how miserable I was until I had something to compare it to, until real happiness crept into my life. It wasn't just the work that made me happy, though. It was Rosie. Working for her, being useful to her, being around her."

"Rosie," he said, his eyes narrowing. "It's Rosie you're in love with?"

"Yes."

"Of course it is. Who else? What an ass I've been! Why did I let you…?" He grew quiet and inscrutable, and then suddenly jumped up, his face set into a horrible glare. "I'll kill her for what she's done to you, that vile, disgusting bitch!" He sputtered and was on his way out the door before I had time to move.

"Jerry," I called frantically, "don't you say a word to her." I ran after him. He was at the front door, pulling on his coat, shoving his wallet into the pocket. He glared at me, nostrils flaring, and said nothing. A gust of cold air raced past me before he left, slamming the door hard on his way out. When I turned around, I saw Amy in the hallway, looking alarmed, holding her empty soda glass in one hand. I attempted a smile, which merely confused her.

She held the glass up to one eye and said, "Watson, something's afoot. Fetch my bag. We must investigate."

Well, that was one way to deal with this, I thought, then slumped into a chair in the living room. The TV was still on. People were laughing.

Amy picked up the remote and shut off the television. "What's going on?" she asked in her regular voice. "What's wrong, Mom? What are you fighting about?"

I didn't answer her, just sat wiping tears off my cheeks.

"He didn't hit you, did he? He looked absolutely crazy."

"No, he didn't hit me. Your father has never hit me. He's

been a good husband."

"What did you say to him?" Now her voice was accusing, realizing that perhaps I was the culprit.

"I don't want to talk about it," I said firmly.

"I wish somebody'd let me in on things," Amy grumbled, walking out.

Back in my bedroom, I phoned Rosie's house. Her voice mail answered, so I left a message. "Jerry knows," I said simply, my voice flat. "Call me as soon as you can."

I had a momentary thought that Rosie might not want me once I was available to her. Such things did happen. Regardless of how powerful my feelings were for her, I still didn't feel that I knew her well. She kept so much to herself. She was a driven, competitive sort of woman. Perhaps it was the challenge that she'd been interested in, after all. Well, I thought, I hope that isn't the case, but, if it is, then I would carry on without her, somehow. I felt a strength of conviction that was unfamiliar but reassuring. I took my wedding ring off my finger and put it in my jewelry box.

I lay in bed in the dark for over an hour, unable to relax. Jerry wasn't a violent man, I reminded myself. He'd never hurt a woman. He probably wouldn't hurt himself. God, I didn't want to tell him. What a nightmare he must be going through. At midnight, the phone rang. I was still awake and Jerry was still out. I answered midway through the first ring, hoping Amy was asleep. It was Rosie. "I just got home. Are you okay?"

"I'm okay, but Jerry isn't. When I saw him last, he was threatening to kill you."

"He won't, will he?"

"No," I assured her. "Maybe I should come over in case he shows up at your house, though."

"It's too late to go out tonight. Don't worry about it, love. I'll be fine. I'll call you in the morning. By the way, congratulations. That was a big step. I'm proud of you."

I fell asleep at some point because the phone woke me. I glanced at the clock. It was six thirty. It was Rosie again. "I got a call from your husband," she said. "He was drunk. He yelled obscenities at me."

"Oh, I'm sorry, Rosie."

"That's okay. I can handle it. After he calmed down, we had a long chat. In the end he was sobbing. I told him to take a taxi home and get some sleep. I just got off the phone with him and thought you should know in case he doesn't show up soon. He said he was outside Bernie's Tavern in his car. Apparently he'd just been sitting there since they closed. I made him promise me he wouldn't drive. I called him a taxi, so I'm hoping he took it."

Shortly after I hung up, Jerry stumbled in. He dropped his coat on the floor and lurched past me, not looking at me. Amy stood in the hall and watched him go into our bedroom. He had forgotten that he was sleeping in Bradley's room. I saw a taxi out front, pulling away.

Amy had her arms crossed over her chest. Her pose was a challenge. "Okay, Jean," she said authoritatively, "it's time you started talking. I have a right to know what's going on. I live here too."

"Yes," I said, resigned, "I suppose you'll have to know eventually. How about after some coffee? It's been a rough night."

Amy made the coffee for a change, then sat with me in the kitchen for one of the most ominous discussions we would ever have. How does one do this, I thought. She waited patiently.

"What I have to tell you," I began, then stopped, unable to look at her. "I mean, this is really hard."

"Mom, is somebody dying?"

"No, no, nobody's dying. It's not quite that bad." Okay, just out with it, I thought. "I've fallen in love with someone else. I'm going to leave your father."

She looked at me in astonishment, as though trying to read me, as though she hadn't noticed me before. "Oh, my God," she said, but not in the way she usually said it with tremendous emphasis on each word. This was a more natural response.

"A woman," I said, feeling sort of frantic to get it out. "I'm in love with a woman."

Amy stared, her mouth open. Then she blinked at me and shook her head. Say something, I thought.

"Are you serious?" she asked at last.

I nodded, realizing that I had not seen such a sober look on her face for years.

"Who? Who is your, uh…"

"GF?" My attempt to rouse her out of this uncomfortable solemnity didn't work. Her expression didn't change. "Rosie," I said.

Her eyes widened. She stared at me, unbelieving.

"I'm sorry, Amy," I said, finally, just to break the silence.

She shook her head, obviously distraught. "Mom, how could you?"

She got up suddenly and ran out of the kitchen. I sat where I was, my life shattered around me. I drank my coffee absentmindedly, feeling helpless. I had hoped that Amy would be sympathetic, somehow. What did you expect? I asked myself. That she would be happy for you? This is her family you're tearing apart. A half hour passed and I didn't move. I just sat staring at my hands on the table.

And then, unexpectedly, Amy returned. She poured me another cup of coffee and sat next to me. "Let's talk," she said in a mature tone of voice, settling in and looking at me with a frank and open expression. "So what are you going to do about it?"

I sighed. "Start a new life, I suppose."

"No shit? At your age?" I smiled slightly, but didn't answer. "So you're gonna unload Dad? We're gonna be a broken home? I'm glad this didn't happen when we were little. Then we'd be like that kid in the book, I don't remember her name—April, Tiffany, something like that, Has Two Mommies."

"Heather," I said, absurdly pleased that I finally got a literary reference that she didn't know. The horrible thought that it could have happened before, when my children were little, caused me to shudder.

"Wow, Mom, I just never imagined…I never thought you,

well, you know…well, you're my mom, you know what I mean?" She shook her head. "Poor Dad."

Amy and I sat and talked for a couple of hours. At first I was reluctant to answer her questions, but after a while it felt good, like a release valve opening. It was strange talking to my daughter about something this private, but, fundamentally, we had a good relationship, and I was grateful for that.

"I'm not a virgin, Mom," she told me as the morning wore on.

"I'm not surprised."

"I was seventeen."

"Jeffrey, right?"

She grinned. "Did you know?"

I shook my head. "No, but I suspected. Why didn't you tell me then?"

"I don't know. Maybe I thought you'd freak out or something. Or put me in a chastity belt. I guess I didn't think you and Dad could handle it. You know, you don't think your parents have the same kinds of feelings you do because they don't really let you see it, do they? They pretend to be so, like, whatever, you know. Like you, Mom, all in love like this. It's sort of amazing to see wild and crazy in your parents. Like you can't help yourself, it's bigger than both of you. That kind of thing, at your age. Awesome."

I felt better. I smiled at my daughter. "I hope you're careful," I said. "About sex."

She nodded. "For sure." Then she winked at me. "You too."

I was incredibly relieved to see that Amy wasn't going to condemn me. She was turning into a beautiful human being and more mature than I had ever given her credit for. She seemed to understand exactly what was going on here. Her instincts were good, even if her ability to articulate them was less than impressive.

After a lull, Amy nodded, gazing at me across the table. "Rosie, huh?" she said. "Wow."

She took the coffee cups and rinsed them at the sink. Then she came up behind me and threw her arms around my neck, hugging me. For the first time in quite a while, I felt hopeful about the future.

"What do you say we go pick up your father's car?" I suggested.

# Chapter Sixteen

I remembered wondering about the idea, in the abstract, of living alone, when I was house-sitting for Rosie. Now I was going to find out what it was like. It was frightening. It was exhilarating. I rented a cheerful, west-facing apartment in mid-town and, within a week, had moved my essentials into it and had a functioning living space. I didn't bring much, very little furniture, in fact, only a two-person dining table, two chairs, one easy chair and a nightstand. The only thing I bought was a bed.

Thankfully, there wasn't much conflict with Jerry over possessions. The most difficult thing would be photos. Amy had volunteered to have duplicates made of all of those taken prior to the digital camera. Jerry, understandably distressed, claimed he didn't care about them. "What good are photos?" he railed, "when you're destroying my life? They're just reminders of what you're taking away from me." But I knew he would want them some day. They would be less painful some day, for me too.

This wasn't an automatic decision, this apartment. In fact, it wasn't really my decision at all. I had assumed that when I left my marriage, I would move in with Rosie and we would begin our idyllic life together as a couple. She, however, saw things differently.

"I think you need to be on your own for a while," she said. "Leaving your house was just the first step. There's more to leaving a relationship than that, especially such a well-entrenched one. I hope you understand."

"No, I don't understand. I want to be with you. That was the whole point."

"You've never been on your own. Everyone should know what that's like. It all sounds silly, I'm sure, but I think this is going to be a really valuable experience for you, and a necessary one. I'd rather you came to me when you weren't running away from something else. That way, it will be a real choice you make."

I really didn't understand, but there wasn't much I could do about it. Although it felt like rejection, she assured me that it wasn't.

Regardless of where I moved to, I knew that moving was the right decision. Jerry and I had nothing to hold us together but the past. Once I had finally made and acted on the decision, it had been much easier than I'd ever expected. Far from stepping off a cliff into a freefall, as I'd imagined, it was more like stepping onto terra firma. As soon as it was done, a serenity descended over me. For the first couple of days, all I felt was relief.

Amy, assuming the role of emotional nursemaid to her father, had become a sort of rock for us both. She even attempted to cook for him a couple of times, which went to show how sorry she felt for him. She helped me unpack and set up my new living space, presenting me with the most cheerful of demeanors throughout. Whatever her own heartbreak was over this family disaster, she kept it out of our sight. Very thoughtful, I realized, and probably rare under such circumstances.

Just as I got settled, the day that my new bed was delivered and set up, in fact, Rosie left town to attend a political convention in San Diego with our new mayor.

"Bad timing," I said to her over the phone as she packed her suitcase.

"Yes, I'm aware of that," she said. "Can't be helped."

"You're going to miss our Chinese visitors. I'm going to have to deal with them all by myself."

"Oh," Rosie said with a laugh. "I thought you were going to say you wanted me to help you break in your new bed. But it's all about work with you, isn't it?"

"The other goes without saying. I can't wait to get my hands on you again. But this Chinese thing is scaring the shit out of me. I thought you'd be here."

"Well, the dear boy needs me. He's a little unsure of himself."

"He's not the only one," I said. "You're going to be running the city whether you're mayor or not, aren't you?"

"Mike needs some help right now, but he'll find his footing soon enough. He's a good man. Oh, and he says the doll museum deal is all but signed thanks to you. He told me to relay his appreciation."

"That's great."

"Yes, it is. Excellent work. And my other news is that I got a letter of apology from Tanya. Must have nearly killed her to write it." Rosie laughed. "I'll show it to you next time you're over."

"Congratulations. You'll withdraw your ultimatum, I assume."

"Oh, sure. I don't think she'll be giving me any more trouble, at least for a while."

"Rosie, call me whenever you can the next couple of days. I'm sure I'll be in the middle of a potential disaster every hour."

"Don't worry, Jean. You'll do fine. You can handle it. I could tell by the itinerary you drafted that you know what you're doing. Just don't forget about political ideologies, that's all. And I think I will be able to be here for the last day anyway. We're flying into Sacramento early. If you schedule the museum tour for afternoon, I can make that. Which I'd like to."

"Okay. I'll count on that, then."

"And once our visitors have left, I expect an invitation to your

184

new place."

I could hardly wait for that day myself. It had been a long time since that blissful night in San Francisco, so long, in fact, that it had taken on a dream-like quality. I knew that it hadn't been a dream, though, no matter how fantastical it appeared in my memories. I longed for something more mundane between us, something run-of-the-mill, if that was possible. I had trouble imagining run-of-the-mill where Rosie was concerned, but I needed to get there, somehow.

The Chinese team arrived as planned, four middle-aged men and their female interpreter, a round-faced woman with a perpetual smile who spoke extremely rapidly in Mandarin and extremely slowly in English. Her English name, she told me, was Cindy. I had to stick with them eighteen hours a day, arriving at their hotel at six in the morning to be sure to be there to accompany them to breakfast. Because of the language barrier, it was an interesting experience. There was a lot of laughing on both sides of the conversation, though often neither side really understood the joke.

I arranged for a gigantic gift basket of local fruit to be delivered and waiting for them in their hotel suite upon arrival. I took them to the symphony, on a riverboat trip through the delta, on a tour of the university, and showed them all around town, of course, including our small Chinatown. Things seemed to be going fine. During lunch both days, I called Rosie and we relayed the details of our two separate adventures. On the third and last day, for our tour of the museum, Rosie met us there as she had promised. It seemed to me that every time she was out of my sight for a few days, I forgot how lovely she was until that moment she came into view again. This time was no exception. I'm sure it showed on my face when she walked up the stairs and into the foyer. After a brief look at me, a wide grin broke out on her face.

Our Chinese visitors politely accompanied us through the displays showcasing Weberstown history, and then through the art galleries, including Rosie's pride and joy, the portrait gallery, which was the newest permanent exhibit and contained a gold plaque just inside the doorway that read, "This exhibit was made possible through the contributions of Rosalind Monroe, Dr. Chandra Patel and Kenneth Sturtevant."

The museum had one room with artifacts recovered from the early Chinese settlements in the area, so Rosie steered us through that next, explaining to Cindy that our Chinese heritage was deeply-rooted and highly valued. Cindy, observing the displays of old Chinese coins and flatware, laughed. "Eighteen-forty-nine!" she exclaimed. "You think that is old?"

Rosie shrugged. "It's as old as we've got," she said. "For California, it's old."

Cindy turned to her countrymen and explained to them what she was chuckling about. The four of them broke out into a joint chorus of good-natured hilarity, pointing at our "old" Chinese artifacts.

"You come to Xi'an," Cindy said. "I will show you myself what is old."

"You mean the terra cotta warriors?" I asked, remembering this from my art history class.

Cindy nodded in an exaggerated fashion. "Yes, yes. You must see those. Those are old."

"That's for sure," I said. "Third century BC. That would be something. But you know what I'd really like to see? Some of those three-legged bowls, those Shang dynasty bronze dings. I've only seen pictures, but I just love those. And they're a lot older than the warriors."

I noticed that Rosie was staring at me in surprise, but I wasn't sure why. Maybe I had made some kind of *faux pas*. But Cindy was nodding emphatically and did not seem at all put off. "Oh, then you must come to Shanghai Museum," she said. "Not only can you see them there, but the entire museum building is shaped to resemble a ding vessel."

Cindy turned to explain to the others what we were talking about, and I stepped over to Rosie and whispered, "Did I say something wrong?"

Rosie shook her head, her expression full of affection. "Not at all. You're doing everything right."

Although I was utterly exhausted from these three days, as soon as I returned from the airport after dropping off my visitors, I immediately began to plan for Rosie's first visit to my apartment. I invited her over for Saturday night, then made vegetable lasagna with three cheeses and a green salad. During the layering of the zucchini and cheese that afternoon, I felt like there was no way I would be able to eat anything. My stomach was turning cartwheels all day.

Rosie arrived on time with a bottle of Riesling and a broad, mischievous smile. After she stepped into the apartment, I took the wine from her, feeling oddly shy and a little insecure.

As she gazed over my space, she nodded. "Nice. Bright," she said. "Cheerful. I love the window seat and skylights. A little sparsely furnished, but that can be remedied over time."

For how long, I thought, are you going to leave me languishing here. I put the wine in the refrigerator, then said, "Would you like the grand tour?"

Just as I turned toward the doorway separating the living room from the bedroom, Rosie caught my arm and pulled me toward her. "Come here," she said. "I can't wait any longer." She kissed me urgently, one arm firmly around my waist, one hand gripping the back of my neck. She was apparently not feeling the least bit shy. I let myself fall into her, closing my eyes and feeling the marvelous sensation of her mouth on mine. It was reality, after all, my memory of how completely she owned my body. We stood together, kissing one another for several minutes, until she said, "Do you have a bed in this place?"

I took her hand and led her through the doorway into the bedroom. There was almost nothing in this room either except the bed, the nightstand and a portable CD player providing a soft background of classical piano. On the nightstand and windowsill, I had placed a few candles, already lit.

"This is my favorite room in your apartment," Rosie said, sitting on the edge of the bed. She reached over and grabbed me by the waistband of my jeans, pulling me roughly between her knees. Her eyes were dark, flashing with desire. "Will dinner be ruined if it has to wait a while?"

I shook my head. "Dinner has always known that it was the second course tonight."

Rosie grinned and pulled me onto the bed. Dinner waited patiently under a foil cover in the oven as we renewed our acquaintance with one another.

Afterward, I lay with my arms wrapped loosely around Rosie's naked body, my cheek pressed against her back, chin still wet. The heat of passion was wearing off and the chill of the night was beginning to creep over me. But I didn't want to move, not even to pull up a blanket.

I felt like I'd always been here with this woman in my arms, that this was right, that this was me. "I still can't believe that this could happen at my age," I said, sliding my hand over the curve of her hip.

"You're not alone," she said. "There's even a support group, as a matter of fact, called Late Bloomers."

"Really?"

"Yes, composed of women like yourself, women who led exclusively heterosexual lives into middle age and beyond."

"It happens that often?"

"It's not as rare as you'd think."

"What about you, Rosie? When did you first suspect?"

She rolled over to face me. "A very young age. All my adolescent crushes were on women—a sixth-grade teacher, a movie star, my best friend. I guess I just passed that off as unremarkable, since they were innocent and, as I understand it, not so unusual even for the 'normal' girls. I dated boys and went to the prom and did all the things you're supposed to do, and married David Lamont, of course. But I think I knew all along. Once I admitted that, there were no more men. I am most definitely not bisexual."

"What about me?" I asked.

"Nor you. You're a late bloomer." She smiled fondly at me in the flickering candlelight. "But oh, what a beautiful bloom!"

# Chapter Seventeen

On one of my trips to my old house to get some things, I noticed Abby in her driveway taking grocery bags out of the trunk of her car. She looked up and saw me. I called a greeting to her, and she granted me a nod of her head, but said nothing, and then turned away. Okay, I thought, resigned, it's started.

Amy was in the living room, talking on her cell phone, the ear buds of her MP3 player in place in her ears. How does she do that, I marveled. She got off the phone when she saw me.

"I just saw Abby," I said. "She wasn't especially friendly. Why? Did you say something to her?"

"No. But I sort of told Lisa." Amy pulled the ear buds out of her ears.

"Oh, Amy, for God's sake. Don't you have any sense? You tell one person, they tell two, and pretty soon everybody knows."

"Geez, Mom, I wouldn't want to be something that I was ashamed of."

Was I ashamed? I still hadn't told my parents. All they knew was that I'd left Jerry. They didn't know why.

"How's your dad?" I asked.

She frowned. "He pretty much sits around sulking. He thinks you'll come back."

"Does he?"

"Yeah. He's convinced himself of it. You won't, will you?"

"No."

"That's what I told him. He says he knows you better than I do. He says you're just having a mid-life crisis and you'll come to your senses soon. He says he's going to just wait it out."

I made sure I was out of the house before Jerry came home. I didn't want to see him. He would just make me feel bad like he did during the emotionally draining phone calls that he made to me several times a week.

I had been fairly successful at avoiding him in person up until now, but I knew I would see him Thursday night, the opening night of Amy's play. The possibility of seeing Jerry, though, wasn't the greatest source of anxiety for me that night. This would be the first time Rosie and I went out to a public event as a couple, and that seemed like a pretty big deal to me.

We entered the theater fifteen minutes before curtain time. Just inside, Rosie was approached by an eager young man who shook her hand. Then we were surrounded by a group of people. Rosie introduced me to them one by one as "my friend, Jean." They'll put two and two together. There's no going back now, I thought. Rosie knew almost everybody in town, and certainly everybody knew her. It would be like that wherever we went. There was not going to be any hiding with her. She was right. She was as far out of the closet as it was possible to be.

In this venue, though, it wasn't just Rosie who knew people. There were people here I knew as well, people I'd known for a long time who would suddenly be looking at me in an entirely new way. One of these was Laura Ramsey, the mother of Amy's best friend Wendy. Wendy, who had been friends with Amy since second grade, was also in the play. Laura and I knew each other well, had often found ourselves sharing parental responsibilities at school as our daughters grew up, and had even occasionally socialized together as couples with our husbands. I knew Laura was in the audience tonight and I knew that she, more than most people, would be likely to know the details of my situation. As we stood at the back of the theater, I scanned the seats below us to locate anyone I knew. I wasn't ashamed. I knew that. But it was still scary to hold yourself out there, inviting disapproval.

Rosie was so involved in conversation that I ended up going ahead to our seats alone, the orange plush orchestra seats ten rows back from the stage. As the houselights went down, Rosie slid into the aisle seat beside me and gave my hand a squeeze. I waited impatiently for Amy to come on stage. When at last she did, in full costume, I didn't recognize her until Rosie jabbed me in the arm. Amy wore a gargantuan eighteenth century outfit of petticoats and satin. Her breasts were constricted and pushed up into the open bodice so that they looked huge. On the left one, a dark mole had been penciled in. She wore a white wig of monstrous proportions and carried a fan. I finally recognized her under the gaudy makeup. Yes, she was in there. Amy was hilarious. She stole the show, and it wasn't just her mother who thought so. The crowd roared every time she spoke. Of course, the playwright had something to do with that, but you couldn't discount delivery.

At intermission, Rosie and I stepped into the aisle to allow others to exit our row. That's when I saw Laura coming up the center aisle toward us. I swallowed hard as I waited for her to see me. When she did, she smiled. I smiled. She approached us.

"Hi, Jean," she said. "Both the girls are doing great, don't you think? Amy's cracking me up."

"Yes," I said, "I'm enjoying it quite a bit."

Now Laura turned to look calmly at Rosie, and it was time to introduce them.

"I'm sure you know Rosie," I said. "Rosie, this is Laura Ramsey, Wendy's mother. Wendy is the one playing Julia."

"Yes, of course, I know Rosie," Laura said. "She's a local celebrity. But we've never actually met."

As Rosie exchanged pleasantries with Laura about the play,

I tried to read Laura's mind. She remained inscrutable. She may as well have been a Stepford wife. Not a word about Jerry, my broken marriage or my shocking relationship with the woman she voted for last November. After a few polite minutes, Laura excused herself with, "It's nice to see you, Jean. There aren't so many opportunities for running into each other as there were when the girls were younger. And, Rosie, I'm glad to meet you, finally. I was truly disappointed that you didn't win that election."

She moved up the aisle and out into the lobby as I sighed deeply. So that's how it was going to be with those who were of a refined temperament. They would be polite and pretend that nothing had happened, but they would be distant, perhaps even disdainful under their unruffled veneer. I felt a little broken as I took my seat for the second act.

When the play was over, Rosie and I went to meet the actors in the lobby. Amy came out still in costume. When she saw me, she made her way over and touched her lips first to one of my cheeks, then to the other, in European fashion. With the wig, she stood well over six feet tall, but wasn't slouching at all. Apparently it was okay to be remarkably tall while in character.

"You were fantastic," I said. "And you look grotesque."

"Thanks, Mom. This is so much fun. What did you think, Rosie?"

"The best Mrs. Malaprop I've ever beheld." In a high-flown voice, Rosie said, "The audience couldn't insist you. They were demented."

Amy giggled, then slapped Rosie playfully with her fan. There was genuine affection between those two. When you thought about it, they had a lot in common. Both were extremely comfortable in the spotlight.

While we were laughing over the performance, Jerry walked up, his hands in his pockets, an unconvincing smile on his face.

"Terrific job, princess," he said, hugging Amy. Then he turned to me and said, "Hey, Jeannie." He looked at Rosie, but did not greet her.

I nodded, feeling awkward. What a strange thing this was, I thought, to cut yourself loose from a person you had loved all of your adult life, a member of your family, the person you had always identified as an essential element in your world. I felt Rosie's arm slide around mine and tug on me slightly. Was she afraid that Jerry had some power over me still?

I gave her a reassuring look and said my good-byes to Amy and Jerry. They went home to my old house and I, after kissing Rosie good night in her car on my street, went into my oppressively silent apartment.

Although my work days were exciting and involving, I hadn't yet learned what to do with myself on weekday evenings. If it wasn't for school two nights a week, it might have been unbearable. I ended up buying myself a computer, television and DVD player, objects to distract me from the quiet. And I was on the phone a lot, every night to Rosie, and frequently to Faye and my mother, who weren't used to hearing from me so often, so our conversations were usually dull and repetitive.

And, of course, Jerry called too to convey his current state of despair or reminisce about the good old days. I understood his strategy. He was trying to show me the value of what I was walking away from. But what he didn't seem to realize was that all of the pretty pictures he was painting for me were from a long time ago.

Although he didn't often mention Rosie, he made it clear that he didn't believe I was in love with her. He thought I had deluded myself about that as a way of escaping my marriage. And because of that, he still thought the real problem, whatever it was, could be fixed. He frequently asked me what it was that I was unhappy with, what he could do to make things better, would I please go to couple's counseling.

These calls with Jerry usually ended with him saying, "I love you, Jeannie," before hanging up. Oddly, that always felt like an accusation. I found myself less and less willing to answer and sit through these calls. They seemed unproductive, more like rubbing salt in the wound than contributing to the healing process. I started to screen my calls and avoid picking up for Jerry.

And I tried not to dwell too much on what was happening in my old house while I was sitting alone eating chow mein out of a take-out box. But soon Jerry and Amy would be joined by Bradley, and I found it impossible not to think about that. Bradley's homecoming would be reality slamming into us all like a careening big rig. It was supposed to have been a reunion for our family. It couldn't help but fortify the feeling that we were now destroyed. I hated to think about the pain my boy was about to face, the pain I was going to cause him.

On the day of Bradley's return, Amy was picking him up at the San Francisco airport. It would fall to her to tell him the state of affairs. We had given him advance warning that I had left Jerry, but that was the extent of it. I didn't know how Amy would tell him the rest and didn't ask her. Bradley wasn't like Amy. He was a serious young man who found it tough to compromise his ideals, a quality I admired in him but which would make it unlikely that he would accept the news easily.

At six o'clock on the day of his return, I called Amy from my apartment. "Did everything go okay?" I asked.

"Well, I got Brad, if that's what you mean. He's home."

"That's not what I meant."

"I'm afraid he freaked out, Mom. Big time!"

"Weren't you tactful at all, Amy?" I asked. "Do you always have to be so blunt and inconsiderate?"

"How can you tell your brother that your mom's a lezzie with tact? Besides, I did it as gently as I could. He's shut himself in his room. Hasn't come out since we got home."

"Tell him I want to talk to him." Amy was gone for several minutes.

When finally she returned, she said, "He won't come. He doesn't want to talk to you. He says you're sick. I tried to tell him how cool Rosie is, but he yelled at me and said I was as sick as you are."

I was devastated. I spent an hour sitting in the dark, sobbing,

194

until the phone rang. It was Rosie. She could tell, most likely, from my voice that I had been crying. "Bradley didn't take it well?"

"He wouldn't even speak to me on the phone."

"Give him some time. After all, you've dumped a lot on him all at once. He loves you. He'll come around."

"But what if he doesn't? What if he won't speak to me again? What if he won't let me see my grandchildren?"

The next day I called the house again. Amy answered and reported that Bradley would still not come to the phone, and that his message to me was that if I came home and promised to get counseling, he would do his best to forgive me. "Sorry, Mom," she said.

"Thanks for trying, honey," I said weakly, and then spent another evening in tears.

The next day, Rosie invited me to lunch. Our restaurant conversation revolved mostly around the situation with my son. She tried to comfort me at first, but by the end of the meal, she had moved on to a different approach. Maybe she just got tired of telling me everything would work out, or maybe she wanted me to buck up and prepare for the horrible possibility that Bradley was not someone who could be won over after all.

"You knew there would be sacrifices," she said.

"I knew I was losing a husband," I said. "I didn't expect to lose my son."

"It happens," Rosie said. "Happens all the time. In any family with a gay person, there are going to be family members who just can't accept it. If you're lucky, there aren't very many of those."

Somehow I managed to quit thinking about myself for a moment. "Rosie," I said, "is there someone like that in your family?"

"My mother," she said, solemnly. "She never forgave me."

"Didn't your mother die not too long ago?"

She nodded. "That's the worst of it. Three years ago. No matter what I accomplished, none of it meant a thing to her. Everything was completely overshadowed by her condemnation of my lifestyle."

My God, I thought, how sad. Was that what all of this over-achieving was about, after all, the search for that elusive parental approval? We talked for a while, then, about Rosie's family and her lifelong and ultimately unsuccessful attempt to win back her mother's love. I was glad she was talking about it, that she felt enough trust between us to reveal the most vulnerable of wounds, but it left me more fearful than before. If a mother could reject a child for this, then certainly a child could reject a mother.

In the midst of my heartache over Bradley came Jerry's ultimatum. I had until the end of the month to make my final decision. It was late February. Winter was over and the trees were preparing their blooms. He would take me back if I came to my senses before then, but he had a life to live too and couldn't wait indefinitely. I suspected Bradley of having a part in this latest move. Give her an ultimatum, Dad, and force her hand. They were ganging up on me.

When I told Rosie about Jerry's ultimatum, she said, "I know how upset you are about Bradley. You can go back if you want to. It sounds like they would welcome you back."

I could see the fear in her eyes. "No, I can't," I said firmly. "I'm not going back."

She was still unsure of me, I realized. She didn't know if I was going to make it. I was a would-be track star running hurdles. Any one of them could knock me out of contention. I remembered when she wished she'd met me two years into the future. In two years, I wondered, will I have cleared all the hurdles? And was that possible if my son would never speak to me again? This was an unexpectedly high hurdle.

Considering that Rosie had these doubts, I was glad that she wasn't a witness to the endless drama that took place in my apartment on the telephone or just by myself with my frequent tears over the shipwreck of my family. She had glimpses of it, especially because of Bradley, but I was shielding her from the bulk of it, presenting my best and happiest self to her when we were together. That wasn't difficult, though, because I really was my best and happiest self with Rosie.

Jerry's deadline came and went. His calls became less frequent. Bradley got his own apartment and a job at the *Sentinel* as a stringer. That was perfect, I thought. I had still not seen him or even spoken to him. Amy had kindly e-mailed me a couple of recent photos which were taped to the wall at my office. He looked more like a man than ever. The traces of boyhood on his face were diminishing. But he was otherwise as I remembered him, a tall, looming sort of boy with sandy hair, a ruddy complexion and a red mustache. He looked like neither Jerry nor me. He looked like my grandfather. But that was the extent of the resemblance. My grandfather was a zany Irishman, full of mischievous good humor, who took absolutely nothing seriously.

One of the photos Amy sent was of Bradley and his new girlfriend, Brenna. She was stunning with a thin face, high cheekbones, long auburn hair and a lightly-freckled complexion. They looked quite natural together. Would I ever meet her, I wondered, imagining red-headed grandchildren.

As spring bloomed, my life began to settle into a routine of sorts, but a routine unlike anything I would ever have called "routine" before. My comfort level at work was increasing rapidly. I began to rely on myself more and more and generate new projects for the Partnership on my own, like the industrial park that, two years after being built, still sat eighty percent unoccupied. This was the sort of disaster which discouraged developers from speculating on such projects. Was this something I should get involved in, I wondered. The limits of my job were undefined. This was, perhaps, a real estate problem and out of my sphere. Then again, if the property could be leased, new businesses would come, new jobs would be created.

I amused myself by imagining bursting out of a telephone booth in blue tights and a cape, bellowing, "This is a job for Jean!"

"I think it's just a matter of advertising," I told Rosie. "The site is really ideal, modern and well-equipped. I think the realtor is indifferent, being out of town as they are and having a lot of other properties to tend to."

"What do you recommend?" Rosie asked.

I remembered the first time she'd asked me that question, the night at my first Vision Partnership meeting. Had she any idea that night what a flood she was unleashing? Maybe, in a way, she had. That was also the night she offered me this job, after all.

"I can create a brochure, send it out to targeted companies. There's nothing wrong with the site. I drove out there, scoped it out. It's close to the freeway, reasonably priced. It's just neglected."

Rosie nodded. "Great idea. Pitch it to the others at the next meeting." Rosie narrowed her eyes. "Jean, why do I get the eerie feeling that some day you're going to open up an advertising agency and run me out of business?"

While my work week had become extremely challenging, my weekends had also taken on a completely new flavor. Rosie and I generally spent our weekends together. With Rosie, that wasn't a time to kick around the house in your old clothes. There was always some event to go to, like a fund-raiser or concert or opening night at an art gallery. Or we would volunteer to work on committees for such events, which reminded me a lot of campaigning and could be tremendous fun. And there were a few things that were less demanding, like riding the horses out for a picnic by the river, or even going to the farmers' market, which we tried to do most Saturday mornings. Rosie couldn't believe I'd never been there before. For us, even that was a social event, and it took us a good two hours to get our berries, broccoli and bread because of all the meeting and greeting going on.

Gradually, we were running into some of the same people over and over now so that people were getting used to seeing us together. When I showed up on my own at the farmers' market, because Rosie had been called to a Saturday meeting, the first thing out of everybody's mouth was, "Hi, Jean, where's Rosie?" and that really couldn't have felt any better.

One of the people I ran into, in front of a stand brimming with vibrant citrus fruit, was Tyler Enbright, a young gay man who volunteered briefly on Rosie's campaign in its final days. I had taken an instant liking to him, and had found him more approachable than most of the others. We had spoken only briefly, so I didn't know him well. He was Bradley's age and had grown up in the Midwest where all of his family remained. He was a lithe, fine-featured boy with dark, deep-set eyes. He stood only slightly taller than me. Since the election, I had seen him a couple of times around town. He was selecting limes with meticulous precision when I greeted him.

"Oh, hi, Jean," he said, his face brightening with recognition. And then he proceeded to look over my shoulder for Rosie like the others had.

"No Rosie today," I said. "She's busy."

He nodded. "Gorgeous day, isn't it? And look at these limes. I'm going to make a tart with these, I think. I just love citrus. Last week they had blood oranges and I made the most incredible roasted beet and blood orange salad."

"Oh, right, you're a chef."

"Chef for hire," he said, striking an extremely gay pose.

Tyler and I strolled through the market together, talking mainly about food, until we reached the end of the stalls with our tote bags filled with produce. Because of him, I ended up with a dubious bunch of greens called *gai lan* in my bag. I wasn't sure how I was going to approach that.

"Just treat it like rapini or escarole," he said. My response to this, which must have reflected my clueless state of mind, made him laugh. "Blanch it and throw it in a stir-fry or just sauté it with garlic and olive oil."

"We're definitely going to have to hire you one of these days."

"No charge for friends. I'd love to cook for you and Rosie."

"Either way, I can't wait. Just listening to you talk about food has left me famished."

He smiled warmly. "I'm kind of hungry too. Hey, let's get lunch."

This invitation took me aback for just a moment. Then I

decided that I had plenty of time for lunch before Rosie was due home.

"All right," I agreed.

Tyler and I had a prolonged, fascinating meal during which he made witty remarks about the food, the waiters, the restaurant décor. He was quite a talker, and extremely entertaining. While we ate, he told me a half dozen funny stories about his early, mostly chaste ventures into gayness. I realized that because of his youth and because of my newbie status, we were sort of contemporaries in the gay subculture.

"I heard these old guys talking about Stonewall one time," he said. "One of my first times in a gay bar, actually. I was underage, so I didn't even try to order a drink." Tyler pushed his empty plate to the side of the table. "They said, 'Stonewall started everything, the entire gay rights movement in America.' Well, the only Stonewall I knew was Stonewall Jackson, the Civil War guy, you know?"

I nodded. "Yes, I know."

"So I figured he was some kind of early homosexual pioneer, like the first openly gay military officer or something. I read a couple of biographies of the guy. Not a word about his gay love life, which I figured had something to do with the fact that this happened back in the dark ages. So then, one day in my American history class, as we were covering the Civil War, old Stonewall died of pneumonia and Robert E. Lee's mournful response was, 'I'm bleeding at the heart.' I raised my hand and asked, 'So, was it Robert E. Lee who was his lover?'"

I laughed loudly at Tyler's expression, which was self-deprecating and extremely cute. He shrugged, his eyes twinkling.

"Yeah, it was embarrassing," he said.

"They don't teach you these things in school, do they?"

"You've got to pick it up on your own. I learned quite a bit about the Civil War on my Stonewall quest. Not so much about gay history, though."

As we were both still smiling over this story, my cell phone rang. "Excuse me," I said and glanced at the display. It was Rosie. I answered.

"Hey, where are you?" she asked.

I looked at my watch. It was after one. "Oh, I didn't realize it was so late. I guess you're home, then. I'll be there in a few minutes. I'm just having lunch with Tyler Enbright. You remember him?"

Before leaving the restaurant, Tyler and I promised to get together again. I hoped we would. I had really enjoyed his company.

# Chapter Eighteen

It was partly Tyler's influence that got me thinking more about the history and politics of gay culture, thinking about it beyond the personal, but I had been making tentative forays into this area already on my own. At least I knew that Stonewall had nothing to do with Stonewall Jackson. Having someone to talk to who was in the same boat was an additional impetus, though. Using the Internet, and borrowing books from Rosie's shelves and the public library, I began to educate myself. Tyler and I met when we could to discuss these topics, sometimes at a coffee shop, sometimes at my apartment. Our conversations were intense and entertaining, often accompanied by a delectable treat from his kitchen.

On weekends, Tyler sometimes joined me at Rosie's place and cooked for us, sessions he characterized as practice for his clients. He was an artist in the kitchen, and we couldn't get enough. He loved cooking for Rosie, too, because she was such an enthusiastic recipient.

On one such Saturday in March, Rosie and I sat on her back

porch with two tall glasses of iced tea while Tyler was inside preparing us a Spanish feast of paella.

"It smells heavenly already," Rosie said, closing her eyes.

I agreed with a murmur, looking lazily out across the yard to the field where Vita and Violet stood grazing on spring grass.

"You remember Sue?" Rosie asked.

"Yes," I said, thinking, how could I forget that cute little minx?

"She's invited me to a party, an anniversary party."

"Anniversary of what?" I asked suspiciously.

"She's been with her girlfriend Dena two years next weekend."

"Do you want to go?"

Rosie nodded. "Yes, I do. I was wondering if you would want to go too."

"Do you want me to go?"

"Are you kidding? I'd love to show you off. I just don't want you to feel uncomfortable. Sue's been cut off from her family completely. This will be exclusively lesbians."

"I'd like to go," I said. Uncomfortable or not, I had to jump into this some day. And I didn't really want to let Rosie loose unchaperoned among a group of women whose common ground was their sexual preference for their own kind, especially if Sue was one of them. She could still be doting on Rosie, despite this girlfriend of two years.

"Ladies," Tyler called through the kitchen window, "dinner is served! Who wants sangria?"

So it was settled. Rosie was going to bring me into the inner circle. I became more nervous as the date approached and started asking questions, like what should I wear.

"Just dress casual," she said "Whatever you're comfortable in."

Right, right, I thought. She wasn't being very helpful. "What sort of thing will happen at this party?" I asked. "I mean, what activities. What will we be doing?"

She looked at me brightly, raised her eyebrows, and said,

"We'll talk, have some food and drink, and then…well, we usually play a few party games. Our favorite is naked Twister, but the way we play it is a little harder than the conventional way because you don't just have your hands and feet on the colors." She was gesturing with her hands in a way that I couldn't make any sense out of, and I was suddenly assaulted with images of naked women's bodies all twisted together in a pile, and I felt my legs start to tremble. "Oh, I can't describe it," Rosie said. "It's hilarious, and it usually ends up in an all-out orgy, as you can imagine." She stopped gesturing and looked at me. "Oh, sweetie," she said, slapping me on the back, "you've gone all white. Hey, it's a joke. Sorry, I didn't realize you were that scared. Believe me, there's nothing to be afraid of."

I started breathing again. "No naked Twister?"

"Of course not. Maybe this was a good idea after all. Maybe we can dispel some of the stereotypes lingering in your mind." She looked like she was trying not to laugh at me.

Sue and Dena lived just outside of Angels Camp. It took us over an hour to get there and when we arrived, there were several cars parked in front of a small house inside a split rail fence. Before ringing the bell, I buttoned the top button on Rosie's shirt, hiding her lovely cleavage. She widened her eyes at me. The door was opened by a woman in jeans and a T-shirt bearing the words, "She Wears the Pants, but I Wear the Strap-On." Rosie shrieked with laughter. If Amy had been standing beside me, I would have now been saying "OMG!" The woman in the doorway was thin and lanky, about sixty, with dark gray hair cut in a short, spiky style.

"Hi, Rosie," she said, opening the door wider.

Rosie hugged her, saying, "Jo, how's the turkey business these days?"

"Oh, it couldn't be better. Just great." Jo turned to me and arched her eyebrows. "Rosie, is this your girlfriend?"

"Jo, this is Jean," Rosie said, looking proudly at me.

"Ummm," murmured Jo, biting her lower lip. "I heard she was cute, but, damn! Come with me, sweetheart." Jo slung her arm around my waist and pulled me inside. Rosie winked at me and followed us in. Jo introduced me to several of the twenty or so women in the house. While she was briefly distracted, I said quietly to Rosie, "Turkey business? Is that some kind of euphemism or something?"

Rosie laughed. "No. Jo raises turkeys. She has an organic turkey farm." Rosie leaned her head against mine, saying, "Not everything is a sexual innuendo."

Rosie took our lentil salad into the dining room while Jo continued introductions. I saw that there was a couple there I knew, Ginny and Aura.

When Ginny saw me, she smiled wide and hugged me. "Jean," she exclaimed, "you and Rosie? Wow. I didn't see that coming. How've you been since the election?" Chatting with Ginny, I recognized that she spoke to me much more intimately and affectionately than she had before. We were sisters now. And that's how it seemed with all of these women. They had a kinship with one another. Even Aura was now my friend.

Jo then introduced me to her partner, Helen, a woman about her own age, and I learned that they had been together for thirty-three years. Now those two probably had some stories to tell, I thought, awed. I remembered Rosie's CD with the label, "Helen, 1995."

"Are you a musician?" I asked.

She smiled. "I'd like to think so. Has Rosie played some of my work for you?"

"I've heard a couple of songs. Really beautiful."

"Thank you. Maybe later you can hear us in person. Everybody's here tonight, so we might have a little jam session later on."

"Oh, you're the jazz band, then?"

"Yes. Jo and I, Ginny and Rosie."

After I'd met everybody in the front room, Rosie reappeared at my side with a glass of wine.

"There's Sue," Rosie said, indicating a woman identical to the photograph on Rosie's dresser. I realized with dismay that whatever had transpired between Rosie and this girl was not in the distant past after all. Rosie moved toward her with me in tow. When Sue looked our way, she smiled in recognition, then broke through the circle of friends she was engaged with. Rosie released my hand to greet her. They hugged each other close and tight, Sue's head nestled under Rosie's chin. Rosie's eyes were closed, I saw, and she looked like she was holding a beloved child. Don't be jealous, I warned myself. At last they moved apart and Rosie introduced me.

As the evening progressed, I relaxed more and more. Rosie, as always, was at home in a crowd. Much of the time I was beside her, doing my best to make her proud. Tonight, in everyone's eyes, I was her mate. And she was mine, I realized. Rosie belongs to me, I thought, triumphantly, so the rest of you sad lot just crawl into a corner and die.

But Sue and Dena, at least, didn't seem too envious. They were affectionate with one another, touching and kissing, and jointly holding the knife that cut the cake. Okay, I thought, so maybe everybody isn't after Rosie.

After getting a plate of food, I went and sat in the living room to eat it, leaving Rosie in conversation with Jo. Rosie moved easily in all of her worlds, despite the huge differences between them. She adapted so gracefully, could talk to anyone, and seemed to really enjoy people in a way that left them feeling good. She was a genuinely warm person. No wonder I fell in love with her, I thought. And Sue over there. And Tracy, and who knows how many others.

Sue was sitting on Dena's lap in the dining room. They were eating from the same piece of cake, Sue working the fork. I watched, thoughtful, as Sue and Dena kissed. It was strange watching two women kiss. When one of them is you, you just do it, you feel it, but you don't see it. It doesn't feel strange. The strangeness would wear off, I thought, in time. It was strange because it was new and because all my life I was on the other side. I've crossed over the boundary of another world, like an alien visitor to this planet of Lesbiana.

"Hi," someone said, startling me. I looked up to see a young woman with one of those modern hairstyles, cut close on the sides and back, longer on top. Her hair was bleached blond, but just on the top, with the back and sides dark brown. She wore dark eye makeup. She looked exotic, harshly sexual. Heavy gold-colored bracelets adorned her wrists. In one ear she wore a huge gold hoop, and in the other a diamond stud.

"Hi," I said.

"You're with Rosie, aren't you?" she asked, sitting beside me. I nodded. "I'm Cherise."

"Jean," I said.

"How long have you two been together, Jean?"

"About four months." Cherise made me uncomfortable.

"Oh, not long, then. Although with Rosie four months is really an accomplishment, I guess."

"What do you mean?" I'd grown defensive.

She shrugged. "Oh, you know, so often these things are over before you know it. Don't you think it's wonderful that Sue and Dena have made it this long? Two years, and they're still in love. I'm so happy to see it. Sue deserves this." Cherise gazed silently at Sue for a moment, then turned to me and said, "I thought she'd never recover after Rosie dumped her. The poor child was a mess. And to make it worse, Rosie had broken up a perfectly fabulous relationship to get her. Mine." Cherise scowled. "Sue and I were together for four years before she met Rosie. And, then, those two, it was less than six months and it was all over. Rosie's one of those people who burns hot and bright and burns out fast."

I said nothing, unsure of this woman's motives.

"Did you leave behind a woman with a broken heart?" Cherise asked.

I thought of Jerry. There was Rosie across the room, gesturing emphatically to punctuate her conversation, burning hot and bright. "No," I said.

"That's good."

"Sue seems to like Rosie well enough, still," I said.

"Yes, but Sue is like that. She doesn't hold grudges. She's got a big, open heart. In some ways, she's like a child. She forgives people. And there's no doubt that Rosie never intended to hurt her. Rosie's not intentionally cruel. She just gets tired of people fast. She's very intense." Cherise paused, watching me. "Oh, look, Jean, I didn't mean to worry you. Rosie's great. Enjoy her while you've got her. And, who knows, maybe you're the one, right?" Cherise slid out of the chair and was gone.

I became morose. I began to wonder if I was the latest in a string of hot flashes. I looked around the room, wondering how many of these women Rosie had slept with? How many of them knew about that spot behind her ear? Rosie was mad about me today, but in a couple of months, would she become bored and move on? I began to wonder how I ever thought I could keep Rosie's interest. She was vibrant and witty and popular. What did she possibly need me for? She'd given in to me because I had aggressively seduced her. She hadn't even wanted me in the first place. And wasn't she even now keeping me at arm's length by insisting on living apart?

Ginny came over and sat beside me. "How are you doing?" she asked. I noticed she was wearing the brown pants of her UPS uniform, but her shirt was blue chambray, tucked in neatly and adorned with a handsome bolo tie. Her blond hair was in a ponytail, as usual, but she wasn't wearing her customary ball cap.

"Okay," I said, no longer sure. "I'm adapting."

Ginny nodded thoughtfully. "I guess Rosie's your first, right?"

My first? Did everybody just assume that Rosie and I were a spring fling? Is that how it was with lesbians? I remembered Jo, then, the turkey farmer, and her partner of thirty-three years. That was some comfort.

"Ginny," I asked, "what do you think of Rosie?"

Ginny looked at me suspiciously. "Why do you ask?"

"I just wondered what she seems like to people who aren't insanely in love with her."

Ginny laughed, glanced over at Rosie, and then looked back at me. "She's the best, Jean. Hang on to her for dear life."

"I don't want to feel that desperate."

"I didn't mean it like that. I just meant she's very special. And she adores you, you know. She was just telling us about the incredible job you're doing for the Vision Partnership." Ginny leaned closer. "I've never seen her so happy. You're not the only one who's insanely in love."

Aura was suddenly behind Ginny, flinging her arms around her and pulling her away from me, nearly knocking her off her chair. Aura was wearing the same tank top and vest I was used to seeing her in. It was her costume, I guessed. She narrowed her eyes at me and pointed her index finger, saying, "I've got my eye on you." I was close enough to her this time to see that the tattoo on her neck was a pair of interlocking female gender symbols. How bold, I thought, impressed.

Ginny, recovering her balance, said, "She's just messing with you, Jean."

Aura's expression widened into a grin. She was awfully cute. Maybe not so scary as I had originally thought. Aura leaned against Ginny affectionately.

Rosie appeared, then, with a flushed face, and sank down on the chair next to me. She put her arm around me and said to Ginny. "So, are you ready to get out that Twister game?"

Ginny looked confused.

Rosie said, "In-joke," grinning at me. Then she kissed me on the mouth for all the world to see. Well, not quite all the world, just the inhabitants of Lesbiana.

"Ginny," Rosie said, excited, "time to jam."

Ginny nodded. "I'll get the Colonel and Jo."

"I hope you don't mind, sweetie," Rosie said to me.

"Of course not. I'm looking forward to this. But who's the Colonel?"

"Helen. She's retired military."

Rosie got her saxophone out of the car and we rearranged the furniture so the four of them could set up in the living room. The rest of us gathered around to provide an audience. The Colonel, on the guitar, seemed to be the leader of this troupe. Jo was the fiddle player. They started off with a raucous Dixieland number. I sat beside Sue, who was tapping her foot and slapping her knee in time with the music.

"They're great!" I said to her when the song was over.

"Oh, sure. Do you play an instrument, Jean?"

I shook my head. No, I thought, I'm not musical either. There were so many ways in which I must be inadequate as a partner for Rosie. I was reminded of what Cherise said about these things being over before you knew it, and the phrase "six months" hung over my head like a noose.

The band played something more traditional for their second song, a slow and heavy-on-the-sax version of "Summertime." It was languorous and seductive. Rosie, who was already flushed from wine, was even redder after blowing her way through the number.

As they prepared for their third piece, Rosie pointed at me and said, "This one is for my beautiful lady, Jean." She winked at me and nodded to the others. They launched into a lazy version of "The Nearness of You."

I was embarrassed, and wondered at Rosie's judgment, considering Sue was sitting right here next to me, but it felt good anyway. Sue didn't seem offended. She beamed at me as though she was happy for me. Rosie kept her eyes on me while she played the last few notes of the song solo, then lowered her instrument and blew me a kiss.

I noticed Cherise standing near the kitchen door, looking disgusted.

The Colonel slapped Rosie on the back and said, "Okay, ladies, let's bring up the tempo." They played "The Lady is a Tramp" then, which everybody seemed to like.

My evening proceeded pretty much like that, swinging up and down. I was hit with too many loaded images, and in the end, I didn't know how to feel. By the time we left, it was almost midnight. Rosie leaned her head back against the seat of the car as I drove.

"Did you enjoy yourself?" she asked.

"Yes," I said. "I especially liked your song dedication. It was touching."

"I'm glad you liked it. I meant every note."

As soon as we'd reached the highway, she was asleep. I tuned the radio into a news channel with the volume low. A few times Rosie woke, startled to find herself moving. Then she'd see me and lapse back into a stuporous sleep. She'd had too much to drink. She woke up when at last the car rolled over the gravel driveway in front of her house.

"Are we home?" she asked, rousing herself. "You're staying, right?"

I nodded. We went inside and got ready for bed. I pulled on a nightshirt and brushed my teeth in the bathroom. Rosie was in the bedroom talking about Dena's party balloon shop, something about advertising. I wasn't really listening. When at last we were in bed, she kissed me and pushed a strand of hair away from my eyes.

"Why so pensive, Jean?" she asked. Then, seeing that I hesitated, said, "It's Cherise, isn't it? I saw her talking to you. She said something to upset you."

"She told me about you and Sue, how you tired of her after only a few months."

"Ah, so that's it?"

"Well, it's scary. I'm afraid the same thing will happen with me. I'm afraid of losing you."

Rosie pulled me closer. "I'm afraid of losing you too. What kind of promise do you want from me?"

Till death do us part, I thought. The same promise I made once to someone. And broke.

"I don't know," I whispered feebly.

Rosie turned my face so that I was looking into her eyes. "I can't help but be a little cynical, Jean. My love life has had its share of disasters. Even so, I'm optimistic about us. I think there's a real chance here for something permanent." She kissed

211

me lightly. "I hope so, anyway."

I tried to smile at her, but I doubt that it was convincing.

"I'm sorry Cherise upset you," she said. "Do you want to hear my side of the story?" I nodded. Rosie cradled my head in her arm.

"You know, the problem with these lesbians is that it's one big incestuous family and we all know everything about each other." Rosie smiled and then settled into her story. "Sue was twenty-three when I met her, in a rocky relationship with Cherise, who is now a high school teacher, and, as far as I know, clean. But at the time, she had a serious fling going with cocaine, and Sue got sucked into that. I met her at the Women's Shelter where I was volunteering when she had pretty much hit bottom. She was estranged from her family, unemployed, a drug addict and had begun accumulating a criminal record. She was a mess, really, and, not surprisingly, suicidal."

"Wow," I said, thinking about how wholesome and well-adjusted Sue had appeared to me.

"I thought she needed some special attention," Rosie continued. "I felt really sorry for her, especially because her parents wanted nothing to do with her. Not surprisingly, she developed a crush on me. I knew she was vulnerable, and I thought it was better for her to love me, chastely, than someone else, someone destructive like Cherise. We were physically affectionate, but it wasn't sexual. She was like a daughter to me. Still is."

I pictured the tender embrace Rosie had given Sue earlier and felt stupid about all of my assumptions and suspicions. Although there were still so many things I didn't know about Rosie's life, the things I did know should not have left me vulnerable to the insinuations of Cherise.

"Eventually, Sue got back on her feet. She got clean, got a decent job. She went on with her life and found someone more appropriate to love. And that's the story. Cherise is a woman with a grudge. She blames me for breaking up her relationship. Now she's trying to ruin mine with you by planting doubt in your mind. You can ask Sue about any of this if you want to."

"No, I don't have to ask anyone. I'm sorry, Rosie."

"It's okay. I hope you'll feel a lot more secure, though, soon. Cherise barely knows me. You can't give much credence to anything she said. And after what I found out tonight, I'm so grateful that she knows almost nothing about me."

"What do you mean?"

"She's a vicious woman, more vicious than I would have suspected. It was Cherise who tipped off Kiester, and it was Cherise who told the press about me and Catherine, and about Sue. She's convinced that Sue and I had an affair, despite what she's been told."

"She would do such a thing for revenge?" I asked.

"Looks like it."

My God, I thought, if I had known, earlier tonight, that Cherise was responsible for causing Rosie to lose the election, what would I have done? Somehow, Rosie, in spite of knowing this, had avoided a scene and had even enjoyed her evening. "What will you do about it?" I asked.

"I told Sue and Dena to let everyone know. Cherise will find that her circle of friends has diminished."

"Woe to the woman who does Rosie wrong," I said, remembering the hapless Tanya Lockhart.

"You'd better believe it," she said. "Let that be a lesson to you. You walk out on me, girl, and I'll have the entire sisterhood down on you. You'll never get laid in this town again."

I nuzzled into her neck, and said, "I love you, Rosie."

"I love you too, Jean. And I'll probably love you tomorrow, so try to relax."

# Chapter Nineteen

It was just a couple of days later that the office mail brought an interesting invitation from the junior college business department. It was addressed to me, as in, "Administrator, Vision Partnership." They wanted me to speak at the college about the work we were doing.

When I turned the letter over to Rosie, she said, "That's fantastic."

"Oh, Rosie, why don't you do it instead? I'm no public speaker."

"They asked for you. And it's not that big a deal. But if you keep this up, you'll be in demand, believe me. Cities all over the country will want you."

"Stop it," I said.

"This is no joke. Somebody who can make things happen like you're doing is a valuable commodity. You're going to get job offers, my girl." She tousled my hair playfully. "Oh, but in the meantime, I think you should probably pick up a business degree of some kind too. You may as well take your career seriously."

Statements like that left me dumbfounded.

I accepted the invitation to speak at the college, the same college where I was taking a class in beginning economics, and grew more and more nervous as the day approached. Rosie helped me with my speech and I memorized everything there was to know about the Partnership. Amy promised to be in the audience. She seemed quite smug to have her mother speaking to her classmates. At least one of my children was proud of me. I was proud of me too.

I stood in front of an audience of about two hundred students, business majors. I had dressed in a conservative knit suit, pants and blazer, a silk scarf arranged in the breast pocket. The students seemed to pay attention, some even took notes. Several times as I spoke, I thought how odd that I should be here, speaking as an expert on these topics. The students, raptly listening for the keys to success, had more education than I did. Would any of them know it? Were any of them my own classmates? I was definitely insecure. Rosie sat in the front row, ready, it seemed, to catch me if I fell off the stage.

"We're talking to a French manufacturing firm," I said, bringing my prepared speech to a close, "about opening up a major west coast distribution center here. I'm optimistic about it. This company will employ at least a hundred people, people like yourselves who ought to be able to work in the community where you grew up and went to school. We want to be sure that when you graduate from this school or from a four-year university, you'll have a good job waiting. That hasn't been the case for a long time. New, high-tech industry hasn't been coming here. I see that changing, right now, right before our eyes."

I concluded by thanking them for their attention and opening the floor for questions. Now I was going to have to wing it. Rosie, I noticed, had a huge Cheshire Cat grin on her face.

"Ms. Davis," asked a young man, "does this school play a part in your plans?"

"Yes, very much so. We've been working closely with the college to make sure that educational programs are in place to support the type of businesses we're attracting. We don't want to be teaching our students skills that aren't needed by the community, so, yes, I've been giving information to the school to help it shape its curriculum. One new class which is a direct result of our cooperative efforts is computer graphic design, which will be offered in the business department for the fall semester. Graphic design is a skill much in demand in the advertising industry and, as in practically every other discipline, there's been a radical shift toward total digitization in recent years." I paused, glanced at Rosie, then said, "You see, we believe very strongly that no part of our community can operate independently. What we're trying to do is draw all factions together so that the right kind of progress will happen. The government has to respond to the needs of business, and business has to participate in the community, and the schools must evolve to support the entire structure. It's a very simple idea, and certainly not new."

The next question came from a woman. "Bringing new business to the area is commendable and exciting, but so many businesses are struggling, shutting their doors. Is your organization involved in any way in preventing this trend?"

"I'm glad you brought that up," I said. "We *are* involved in that." I explained about the Chevrolet dealership that was still operating due to our intervention, and about another business we were helping to resolve a labor dispute. "This isn't always possible," I said, "but we're dedicated to making the attempt. This is hard work. It's harder than most people realize just to get local government and businesses to talk to one another. Cooperation is a new approach for them."

I took about a half dozen questions, and then, running over the time I'd been allotted, brought it to a close. They clapped. Loudly. It was a rush. I stepped off the stage to the side of the room where Rosie greeted me with a rather absurd handshake. Well, it was appropriate for the setting.

"You're marvelous," she said. "I can't get over it. Once you got going, you were just incredible. You sounded like you'd been doing this all your life."

Yes, that's the way so many new things felt these days, like I'd been doing them all my life. It was like I was remembering who I was after having been an amnesiac for twenty years.

Mr. Winkle, the instructor who had arranged the talk, approached and shook my hand. "Quite inspirational, Jean. I'm glad I asked you in. Can I take you to lunch? I'd like to ask you a few questions myself. Rosie, will you join us?"

"I'm afraid I can't. I've got to get back to work. I'll see you later, Jean." She winked and took off.

Suddenly Amy was there, her arms flung around me. "Oh, Mom, you were really good up there. I was so scared you were gonna freeze or flop or sound like a ditz. But you didn't."

I laughed. "What an endorsement."

Mr. Winkle seemed amused. I introduced him to Amy and the three of us went to Risso's for lunch.

When Rosie called me that evening, I was still high.

"I'm so happy for you, Jean," she said.

"I'm sure some of it sounded familiar to you."

"Yes. Now where did I hear this stuff about business and government cooperating before?"

"Okay, so I stole your platform."

"It's in the public domain. I want to see you do more of this sort of thing, out in the public eye, not just behind the doors of people's offices. It's good PR for the Partnership and for the city. I'm really proud of you, you know."

Yes, I knew. And that was probably why I started planning courses for the fall semester which would put me on track toward an MBA.

I was already feeling pretty good about myself when the most extraordinarily uplifting day occurred that same week. The afternoon that Dr. Chandra Patel walked into my office, I didn't immediately recognize her because she was wearing a white lab coat and slacks and I had only seen her before in elaborate costumes. But as soon as she smiled at me, I knew who she was.

"Jean," she said warmly, "I've come to ask you a favor."

I bolted from my chair and stepped toward her, taking her extended hand, which, it seemed to me, she expected me to kiss rather than shake. So it ended up being a limp grasp instead. I don't know if it was the idea of her money or her regal manner, enhanced by the British accent, that intimidated me, but I was never relaxed in her company. I knew my voice sounded unnatural as I said, "Dr. Patel, welcome. Have a seat."

"No, no," she said, waving the air. "I'm just here for a moment. It's my lunch hour."

"Well, what can I do for you?"

"My tax man is after me for receipts. I know you sent me a beautiful package after the election, but I'm hopeless with paperwork. Everything gets lost. I should have sent it on right away, but I didn't. So I'm hoping you can lay your hands on that again for me and send it directly to my accountant." She handed me a business card. "This is his card. A fax will be sufficient. He's expecting it."

"Yes, no problem. I know where the file is."

"I know it isn't your job anymore, being Rosalind's campaign manager, but I also knew that you were my best chance for the information. You're so efficient and I'm so disorganized. Money matters!" She made a sputtering sound to indicate that money matters were of no interest to her, which I was certain was not even a little bit true.

"You didn't have to come over for this," I said. "You could have just called."

"Yes, I know. But I wanted to see you in person." She looked directly at me and smiled slyly, her dark eyes bright and expressive. I watched her gaze slide down from my eyes to pass over the length of my body. Oh, my God, I thought, suddenly grasping her unspoken message. When our eyes met again, she knew that the message had been received.

"I heard you left your husband," she said simply. "Are you seeing anyone?"

My tongue felt like it was nailed to the inside of my mouth. When I finally coaxed it to move, my voice came out at an oddly high pitch, almost a squeak. "Yes, I am." Her expression turned into a pout, an exaggerated look of disappointment. "Rosie," I said, "I'm seeing Rosie."

She clapped her hands together and shook her head. "Oh, that woman is always one step ahead of me. If it was anyone else, Jean, I'd take you from her without a qualm."

Well, I thought, I might have something to say about that.

"But Rosalind is my dear friend, as you know." Dr. Patel took another business card from her jacket pocket, reached over and tucked it into the waistband of my pants with deliberate slowness. "File this some place where you won't lose track of it. This has my personal number on it. If you should ever find yourself not seeing Rosalind, please call me."

Her expression was seductive as she turned and left the office. I stood dumbly where I was for a couple of minutes, watching the door. And then I looked at the card at my waist and took it between my fingers. Eventually, I ended up back in my chair, but it was quite a while before I could get back to opening the mail, which is what I had been doing before this most bizarre incident occurred. And even when I got back to it, my fingers were stupid, fumbling to open an envelope with a foreign stamp. Noticing the return address and the company logo on the letter inside, though, abruptly broke the spell I was under.

The letter was from the French company I had been trying to persuade to set up shop in Weberstown. Written in English, it was an invitation to come to Paris to tour the parent company and to discuss the details of our proposal in person. The invitation was for myself and anyone I felt would be qualified to contribute to the discussion. Thrilled, I immediately called Rosie and read the letter to her over the phone.

"They're serious," she said. "This is going to be a big one for you, Jean. Who's going?"

"I am," I said triumphantly. "I'm going to Paris! It's my deal, so I'm going."

Rosie laughed. "Well, yes, of course you are. I'm glad to hear you say it. I meant, who are you taking along? You'll need some city official, probably."

"Oh, sure."

"Think of it, Jean, Paris! Oh, how fantastic for you! And you can bill the whole thing to us. Drinking wine like water, walking down the Champs Élysées, sipping an aperitif at La Tour d'Argent."

I closed my eyes, trying to imagine myself making business deals in Paris. "Rosie," I said, "come with me. Of course you have to."

"In what capacity?"

"Advertising agent. Director of the Partnership. My special friend." I was getting hyped. "You could tell them about advertising their product, about the U.S. market, consumer tastes, all that jazz. And you speak French! Come, please."

"It will depend on when it is."

"You set the date," I countered. "Oh, come with me, Rosie. Imagine the two of us in Paris, walking arm in arm down the Champs Élysées, drinking wine like water. Without you, what kind of romantic holiday would it be?"

"A business trip," she said bluntly. Then she laughed. "Okay, love, I'll see if I can swing it."

We talked for a few minutes about the delights of Paris before I remembered Dr. Patel's visit. "Oh, Rosie," I said, "you won't believe who came to see me earlier. This has been a crazy day!"

I told her about the visit, in detail.

"Why that sneaky thing," Rosie said. "I had no idea she had even noticed you."

"Me neither," I said, astonished all over again.

"Well, how did that feel, Jean?"

"Thrilling! Sorry, Rosie, but I can't help it. I've never had a woman make a pass at me before."

"It's okay to be thrilled, especially when it's such an enchanting, accomplished woman. Just so long as you turned her down."

"Of course."

"Quite a day you've had," she said. "Quite a life you're forging for yourself, actually. I have to admit that I'm sort of envious. Not because of Chandra, but because of the excitement of all of these new things, all the possibilities."

"No need to be envious, Rosie. You're right here with me."

"Yes, and it's a joy to observe, believe me, but it's happening to you. Well, you're making it happen. That's the thing, really. Let's go out tonight to celebrate. We can talk about where we'll go in Paris."

"Oh, Rosie," I said, "I can't go out with you tonight. Tyler and I are going to a gay and lesbian film festival in the East Bay."

"No problem," Rosie said. "We'll celebrate tomorrow or the next day, whenever we can manage to get together. I'm glad you and Tyler are enjoying one another's company so much."

After Rosie consulted her schedule, I arranged the meeting with the French CEO for May 28 and 29. My birthday, my forty-first birthday, was May 27, the day after our scheduled arrival. We were going to be in Paris on my birthday. Doesn't get much better than that, I thought.

I asked Harry Stone of the labor relations board to come too, and he agreed. The three of us would be the team. We would be gone a week, which would leave us free from business for at least four days, free to explore Paris. Amy agreed to take care of the horses and cats. She wanted to go with us, of course.

"Next time," I told her, as parents do, but this was for real because I was beginning to understand that there would be a next time, that there would be a lot of adventure ahead. Even so, this first trip to Europe was a pretty big deal to me, and I was so glad Rosie was coming too. Can all of this really be happening, I wondered. When Faye handed me an envelope with boarding passes, Métro pass and itinerary, I knew it was for real. May 25, it said, SFO to CDG, next day arrival.

"You're going to love it," Faye said. "I stuck a little wallet card in there with a Métro map on it. That's how you'll be traveling around the city. Good luck with that business deal, by the way."

"Thanks, Faye," I said, tucking the envelope into my bag. "Could you ever have imagined that I would be going to Paris to broker a deal like this?"

Faye shook her head. "No, definitely not. Jean. You've been nothing but surprises to me lately." She stood and gazed at me thoughtfully. "It's taking some getting used to, and not just the idea of you and Rosie either, which is plenty to get used to all by itself." Faye came out from behind her desk and gave me a warm hug. "I want you to know that I'm happy for you," she said. "And you should be happy for me too." She held out her hand to display a showy solitaire diamond on her ring finger which I had somehow overlooked while she was making my reservations.

"Faye, you're engaged?"

She nodded. "You're not the only one making big changes."

I hugged her again. "Yes, of course I'm happy for you!"

"Let me walk you back to your office," Faye said excitedly. "We can talk about my wedding. I want you to be my maid of honor, of course. I'm thinking October." She locked her office behind us as we emerged onto the sidewalk. "Or, maybe, if you and Rosie are ready, we can make it a double wedding or a double commitment ceremony, or whatever you call it! How about that, Jean? Just like we planned when we were sixteen, remember?"

I laughed. "Not exactly just like it."

"Oh, well, close enough. What's twenty-five years, more or less?" Faye's eyes sparkled with mischievous delight. "Can you imagine?"

"You're nuts," I said, "even if Rosie would go along with it."

"Why wouldn't she?"

"Rosie's afraid, I think, to even imagine the future. These sorts of ceremonies are all about a belief in just that, your future together. Besides, she's come right out and said that marriage is not for her, and I don't see why she would feel any differently about a commitment ceremony." We had arrived at my office door. "It's a wild idea, Faye, but I'm sure your family will be much happier if we don't realize our teenage fantasy of a double wedding, under the circumstances."

After congratulating her again, I said good-bye to Faye and settled back into my work day, musing over her crazy idea. I didn't care about a ceremony. I had done it once. All that mattered to me was that Rosie and I were together and we were happy. Still, it was a funny idea, and the image of Faye's parents sitting through such a ceremony made me chuckle. Her brothers, too, all older than Faye, looking like jocks and lumberjacks—well, her family would certainly boycott such a thing *en masse*.

And what about my family, I thought. Outside of Amy, I wasn't having much luck on that front. I still hadn't spoken to Bradley, and I couldn't muster the courage to talk to my parents at all about my situation. In phone conversations with my mother, the subject of Rosie was carefully avoided. I knew she knew the truth because Amy told me that remarks had been made, but neither of us spoke of it. I was afraid to discuss it with her. It was easier to pretend there was nothing to discuss. But that was getting increasingly uncomfortable.

"You can't really have a meaningful relationship of any kind," Tyler said during one of our many talks on this subject, "if you keep pretending. It's like the whole Don't Ask, Don't Tell policy. It's such a pile of shit. If you don't mention it, it doesn't exist. Bull crap! The fact that they can make a national policy out of that kind of flimsy lie is absurd."

"You have come out to your parents, haven't you?" I asked.

"Oh, sure. When I was fifteen. I was in a cold sweat for days beforehand, working up the courage. When I told them, my father went berserk and demanded that I recant and my mother broke down and wept. But I was so relieved because at least I had said it, you know."

"And they recovered?"

"They recovered completely. So completely that they forgot. I had to keep telling them, over and over, and they just stared blankly like they didn't see me. And my mother kept inviting girls over for me to meet. Once she even devised some ridiculous scheme to leave me alone in the house with this girl, this skank, thinking that hormones would take over and I'd be cured. To this day, they still don't acknowledge that I'm gay. They tell lies to relatives and they avoid certain subjects. If they talk about homosexuality at all, they do so as if it has nothing to do with them, like an abstract idea or something that happens in other places, to other people. Right in front of me! It's much easier just not being around them."

"That's too bad," I said.

"Yes, well, I've adapted. I have a new family now." He smiled at me. "You know, if everybody got to pick their own family members, they'd never pick the same people God stuck them with."

True, I thought, laughing. One thing Tyler and I had discovered, personally and through our research, was the pain and damage that silence could inflict. You didn't have to tell the whole world if that was too difficult, but you did at least have to tell the people who loved you. What was the point of being loved, after all, by someone who didn't know who you were?

When my mother invited me for Easter dinner, I accepted, but after hanging up the phone, felt frustrated with myself. I called right back and said, "Mom, does your invitation include Rosie?"

"Well, dear," she began, "your father doesn't like to have strangers around. You know how he is. Just family for holidays."

I was feeling particularly reckless. "Rosie shouldn't be a stranger to you. We come as a package."

"Your father won't like it."

"Don't use Dad as an excuse. Do you want us to come or not?"

She stuttered momentarily, then said, "Yes, of course. Don't get upset. Of course she can come."

"Fine," I said a little too harshly.

Easter—or the vernal equinox, as Rosie called it—at my parents' house was going to be a significant event. This would be the first time Rosie had come into contact with several members of my family, including Bradley who, Mom assured me, would be there with his girlfriend Brenna.

"Calm down," Rosie said as I chattered on about whether we should have put miniature marshmallows in the ambrosia salad after all. I turned down the quiet street where my parents lived, a neighborhood shaded by giant old elm trees.

"My mother thinks she's a gourmet cook ever since she

developed the habit of putting together incongruous ingredients like cinnamon and chicken livers. That was how she dealt with *her* mid-life crisis. Sorry to put you through this, Rosie."

"Don't worry. The worst that could happen is a nasty fight in which a hotheaded family member pulls out a shotgun and wastes a few of us." An image of Dad's fully stocked gun cabinet came to mind. I stiffened. Rosie slapped my shoulder. "Laugh. It's a joke. And, believe me, this is going to be a breeze compared to when I take you to meet my family."

"Oh, God," I said.

When we arrived, Amy's Honda was already parked in the driveway. Rosie, seeming carefree, grabbed the salad bowl and jumped out of the car. "Nice place," she observed. "I like this part of town. It's got character. It's not row after row of houses with the same front door and false brick facing around the garage."

Amy came bursting from the house and skipping toward us. "Hi, guys." I hugged her. Rosie hugged her with her free arm.

"Grandma's nervous," she whispered to me.

"Me too," I said. "Is Bradley here?"

"Not yet." Amy forged the way into the house where my father lounged in his La-Z-Boy recliner. He pulled himself up to meet Rosie. His smile was forced. What a day this was going to be.

My mother, when we approached her in the kitchen, didn't even try to disguise her disapproval, though she may have thought she did. She wiped her hand on a towel before extending it to Rosie with a formal, "How do you do?" I was mortified.

"I'm so glad to meet you," Rosie said. "What a lovely kitchen. Oh, and that aroma." Rosie sniffed the air. "Enticing. Ham, obviously, but something else. What is that smell? Very familiar. Is it mustard? Did you put a mustard paste on that ham?"

"Why, yes," my mother said, brightening. "It's a mustard and roasted garlic paste, in fact."

"My grandmother used to bake ham just that way. I haven't had it for decades. What a treat!"

That's right, Rosie, aim for the tender spot, you old

politician.

"Isn't that interesting?" Mom said. "Where was your grandmother from?"

I left Rosie to charm my mother, relaxing a bit. Could she pull it off? I went out into the backyard to pet the dog. They'll like her if they give her a chance, I told myself. Everybody does. Amy came out and positioned herself on a chaise lounge, sunglasses on, arms and legs bare. "You shouldn't lie in the sun," I said. "You know how dangerous it is."

"I've got sunscreen on, Mom. Chill. I've got to get a head start on summer." Amy rolled up her shirt so her stomach was exposed to the sun. "Now," she said, "if I were going to the south of France like some people I know, I could get a whole-body tan lying naked on the beach."

"I'm not going to the south of France. I'm going to Paris."

"Speaking of Paris," Amy said without looking at me, "do you know where that old saying comes from, 'We'll always have Paris'?"

That old saying, I thought, amused. "Yes, as a matter of fact, I do. And I guess you do too, now that you've seen the movie."

"Dad thinks we ought to watch *Gone With the Wind* next."

"Interesting choices he's making for you. And that's a good one since you are so fond of saying, 'Frankly, my dear, I don't give a damn.'"

"Is that from *Gone With the Wind*?" she asked. "Who knew there were all these cool old movies where characters repeat all my catch phrases?"

I laughed and then remembered the ordeal I was about to be faced with. "What is your brother's state of mind about me lately?"

"We've had some talks. He's trying to deal with it. I think I've convinced him that you're not coming back. Yes, I think we've got him successfully through the denial phase." Amy spoke with her idea of a German accent. "The boy is suffering from what he perceives is a rejection by the mother, a rejection of the masculine lover, ergo, the son. He is further confused by the conflict of

226

viewing his mother as both the nurturing teat and the…" In her own voice, she said, "Ah, well, let's not go into that."

"Why don't you take anything seriously?"

"Because it's so boring. Besides, you wouldn't like it, would you?"

I considered that for a moment, then said, "Probably not."

"He was at school the other day, you know, when you gave your talk."

"He was?"

"Yes. He wanted to see you, but he didn't want you to know he was there."

"Did he say anything about it?" I asked anxiously.

"He said he didn't recognize you, like you weren't his mother at all."

I sighed. "Great."

"But I told him about our lunch afterward, how excited you were. And I told him that maybe you weren't the same, but you were really happy now, and that was better, at least for you. I think maybe that made an impression on him. I mean, like, he couldn't really want you to be miserable, now, could he?"

One would hope not. So, I was really happy now? I smiled to myself. Yes, for the most part. Things had just been getting better and better.

I inspected my mother's flower beds for insects and diseases, finding them in good shape except for a few aphids, which I flicked off with a fingernail. When I got to the blooming freesias near the kitchen window, I heard Rosie's laugh from inside, and then Bradley's deep voice. My heart quickened. I hurried inside to find Rosie and Bradley sitting at the kitchen table in conversation.

Bradley was a big, bristling young man, healthy and beautiful. It had been so long since I'd seen him and the photos had been an inadequate preparation for the real thing.

"In the Czech Republic I actually ran into a guy I knew," Bradley was saying. "There are Americans all over the place in Prague. Just hanging out."

"The new expatriates," Rosie said, nodding.

227

"How long since you've been to Paris?" Bradley asked.

"The last time I was there was about five years ago. It's good to go back after you've already done all the tourist things so you can absorb the spirit of a place. On my third trip to Paris I spent one day just strolling through the Bois de Boulogne pretending I was a native out for a Sunday walk."

I stood in the doorway, incredulous.

"I did that too," Bradley said with enthusiasm. "I pretended I lived there, imagining what it felt like for the people who really did, trying to imagine myself living a completely different life from my own." Rosie turned to look at me and Bradley followed her gaze.

"Mom," he said tentatively, rising. I held out my arms. He approached and hugged me wordlessly. When he stepped back, his face was serious, emotional, with that familiar tell-tale quiver at the left side of his mouth. He didn't know what to say. Me neither.

"I got you something," he said at last and pulled a small package from his shirt pocket. "For your trip to Paris."

Under shiny paper was an electronic device about the size of a checkbook calculator. "What is it?"

"A French language translator," Bradley said, taking it from me. He demonstrated. "Look. You type in a French word like 'amour,' and it gives you the English equivalent." He held it up so I could read the LCD image. "Love."

My eyes misted as I took the device.

"Or you can translate an English word into French," he said.

"Well, this ought to come in handy. Merci beaucoup."

I met Brenna, then, who was a warm, lovely girl with an elegant carriage. "I'm so glad I've finally gotten to meet you, Jean," she said. "I wish it could have been sooner, but Brad's been sort of stubborn about it."

"Yes," I said. "Perhaps understandably."

She nodded. There was strain among our little group during dinner, but the worst was over. Bradley had forgiven me and was trying to overcome his unease. And Mom and Dad, once they'd met Rosie and realized she was such a regular person, managed to relax a bit. Rosie dominated the evening, of course, talking politics with Dad, swapping traveling horror stories with Bradley. I heard her welcome laugh frequently.

My mother was impressed with Rosie's appetite, for she was never shy about eating, and the ham with the mustard paste was a big hit with her. We downed a couple of bottles of wine while we ate, and everyone was feeling a little friendlier, it seemed to me, as the meal wore on.

"I didn't vote for you," Dad told Rosie as we were finishing dinner. "Do you know why?"

Oh, my God, I thought. I can't deal with this. How can he be bringing this up? "Dad!" I barked, coming out of my chair.

Rosie held up a hand to me and gave me a look that said she had it under control. "Yes, I know why," Rosie said with mock antagonism, pausing for dramatic effect. "Because of my criticism of the city manager."

"How'd you know that?" he asked, astonished.

I let myself fall back into my chair, my pulse returning to normal.

"Because I happen to know that the two of you are friends. He told me so when I introduced him to Jean. You were in the Navy together."

Dad snorted, then grinned and pushed himself away from the table. "Hey, Bradley," he said, "come on out to the garage. I want to show you my new rod and reel." The two of them left together and Amy excused herself with the intention, I was sure, of calling her boyfriend.

"Well, Rosie," said my mother, "I *did* vote for you."

"Oh, thank you," Rosie replied.

My mother stood a little unsteadily and began to stack the plates. "I thought, what difference does it make who she sleeps with anyway? Nothing to do with running the city."

"That was very forward thinking of you," Rosie said, handing her plate over.

"Yes, well, that was before I knew that you were sleeping with my daughter, wasn't it?"

My mother cackled loudly as though she had made the best joke of all time and took her stack of plates into the kitchen.

Rosie looked at me, her eyes open wide. I looked at Brenna, who was trying desperately to suppress a laugh. I just shook my head.

After dinner Rosie helped my mother clean up in the kitchen, and I could hear them arguing from the front room about spaghetti sauce with unnecessarily loud assaults on each other. "If you put in mushrooms that big, they just sit there like ugly lumps," Mom was saying. "Everything should be small so it all blends into a sauce, not like a salsa, for crying out loud."

"If you cut them that small," Rosie said, "you can't taste them. Besides, they'd disintegrate after all those hours of simmering."

They seemed to be enjoying themselves. Rosie had intuited a basic truth about my parents to help her ingratiate herself with them—they liked to argue.

Bradley and I talked about his trip and about his plans for the future, which, I was happy to hear, included returning to college to finish his degree. Whenever Rosie was near me, regardless of what she was doing, he tensed slightly as though he was afraid he might witness some affection between us. We carefully avoided touching one another. We obviously had some distance to go, but it was a promising start. He was trying.

Later, when dinner had sufficiently settled, I helped Mom serve up dessert.

"Rosie's okay," she said, slicing a strawberry pie into eighths.

"Thanks. I really appreciate that. And everything. I know it's awkward."

"I guess you two are like a real couple, then?"

"Uh, I'm not sure what that means but, yes, I guess so." I lined up small plates and filled them with wedges of pie.

"Then why aren't you living together? If you lived together, you could share expenses. Do you know how much money you're wasting living in two places like this?"

I was momentarily stunned, as I wasn't expecting the conversation to go in this direction. "I'm making plenty of money now. You don't need to worry about that."

"Well, that's good."

Plopping Cool Whip on the pie slices, I thought about her question. "I'm glad I got my own place, though," I said. "I've been enjoying the independence of it. Just taking care of myself for a change."

"It's kind of lonely, though, isn't it?"

"Sometimes it is. Not so bad now as it was at first. When you live with other people, you're always responding to them responding to you. You get an experience of yourself that's a sort of reflection of what they see. So you're a mom or a wife. When you're just with yourself, you don't have the luxury of the ready-made point of view. You have to experience yourself on a different level. And I have to say that I'm enjoying the woman I'm getting to know. She's so full of vitality, for one thing."

I looked up from the plates to see my mother looking thoughtfully at me. "You've really changed, haven't you?"

I nodded. "In a good way, I hope, Mom."

"Well," she said, suddenly boisterous, flinging her arm into the air, "I never thought Jerry was any good for you anyway."

I stood there flabbergasted as she picked up two plates and flounced into the dining room, saying, "Rosie, how about dessert? You'll never guess what I put in this strawberry pie."

Shortly after that, the party broke up. Bradley left first. At the door he kissed his grandmother goodnight, then turned to me. "Love you, Mom," he said. I squeezed him tightly. By the time Rosie and I left, I was exhausted. It had been an emotional day. Another hurdle had been cleared—parents, family gathering. It could have been a lot worse.

"What did I tell you?" Rosie said on the drive home. "Your family loves me."

"Everybody loves you."

"That's true. Your mom's a riot. I like her a lot."

I shook my head. "You never can tell."

# Chapter Twenty

When I first moved to the apartment, I resisted buying anything for it. I thought of it as a brief stop on my way to something else, but, gradually, it was feeling like my sanctuary, that proverbial room of one's own. It was Tyler who got me started personalizing the place when he arrived one evening with an armload of towels, a shower curtain and throw rugs, saying, "I can't bear your bathroom for another day! All those mismatched things you brought over from your old house, it's too wretched. I refuse to pee in a room with no color scheme."

I had to admit that the bathroom was a whole lot more inviting when he had finished with it. So I bought some artwork for the walls and a few pieces of furniture, and I let the place evolve into something uniquely mine. I began to feel safe and contented there. And I quit asking Rosie when, if ever, she thought we might live together. It had seemed urgent to me in the beginning, as if I had to move into her house to secure our relationship. But that would have been no real security, of course. She knew that. She told me the joke about how lesbians show up on the second date with the U-Haul. The things you do in haste, out of fear, don't hold up, she said. In February, it had hurt my feelings, but in May, I had to agree that no harm had been done to our relationship by this arrangement. We were fine. We were great.

One of my most cherished new possessions, an object I put up a special shelf for, was a three-legged bronze bowl, a reproduction of those exquisite old dings. It had recently arrived on my doorstep from Beijing with a note from Cindy, thanking me for making her feel so welcome in our city and inviting me to come to visit her in China. The note also hinted that I would soon be doing business with her colleagues, who had been favorably impressed by their visit. That might occasion a trip or two to China, I thought, extremely satisfied with myself. France, China—where to next?

When I first took this job, I had envisioned it as a high-class secretarial position, but it had turned out to be so much more than that. That was my doing, Rosie told me. All of the partners were astonished at how completely I was running the organization. They were just sitting back enjoying the ride. When Rosie told them about the likelihood that this French deal was going to materialize, they voted to give me a substantial raise because they too had originally envisioned the position as a glorified secretary.

So things were going fantastic on both personal and professional fronts. I was no longer just waiting to move in with Rosie. We didn't have to live together to have a life together. I was willing to wait, indefinitely, if necessary, if that was the only way she could deal with her fear of the future. In the meantime, I contemplated the possibility of buying my own house, maybe one of those charming old places near the university with an attic and a sprawling front porch. I was thinking ahead to visions of grandkids on tricycles. I'd need a yard some day. And some day, I mused, when Rosie was too old to throw bales of hay around her barn, I would invite her to come live with me and she would gratefully accept, riding her motorized scooter up my front walk while my great grandkids carried in her luggage.

Financially, purchasing a house wouldn't be possible for a while, but I was saving a good chunk of my salary, so it wasn't unrealistic to plan for it. And there was going to be some sort of settlement, I knew, from my divorce, which I was now ready to set in motion.

Feeling somewhat buoyed by the success of Easter, I arranged to meet Jerry for lunch to talk about what would come next. I had been avoiding him for quite a while, using poor Amy as a go-between when necessary. We were no longer talking much on the phone either, so I wasn't sure what his state of mind was.

He arrived at the restaurant looking neat, but tired.

"How've you been, Jerry?" I asked across a white tablecloth.

"How do you think?" he answered resentfully. "Why did you ask me here?"

Okay, I thought, no small talk. "I'm filing for divorce. I'm meeting my lawyer Thursday. I didn't want you to be surprised by it."

His expression was hard. He was protecting himself from grief with anger. "Is that it, then? You're not even going to try to reconcile? Our life together means so little to you that you aren't willing to make even a little effort?"

"We've been over all of this," I said. "I'm happy with my decision."

"So, twenty-two years up in smoke?"

"Try not to think of it that way. We had a good life together. Now let's move on to something else."

The rest of the meal was a disaster. When he looked at me, it was with disgust. He was gruff and callous. I had underestimated his anger.

"How's your mother?" I asked over a bowl of clam chowder.
"Fine."

Then, as he picked at his salad, I asked, "Do you like Bradley's girlfriend?"

"She's okay." That was practically the extent of our conversation. We each paid for our own meal and left the

234

restaurant together. On the sidewalk, in a shower of spring sunshine, he stared at me coldly and said, "What you're doing is wrong. You've ruined my life and you've humiliated your entire family." Then he turned and walked away.

Although I had managed to be strong enough in Jerry's company, later that night, after dinner with Rosie, I remembered the sneer on his face, the contempt in his voice. I broke down.

"What is it?" Rosie asked, sitting on the couch beside me.

"We lived a lifetime together and now he hates me. You should have seen the look on his face."

She held me and said, "It's still a fresh wound for him. He's not moving on as fast as you are. Don't expect too much, too soon."

I nodded, thinking how true that was. Jerry and I seemed to be living in two different temporal realities.

"Maybe, eventually," she said, "his hostility will subside and you can be friends. And consider this, Jean. You're forty years old. You'll probably live another forty years. You were with Jerry twenty-two. That means that you've got a good chance of being with me longer than you were with him, and you've already started on a whole new set of happy memories."

"Very daring prediction," I said, noting how interesting it was that we were both thinking about being together in our old age. "Very unlike you, Rosie."

"Did it make you feel better?"

"Yes."

"Good. I had to get you in a good mood somehow, 'cause I want to fool around."

I laughed as she pushed me down on the couch and straddled me.

Sometimes I felt that Rosie had given me my life, that I had set it aside somewhere long ago and she had recovered it for me. She said I had found it myself, was still finding pieces of it, and she just happened to be standing alongside one of the big pieces when I found it.

I didn't realize it ahead of time, but of all the hurdles I had to jump on my way to embracing my new lifestyle, the last and biggest of them had nothing to do with friends and family members and their degree of acceptance. It was about my own degree of acceptance. I was beginning to understand, finally, what Rosie meant about the many steps involved. It wasn't just a single change that happened. It was a process, and I could imagine that it could be a long one for some people, spanning many years, even decades.

I didn't know how many steps were involved or even when I had taken one. It was a natural, subconscious progression. But a day did come when I understood that my point of view had indeed shifted, just as Rosie had predicted. That day happened in mid-May when the California Supreme Court overturned the ban on gay marriage. In the excitement that followed that news, I realized that I had, at some point in the last several weeks, identified myself thoroughly with the gay community. This felt personal to me. For weeks, Tyler and I had been reading and talking about gay rights in America, understanding, but not really feeling, that we were a part of it. Suddenly, here it was in our neighborhood, in our time. It wasn't history. It was happening right now. It was history in the making.

I heard the news first over my office radio. Within the hour, there were people congregating in the downtowns of cities across the state, most of them gay men and lesbians celebrating. I was in the process of locking up my office when my cell phone rang. It was Tyler.

"Jean," he said, "I'm on my way downtown. Are you coming? We're going to be dancing in the streets, baby."

"I'm going to get Rosie. I'll see you there. Call everybody."

I rushed downtown to Rosie's office, calling Ginny on the way. She was on her way too, she said. When I arrived at Rosie's office, I burst in, interrupting her conversation with Tina.

"Did you hear the news?" I asked, breathless.

"Yes," Rosie said. "Just a few minutes ago."

Tina nodded enthusiastically.

"Well, let's go!" I said impatiently.

"Let's go where?" Rosie asked, looking perplexed.

"The courthouse, of course. There's a bunch of right-wingers there already waving their one man plus one woman signs and spewing their crap about slippery slopes and what do we do if some farmer wants to marry his pig! We need a presence, a big one, to show that we're celebrating while they are languishing in defeat. We can't afford to be complacent because you know they're going to come right back at us as soon as they get the chance. We have to show everybody how many of us there are and how passionate we are about our rights. I've already spoken with Ginny and Tyler. They'll meet us there and they're rallying the troops. So, let's go, let's get some signs made. Something like, 'Hallelujah, the wicked witch is dead!' Or whatever. Something that the media will want to put on camera. Tina, you have to come too, even though you're not gay. But we won't hold that against you in a time of need. You can't be on the fence here. You have to take sides, and obviously, you're on our side."

Tina looked amusedly resigned. Rosie stood staring at me like I'd lost my mind, a reaction I didn't comprehend.

"Well?" I said. "Are you coming?"

And then I realized that her eyes had teared up. She put her hand to her mouth, obviously overcome with emotion, which seemed a tremendous overreaction to the situation, especially since Rosie wasn't a person prone to that kind of emotional display.

"Rosie," I said gently. "What's wrong? Why are you crying? This is good news. A major victory for our side!"

She nodded her head emphatically as a tear dropped to her cheek. "Oh, yes," she said, sniffing.

And then I understood, by the way she was looking at me with such affection and gratification, that her reaction, these tears of joy, had nothing to do with the court decision. I reached out and pulled her close. She put her head on my shoulder and wept freely.

"I'll go get some sign boards," Tina said, tactfully leaving the room.

After a moment, Rosie lifted her head from my shoulder. I wiped the tears off her face and smiled at her.

"Ready?" I asked.

She nodded, composing herself. "I'm ready."

# Chapter Twenty-One

Rosie and I sat on one side of the plane with Harry across the aisle. We flew overnight with the intention of sleeping, but that had been a too-optimistic plan. Rosie, her hand clasped in mine between us, dozed off for short naps, but I don't think I managed to fall asleep once. I kept thinking how incredible it was that I was here, flying to Paris with Rosie. The events which had led me to this place were still unreal to me. But I thought of them as alien less and less. My new life continued to feel ever more comfortable and grounded.

The flight was tiring and seemed interminable. The trip from the airport into Paris and our hotel took well over an hour. When at last Rosie and I were alone in our room, she kissed me deeply, then said, "Bienvenue à Paris."

"What do you want to do?" I asked.

"I'm very tired, but I don't think we should waste the rest of the day. There are a million things I want to show you. Are you up for a night on the town?"

We cleaned up a bit, then changed into Levi's and walking

shoes. "What about Harry?" I asked on the way out of the room.

"Let him find his own amusement for tonight. He's probably asleep by now anyway. Tomorrow we can all go sightseeing together." In the hotel lobby we pulled on our jackets and went out to face a windy city. It was late in the afternoon already, but the evening lay ahead, an evening of exceptional promise. I had my camera, guidebook, electronic translator, Métro map and some Euros that we had purchased ahead of time. On the street outside the hotel we stood looking up toward the Avenue de la Grande Armée, our destination. I gawked at everything like the neophyte I was, while Rosie led me by the arm to the huge avenue. Despite our long trip, her eyes were bright with a sense of adventure.

We walked along between a mixture of old stone and new glass buildings. After a few blocks, Rosie pulled me to the curb and stopped. I looked down the avenue to where she pointed to see the Arc de Triomphe ahead, that massive ornate landmark which was the first familiar sight, the first proof that I was really in Paris. We headed toward it as though it were a beacon. When we arrived at the hub of radiating roadways, we stood as insects beneath the bulk of the arch. We stayed there in the square for some time, walking around the colossal structure amid honking Parisian traffic.

Rosie quoted interesting historical facts like a tour guide, but without the corny jokes. Then we entered the Champs Élysées and walked toward Tuileries Gardens, past airline offices and embassies from around the world. We walked for several blocks until at last we reached the Grand Palais. Circling it, we saw statues and fountains at every glance. This mix of classical and contemporary was jarring, but enthralling.

We decided to take a break from walking and stopped at a café for some fruit, some *fromage*, a bottle of *vin rouge* and a baguette. A baguette in Paris! I was delighted. Rosie spoke to the waiter and ordered in French. "I'm a little rusty. But they'll get the message. And they appreciate the attempt."

The last glow of daylight disappeared while we enjoyed our meal. Exotic sounds and sights swirled around me. This is so much like a fantasy, I thought, looking at Rosie across the table, it was hard to believe it. But then, life had been like that for me for months now, an incredible, breathtaking idyll that I could barely keep up with. Maybe someday I would manage to catch my breath. I remembered what Rosie had said about living for another forty years, about still having that much time left to forge new memories. If that could happen then this was just the beginning of an entirely new lifetime for the two of us. As she gazed at me across the table, holding my hand, I could believe in that possibility. I hoped she could believe in it too.

Eventually we dragged ourselves back onto the street, leaning against each other for support. "Where to now?" Rosie asked.

"The Louvre is just up ahead," I said, consulting my map. "Closed, of course, but we could scout it out for tomorrow. I know you've been there several times. I hope you don't mind too much going back to all of these places."

"Jean," she said, putting a hand to my cheek, "everything is new to me tonight." She smiled at me fondly. "Besides, what would your art history professor say if he knew you were in Paris and didn't stop in at the Louvre? That has got to be some form of heresy."

We walked with our arms locked together, two lovers moving through shadows and puddles of light on a busy Paris thoroughfare. Our pace had slowed considerably, and we decided that we would ride the Métro back to the hotel when the time came, being much too exhausted to walk. It was late when we arrived at the Louvre, and then moved off toward the Seine. Standing like a magical kingdom before us, Notre Dame rose up from the Île de la Cité, splitting the river around it.

Rosie and I leaned against a railing looking across to the island. The gothic cathedral shone in a bath of bright light, lit up by powerful spotlights at its base. Its central spire shot delicately up into the night sky.

"For two thousand years people have prayed there," Rosie

241

said quietly. "A long history of holiness. The first time I was here I was twenty-six, traveling alone. I was seeing as much as I could as fast as I could, all the usual things. Notre Dame was, of course, on the list. I rushed inside and began checking off things I had read about, the artwork, the statues. I was in the process of taking in the rose windows when I looked up to the ceiling and then out along the interior and had my breath taken away. I had been inside about fifteen minutes, but I hadn't noticed how awe-inspiring, how grand the cathedral was. I had been missing too much. I sat down for a long while, just looking about, imagining what it was like for other people to sit there throughout the centuries, thinking about the vastness of human history. I believe that was a rare, near religious moment for me. How appropriate, don't you think, that it should occur in such a place?"

Rosie's face was illuminated on one side only. The crease beside her mouth was deep. I kissed it lightly. We dropped onto a bench to rest and watched people pass. Rosie put her arm loosely behind me on the back of the bench and we sat close for some time, wordless, watching the light dance off the river.

"Are you happy?" she asked.

"Elated."

Rosie reached into the pocket of her jacket and pulled out a small white box. "Jean, I was going to give you this tomorrow, on your birthday, but tonight seems more appropriate for it. Besides, tomorrow we'll have Harry along."

I took the box, my fingers cold and stiff from the chill of the night. Inside was a ring, an unbelievably gorgeous platinum band encrusted with a row of princess-cut diamonds. The streetlight above our bench caught them in a dazzling shimmer. "Oh!" I said, overcome.

"Do you like it?" she asked.

"Are you kidding? This is the most beautiful ring I've ever seen in my life."

Rosie put her arm around my shoulders more securely. "It's inscribed. Can you read it?"

I wiped a tear from my eye and looked inside the band, turned it to catch the light and attempted to read the inscription. "Jean et Rosie. Heureux pour toujours."

"Well," she said, "the pronunciation is a little off." She read it to me in a way that made it sound much more romantic.

"I don't know the words," I said.

"Look them up."

I took Bradley's translator out of my pack and typed in the two words I didn't know, "heureux" and "toujours." The lighted display came back with "happy" and "always."

I looked up to see Rosie looking tired, but lovingly, at me. "Happy for always?" I asked.

"Yes. Jean and Rosie, happy for always. The French don't really have a phrase for 'happily ever after,' This is the closest I could get. Their fairy tales end with a slightly different sentiment that basically means, 'they lived happily and had a lot of kids.'"

I laughed. Rosie took the ring from me, holding my hand in hers. "Marry me, Jean," she said, sliding the ring over my finger. "Come live with me happily ever after."

My eyes felt hot with new tears. "This is so…" I choked and couldn't say another word.

"Nod if that means yes."

I nodded vigorously. And then I flung myself at her and kissed her passionately, welcoming the now familiar response of my body.

"I'm going to adore looking at your sweet face over my coffee cup every morning," Rosie said, her expression serene.

We kissed again.

"Do you think we'll shock the natives?" I asked, realizing that there were still pedestrians walking by.

"I doubt it. Parisians have seen everything. We didn't invent this, after all." Rosie stood, pulling me to my feet. "It's almost midnight. We should get back. I'm too old for such extravagant hours. Besides, I feel like one of us is going to turn into a pumpkin at any moment."

I knew what she meant. The night couldn't have felt more magical. We walked over to the path beside the river to make our way back. Below us, parked along the Left Bank, a few noisy restaurant boats were still serving meals. The clatter of dishes, music and laughter drifted up to us, distorted by the wind. Among the commotion, my ear picked out a familiar orchestral tune coming from somewhere among the boat population. I tried to focus on it and began to hear the melody.

"Do you hear that music?" I asked, stopping to listen.

"Yes. It's the waltz from *Sleeping Beauty*. Lovely, isn't it?"

*Sleeping Beauty*, I thought. Remarkable.

There was no way I could have been happier than I was at that moment, thinking about the incredible journey I had taken to this place and the marvelous promise of our life to come. The best part of it, though, was seeing the joy in Rosie's eyes and knowing that she, too, was confident about the future, our future together.

I turned to face her and held out my hand, noting the glitter of diamonds on my finger. "Shall we dance?" I asked.

She smiled fondly at me, took my hand and asked, "Who leads?"

# Afterword

May 15, 2008, the California Supreme Court overturned a ban on same-sex marriage as unconstitutional. In November of the same year, voters narrowly approved a proposition defining marriage as exclusively between a man and a woman, taking away the right of gays and lesbians to marry. These two events were only the latest in an ongoing battle over gay marriage in California and across the U.S. As this book goes to print, same-sex marriage is illegal in California, pending a Supreme Court ruling on the constitutionality of the November, 2008 initiative. But in the summer and fall of 2008, an estimated 18,000 same-sex couples were legally married. Jean and Rosie were among those who said "I do."

**Publications from**
**Bella Books, Inc.**
*The best in contemporary lesbian fiction*

**P.O. Box 10543, Tallahassee, FL 32302**
**Phone: 800-729-4992**
**www.bellabooks.com**

WITHOUT WARNING: Book one in the Shaken series by KG MacGregor. *Without Warning* is the story of their courageous journey through adversity, and their promise of steadfast love.
ISBN: 978-1-59493-120-8
$13.95

THE CANDIDATE by Tracey Richardson. Presidential candidate Jane Kincaid had always expected the road to the White House would exact a high personal toll. She just never knew how high until forced to choose between her heart and her political destiny.
ISBN: 978-1-59493-133-8
$13.95

TALL IN THE SADDLE by Karin Kallmaker, Barbara Johnson, Therese Szymanski and Julia Watts. The playful quartet that penned the acclaimed *Once Upon A Dyke* and *Stake Through the Heart* are back and now turning to the Wild (and Very Hot) West to bring you another collection of erotically charged, action-packed tales.
ISBN: 978-1-59493-106-2
$15.95

IN THE NAME OF THE FATHER by Gerri Hill. In this highly anticipated sequel to *Hunter's Way*, Dallas Homicide Detectives Tori Hunter and Samantha Kennedy investigate the murder of a Catholic priest who is found naked and strangled to death.
ISBN: 978-1-59493-108-6
$13.95

IT'S ALL SMOKE AND MIRRORS: The First Chronicles of Shawn Donnelly by Therese Szymanski. Join Therese Szymanski as she takes a walk on the sillier side of the gritty crime scene detective novel and introduces readers to her newest alternate personality—Shawn Donnelly.
ISBN: 978-1-59493-117-8
$13.95

THE ROAD HOME by Frankie J. Jones. As Lynn finds herself in one adventure after another, she discovers that true wealth may have very little to do with money after all.
ISBN: 978-1-59493-110-9
$13.95

IN DEEP WATERS: CRUISING THE SEAS by Karin Kallmaker and Radclyffe. Book passage on a deliciously sensual Mediterranean cruise with tour guides Radclyffe and Karin Kallmaker.
ISBN: 978-1-59493-111-6
$15.95

ALL THAT GLITTERS by Peggy J. Herring. Life is good for retired army colonel Marcel Robicheaux. Marcel is unprepared for the turn her life will take. She soon finds herself in the pursuit of a lifetime—searching for her missing mother and lover.
ISBN: 978-1-59493-107-9
$13.95

OUT OF LOVE by KG MacGregor. For Carmen Delallo and Judith O'Shea, falling in love proves to be the easy part.
ISBN: 978-1-59493-105-5
$13.95

BORDERLINE by Terri Breneman. Assistant prosecuting attorney Toni Barston returns in the sequel to *Anticipation*.
ISBN: 978-1-59493-99-7
$13.95

PAST REMEMBERING by Lyn Denison. What would it take to melt Peri's cool exterior? Any involvement on Asha's part would be simply asking for trouble and heartache...wouldn't it?
ISBN: 978-1-59493-103-1
$13.95

ASPEN'S EMBERS by Diane Tremain Braund. Will Aspen choose the woman she loves...or the forest she hopes to preserve...
ISBN: 978-1-59493-102-4
$14.95

THE COTTAGE by Gerri Hill. *The Cottage* is the heartbreaking story of two women who meet by chance . . . or did they? A love so destined it couldn't be denied . . . stolen moments to be cherished forever.
ISBN: 978-1-59493-096-6
$13.95

FANTASY: Untrue Stories of Lesbian Passion edited by Barbara Johnson and Therese Szymanski. Lie back and let Bella's bad girls take you on an erotic journey through the greatest bedtime stories never told.
ISBN: 978-1-59493-101-7
$15.95

SISTERS' FLIGHT by Jeanne G'Fellers. *Sisters' Flight* is the highly anticipated sequel to *No Sister of Mine* and *Sister Lost Sister Found*.
ISBN: 978-1-59493-116-1
$13.95

BRAGGIN' RIGHTS by Kenna White. Taylor Fleming is a thirty-six-year-old Texas rancher who covets her independence. She finds her cowgirl independence tested by neighboring rancher Jen Holland.
ISBN: 978-1-59493-095-9
$13.95

BRILLIANT by Ann Roberts. Respected sociology professor, Diane Cole finds her views on love challenged by her own heart, as she fights the attraction she feels for a woman half her age.
ISBN: 978-1-59493-115-4
$13.95

THE EDUCATION OF ELLIE by Jackie Calhoun. When Ellie sees her childhood friend for the first time in thirty years she is tempted to resume their long lost friendship. But with the years come a lot of baggage and the two women struggle with who they are now while fighting the painful memories of their first parting. Will they be able to move past their history to start again?
ISBN: 978-1-59493-092-8
$13.95

DATE NIGHT CLUB by Saxon Bennett. *Date Night Club* is a dark romantic comedy about the pitfalls of dating in your thirties...
ISBN: 978-1-59493-094-2
$13.95

PLEASE FORGIVE ME by Megan Carter. Laurel Becker is on the verge of losing the two most important things in her life—her current lover, Elaine Alexander, and the Lavender Page bookstore. Will Elaine and Laurel manage to work through their misunderstandings and rebuild their life together?
ISBN: 978-1-59493-091-1
$13.95

WHISKEY AND OAK LEAVES by Jaime Clevenger. Meg meets June, a single woman running a horse ranch in the California Sierra foothills. The two become quick friends and it isn't long before Meg is looking for more than just a friendship. But June has no interest in developing a deeper relationship with Meg. She is, after all, not the least bit interested in women...or is she? Neither of these two women is prepared for what lies ahead...
ISBN: 978-1-59493-093-5
$13.95

SUMTER POINT by KG MacGregor. As Audie surrenders her heart to Beth, she begins to distance herself from the reckless habits of her youth. Just as they're ready to meet in the middle, their future is thrown into doubt by a duty Beth can't ignore. It all comes to a head on the river at Sumter Point.
ISBN: 978-1-59493-089-8
$13.95

THE TARGET by Gerri Hill. Sara Michaels is the daughter of a prominent senator who has been receiving death threats against his family. In an effort to protect Sara, the FBI recruits homicide detective Jaime Hutchinson to secretly provide the protection they are so certain Sara will need. Will Sara finally figure out who is behind the death threats? And will Jaime realize the truth—and be able to save Sara before it's too late?
ISBN: 978-1-59493-082-9
$13.95

REALITY BYTES by Jane Frances. In this sequel to *Reunion*, follow the lives of four friends in a romantic tale that spans the globe and proves that you can cross the whole of cyberspace only to find love a few suburbs away...
ISBN: 978-1-59493-079-9
$13.95

MURDER CAME SECOND by Jessica Thomas Broadway's bad-boy genius, Paul Carlucci, has chosen *Hamlet* for his latest production. To the delight of some and despair of others, he has selected Provincetown's amphitheatre for his opening gala. But suddenly Alex Peres realizes that the wrong people are falling down. And the moaning is all to realistic. Someone must not be shooting blanks...
ISBN: 978-1-59493-081-2
$13.95

SKIN DEEP by Kenna White. Jordan Griffin has been given a new assignment: Track down and interview one-time nationally renowned broadcast journalist Reece McAllister. Much to her surprise, Jordan comes away with far more than just a story...
ISBN: 978-1-59493-78-2
$13.95

FINDERS KEEPERS by Karin Kallmaker. *Finders Keepers*, the quest for the perfect mate in the 21st Century, joins Karin Kallmaker's *Just Like That* and her other incomparable novels about lesbian love, lust and laughter.
ISBN: 1-59493-072-4
$13.95

OUT OF THE FIRE by Beth Moore. Author Ann Covington feels at the top of the world when told her book is being made into a movie. Then in walks Casey Duncan the actress who is playing the lead in her movie. Will Casey turn Ann's world upside down?
ISBN: 1-59493-088-0
$13.95

STAKE THROUGH THE HEART by Karin Kallmaker, Julia Watts, Barbara Johnson and Therese Szymanski. The playful quartet that penned the acclaimed *Once Upon A Dyke* are dimming the lights for journeys into worlds of breathless seduction.
ISBN: 1-59493-071-6
$15.95

THE HOUSE ON SANDSTONE by KG MacGregor. Carly Griffin returns home to Leland and finds that her old high school friend Justine is awakening more than just old memories.
ISBN: 1-59493-076-7
$13.95

THE FEEL OF FOREVER by Lyn Denison. Felicity Devon soon discovers that she isn't quite sure what she fears the most—that Bailey, the woman who broke her heart and who is back in town, will want to pick up where they left off...or that she won't...
ISBN: 978-1-59493-073-7
$13.95

WILD NIGHTS (Mostly True Stories of Women Loving Women) Stories edited by Therese Szymanksi. Therese Szymanski is back, editing a collection of erotic short stories from your favorite authors...
ISBN: 1-59493-069-4
$15.95

COYOTE SKY by Gerri Hill. Sheriff Lee Foxx is trying to cope with the realization that she has fallen in love for the first time. And fallen for author Kate Winters, who is technically unavailable. Will Lee fight to keep Kate in Coyote?
ISBN: 1-59493-065-1
$13.95

VOICES OF THE HEART by Frankie J. Jones. A series of events force Erin to swear off love as she tries to break away from the woman of her dreams. Will Erin ever find the key to her future happiness?
ISBN: 1-59493-068-6
$13.95

SHELTER FROM THE STORM by Peggy J. Herring. *Shelter from the Storm* is a story about family and getting reacquainted with one's past. Sometimes you don't appreciate what you have until you almost lose it.
ISBN: 1-59493-064-3
$13.95

BENEATH THE WILLOW by Kenna White. A torch that even after twenty-five years still burns brightly threatens to consume two childhood friends.
ISBN: 1-59493-051-1
$13.95

THE WEEKEND VISITOR by Jessica Thomas. In this latest Alex Peres mystery, Alex is asked to investigate an assault on a local woman but finds that her client may have more secrets than she lets on.
ISBN: 1-59493-054-6
$13.95

ANTICIPATION by Terri Breneman. Two women struggle to remain professional as they work together to find a serial killer.
ISBN: 1-59493-055-4
$13.95

OBSESSION by Jackie Calhoun. Lindsey Stuart Brown's life is turned upside down when Sarah Gilbert comes into the family nursery in search of perennials.
ISBN: 1-59493-058-9
$13.95

18th & CASTRO by Karin Kallmaker. First-time couplings and couples who know how to mix lust and love make *18th & Castro* the hottest address in the city by the bay.
ISBN: 1-59493-066-X
$13.95

JUST THIS ONCE by KG MacGregor. Ever mindful of the obligations back home that she must honor, Wynne Connelly struggles to resist the fascination and allure that a particular woman she meets on her business trip represents...
ISBN: 1-59493-087-2
$13.95

PAID IN FULL by Ann Roberts. Ari Adams will need to choose between the debts of the past and the promise of a happy future.
ISBN: 1-59493-059-7
$13.95

END OF WATCH by Clare Baxter. LAPD Lieutenant L.A. Franco follows the lone clue down the unlit steps of memory to a final, unthinkable resolution.
ISBN: 1-59493-064-4
$13.95